## *Opal's Faith*

When the Barnett family reached Wildweed, Arizona, it was around noon on a Thursday. George pulled the wagon to a stop in front of Mayfield's General Store, an unpainted false front frame building with spittoons sitting on either side of the double doors and a crude bench placed under a fly-specked window that displayed a variety of tools. He glanced at his wife and muttered, "Well, honey, we're finally here. Now all I have to do is get directions to the ranch."

"Oh, George, do you think we've done the right thing by coming here?" Gloria asked as she shifted her two-year old daughter in her lap and looked around the small dusty town's main street, plank sidewalks and other false front buildings.

Opal, the eldest of their four daughters, watched her mother's reaction and could almost feel her disappointment in learning this would be the nearest town to their new home. Though they'd seen several towns such as this on their trip to Arizona, they'd all hoped to find Wildweed to be something a little different. Something more like they were used to in Memphis. But seeing the looks on all their faces, she knew it was not to be. This was it.

"Of course we have, dear." Her father's voice brought her back to reality. He went on, "Please try to be positive. We have a ranch that is all our own. It has no bank mortgage like the house in Tennessee. We will eventually have cows and horses and in the meantime, we'll make our own living from the land. I'm sure we'll never have to worry about money again." He gave his wife a big grin and glanced at his daughters as he jumped down. "Don't you girls agree with me?"

"Yes, Papa," the girls riding in the back of the wagon said, but they didn't sound as enthusiastic as they did when they first left

Tennessee to claim the ranch George's deceased brother had willed to him.

When the telegraph first arrived from Arizona informing George his brother had died and left all his worldly possessions to him, most of the Barnett family was elated. Only nineteen-year-old Opal was suspicious and she wasn't sure why.

*Other Works From The Pen Of*

## *Agnes Alexander*

**Valissa's Home**  (Sept. 2013)

Valissa Prescott's half-brother has gambled away her Galveston estate, Hartsong and it's been bought by Nathan Stone a hard-nosed cowboy and businessman who owns several businesses in Galveston. Though she thinks she has three weeks to vacate the estate, he arrives early to claim his property. Without money or close relatives she has no choice but to remain at the house until she finds somewhere else to go.

When she realizes she is beginning to fall for this giant of a man who thinks he can bully everyone into doing his will she tries everything she can think of to get away from him. But the one thing she didn't count on was his smoldering desire to keep her in his home.

# OPAL'S FAITH

**Agnes Alexander**

**A Wings ePress, Inc.**

**Western Romance Novel**

# Wings ePress, Inc.

Edited by: Jeanne Smith
Copy Edited by: Leslie Hodges
Senior Editor: Leslie Hodges
Executive Editor: Marilyn Kapp
Cover Artist: Trishia FitzGerald



Wings ePress Books
http://www.wings-press.com

Copyright © 2014 by Lynette Hall Hampton
ISBN  978-1-61309-679-6

Published In the United States Of America

Wings ePress Inc.
3000 N. Rock Road
Newton, KS  67114

## *Dedication*


For my nephew, Dr. Dan A. Hall
Because he loves all my westerns,
And because I love him

## *One*

When the Barnett family reached Wildweed, Arizona, it was around noon on a Thursday. George pulled the wagon to a stop in front of Mayfield's General Store, an unpainted false front frame building with spittoons sitting on either side of the double doors and a crude bench placed under a fly-specked window that displayed a variety of tools. He glanced at his wife and muttered, "Well, honey, we're finally here. Now all I have to do is get directions to the ranch."

"Oh, George, do you think we've done the right thing by coming here?" Gloria asked as she shifted her two-year old daughter in her lap and looked around the small dusty town's main street, plank sidewalks and other false front buildings.

Opal, the eldest of their four daughters, watched her mother's reaction and could almost feel her disappointment in learning this would be the nearest town to their new home. Though they'd seen several towns such as this on their trip to Arizona, they'd all hoped to find Wildweed to be something a little different. Something more like they were used to in Memphis. But seeing the looks on all their faces, she knew it was not to be. This was it.

"Of course we have, dear." Her father's voice brought her back to reality. He went on, "Please try to be positive. We have a ranch that is all our own. It has no bank mortgage like the house in Tennessee. We will eventually have cows and horses and in the meantime, we'll make our own living from the land. I'm sure we'll never have to worry about money again." He gave his wife a big grin and glanced at his daughters as he jumped down. "Don't you girls agree with me?"

"Yes, Papa," the girls riding in the back of the wagon said, but they didn't sound as enthusiastic as they did when they first left Tennessee to claim the ranch George's deceased brother had willed to him.

When the telegraph first arrived from Arizona informing George his brother had died and left all his worldly possessions to him, most of the Barnett family was elated. Only nineteen-year-old Opal was suspicious and she wasn't sure why.

Maybe it was because Uncle Horace, unlike her father, was always dreaming up some scheme that was going to make him wealthy. Or maybe it was because her father, without consulting anyone in the family, decided immediately that they were going to pull up stakes and move to this place they'd never heard of in Arizona. She wouldn't have been more surprised if he'd said he was moving them to a foreign land. Which from the looks of Wildweed, he had.

Though she suspected the family had fallen on hard times and might lose their home near Memphis unless a miracle happened, Opal wasn't prepared for this. She didn't want to leave Tennessee. She wanted to spend the rest of her life on the Mississippi River where she could watch the big white paddle boats slip by weekly. It was her secret dream to one day ride on one of the giant river boats to the different cities up and down the Mississippi and dress like the ladies she'd seen at the railings. She'd even pretended she was one of them as she'd watched the boats dock at one of the many landings. How could she give all her hopes and dreams up to move to some tiny western town where they would surely run into outlaws, and Indians and dangers around every corner?

But without asking anyone, her father had said they were going west and she felt she didn't have a choice but to go along. Of course, she didn't let anyone know her true feelings about the move. As it had always been, her faith in her father and his decisions was unshakable. She knew he felt he was doing the right thing for the family and she was willing to go along with his idea to move to Arizona, regardless of what she herself wanted. Her family was the important thing.

Within two weeks of receiving the wire, George, his wife, and their four daughters had packed the wagon with furniture, food supplies, and bedding and were headed west. Now that they were almost at their destination, Opal didn't feel any better about the move. She still longed for the beautiful grassy riverbank and the familiar surroundings of Tennessee.

Her seventeen-year-old sister, Ruby, seemed to agree with her and was more vocal about the situation. She pointed to a store three doors down from where their wagon was parked. "Do you see that dress-making shop, Opal? It looks like the only place in town where you might buy clothes," she whispered as they sat in the wagon while their father went into the store to ask for directions to the ranch.

Opal couldn't help giving Ruby, who was always aware of how women should dress, a sad smile. "It's nothing like Memphis, is it?"

Ruby's voice turned sarcastic. "Papa said we might find rich husbands here. I think he may have been wrong."

Though a husband was the least of Opal's goals, she knew one was important to her sister. "I'm not sure we'll find any kind of husband here. Much less a rich one."

"I wish we'd never left Memphis." Ruby sounded on the verge of crying.

"We're here, girls, and we have to make the best of it. I don't want you to upset your father by complaining."

"Yes, Mama." Opal squeezed her sister's hand and sighed, but said no more. What could she say? She'd wished all along that they'd stayed in Tennessee.

In a matter of minutes, George returned from the store. "Mr. Mayfield said the ranch is only about seven miles out of town. That's a blessing. We won't have to come too far for supplies when we run low."

"That's good, dear," Gloria said.

Nobody else said anything as the wagon pulled out of Wildweed. Opal was trying to take in her surroundings. There was a bank, a barbershop, a small hotel, a place that looked like it might be a laundry and then what had to be one of those drinking establishments came into view. She knew this because the tinkling of an out-of-tune piano came from inside. As they drew closer she could see a sign nailed on the wall beside the bat-doors. It read: 'The Cactus Saloon, the best place in Arizona Territory to find women you can't tame and men who keep trying.' Opal had never seen such a thing and her eyes grew wide as she stared at it. Feeling self-conscious for looking at it so long, she let her eyes drop to a couple of cowboys dressed in dirty pants, wrinkled shirts and worn boots leaning on posts in front of the saloon. They both stared at the Barnett family as they passed.

Opal bit her lip and turned her head away as one of the cowboys smiled at her and touched his hat. She'd heard of saloons, but in Memphis they'd been in an area where her father never permitted the girls to go. He said only men looking for trouble visited such establishments.

As they pulled toward the edge of town, she tried to forget the leering eyes of the cowboy who'd noticed her. It was easy when she saw a fuzzy little dog playing with a young boy in front of a blacksmith shop. The little boy stopped his play and stared at the Barnetts. She smiled at him, but he ducked his head and ran into the shop without acknowledging her.

On the ride to the ranch, nobody had much to say. Opal was busy trying to take in the vastness and the loneliness of the Arizona prairie and she figured everyone else was doing the same.

The family was still subdued when they finally reached the ranch; even her father seemed a little taken aback. Though he looked as if he wanted to apologize for bringing them here, he said, "We've arrived, folks."

"It's not much pretty," ten-year-old, Pearl said as Gloria handed the baby to her husband, then climbed from the wagon. Pearl jumped from the back, not waiting for her father to help her.

George handed the baby back to Gloria and walked to the back of the wagon. "Let me help my beautiful jewels out so they can explore our new home."

"Down," two-year-old Sapphire said as she wiggled out of her mother's arms. As soon as her feet touched ground, she called out in an excited voice, "Flower," and headed toward a bloom growing at the edge of the steps to the rundown log cabin.

"Sapphire, come back," her mother called.

The baby turned and gave her mother a puzzled look.

"I've heard there are a lot of snakes in Arizona. I don't want you to get on one in these weeds."

"I'll get her, Mama." Ruby stepped to the ground and let go of her father's hand. She ran to Sapphire and grabbed her little sister's arm. "I'll walk with you to the pretty flower, Sapphire."

Taking her father's hand and climbing out of the wagon last, Opal had to fight back tears when she took her first close look at the small cabin. It appeared like something one might find on one of the poorest farms back in Tennessee. The structure couldn't have more than four small rooms and the front porch was leaning to the left. The yard leading up to the house was almost covered in weeds with strange flowers trying to peep through the overgrown mess here and there.

She let her eyes drift toward a barn which seemed to be in a little better shape. It was big and to the side was a fenced corral, though several of the rails of the wooden fence had fallen sideways to the ground. She figured the nails had pulled loose. A building had been started near the corral, but she didn't have any idea what it was meant to be. Only a few upright logs of the frame were standing. There was an outhouse several yards from the cabin and what looked like it had once been a pig pen off to the right side of it. Behind the house were a chicken coop which was almost falling down, an overgrown vegetable garden and a well. Of course there were no chickens or any other livestock that she could see.

"Well, girls, shall we take a look inside?" Gloria turned to her daughters. "Maybe it'll be nicer in there."

It wasn't. The well-worn sofa was on its side and the two rocking chairs were shoved against the wall. A rag rug had been rolled up and left in the middle of the floor. A small round table sat under the window, but it was bare. Everything was covered in several layers of dust and the floor and walls were dirty.

The kitchen corner of the room held a crudely built table and four ladder back chairs. One with the seat rotted out. Not only was the iron cook stove filthy, it was one of the first models produced. It was waist high, but didn't have a warming oven above it. Opal wondered if it would set the entire place ablaze when a fire was built inside it. She felt a little guilty because she almost hoped it would. Then maybe her father would see the foolishness of leaving Memphis and decide to go home.

Opal looked from the kitchen to her mother and saw Gloria biting her lip. There was a single tear sliding down her right cheek. Moving beside her, Opal said, "I've got faith that it'll be all right, Mama. We can make this place livable. It may take a while, but we're Barnett women. We can do it."

Gloria squeezed Opal's hand. "Thank you, honey. Your faith has given me courage. You're right. It's going to take some hard work, but we can do it. We can't let your father know how we wish he'd never decided to come here. It would break his heart."

"I know. We have to support him."

Gloria patted Opal's arm, removed her bonnet and smiled. "All right, daughters, since we have a lot of work to do before it gets dark, let's get started. Pearl, please go ask your father to bring my trunk in. I have enough aprons for all of us in it. Also ask him to find a broom, a mop and a bucket in the wagon. Opal, please see if the well is safe enough for you to draw some water so we can start scrubbing this place." She looked around again. "I won't trust this stove until it's cleaned and checked out. Your father can check it later, but in the meantime I'll have him build a fire in the yard so we can have hot water to clean. I'll also get the big cooking pot we've used on our journey here and have him set it over the fire. That way we can cook a stew while we're cleaning. Ruby, when Pearl gets back, I'll put her in charge of watching Sapphire. We'll need you to help us with the cleaning. In the meantime, keep a sharp eye on her. You know how she likes to explore new places."

"Mama, this place is awful. There's no way we can get it clean."

"It's not as bad as it looks, Ruby. Now, don't argue with me. Do as I asked."

Ruby looked as if she might cry, but she only muttered, "Yes, Mama."

In a short time the Barnett women began to work in the kitchen, the area they deemed the most important to get clean first.

~ * ~

After getting the things Gloria wanted, building the fire and promising to check out the stove, George unhitched the two work horses and walked them to the barn. He brushed them and turned them into stalls. He was glad there was still some feed left in the loft to give them, but he knew he'd have to go back into Wildweed to get more in a day or so.

While he was in the barn he checked out the structure and decided it was sound. As he came out, he glanced at the corral. It was in pretty good shape, too. None of the fencing that had fallen seemed to be splintered or damaged. It would just have to be nailed back to the posts.

Knowing there was nothing he could do about it at the moment, he headed toward the house. Realizing what miserable shape the cabin was in, he tried to push away the guilt he felt for bringing his family to this godforsaken place. Why didn't he check further before making the rash decision to move? He should have known that anything his brother owned would not be a fit place to bring his wife and daughters, but when he'd first gotten the news of the inheritance, he was thrilled. He felt it was the answer to a prayer. In his mind he could only envision it as a wonderful place where his family could have a real home of their own. One the bank wouldn't ever be foreclosing on.

Of course, he'd never told his family they were on the verge of being put out on the street in Tennessee. He'd secretly been scouring the county to find a job so they could pay the back taxes. It had been to no avail. Mr. Dilworth's threat was proving to be true. There wasn't much demand for a bookkeeper who had been fired. The fact that the bank let him go because he was questioning some of their dealings he considered unlawful, didn't matter. Even the sheriff had laughed when George tried to tell him what was going on. "You know Mr. Dilworth would never abide anybody doing such a thing in his bank, George. I'm surprised you even mentioned it," the lawman had said.

Of course it wasn't long until Dilworth had heard about his visit to the sheriff's office and demanded his resignation. His parting words still rang in George's ears. The overweight man with a full beard had leaned back in his chair, crossed his arms across his huge mid-section and said, "I'm surprised you'd do this to me, George Barnett. I intend to see that you'll never find another job in banking in Memphis or even in the whole state of Tennessee. Nobody tells lies about Elroy D. Dilworth and gets away with it." He'd then laughed a sinister laugh and added, "Even if the lies were true."

George was thankful he'd suspected what might happen and had managed to take his savings from the bank before his dismissal. It wasn't a lot, but added to the amount they'd gotten for selling the furniture they couldn't bring with them, it would get them by for a while. Until he could make this ranch support them, anyway.

Going back to the wagon, he found the box which contained his tools. Pulling them out, he went into the house. "I thought I'd go ahead and check the stove for you. Then I can start unloading the rest of the furniture."

"Thank you, dear. Just be careful. I scrubbed the floor in that part of the kitchen and it's still wet."

He looked around the room. "I'm amazed at what you've managed to accomplish in such a short time."

Gloria smiled. "It's beginning to look better in here already. I sent Opal and Ruby into the bedrooms to drag out the mattresses. I'm sure they need a good airing if they're even useable."

"Where are Pearl and Sapphire?"

"They're picking flowers in the back yard."

He nodded.

"Before you start on the stove, will you get the curtains down from the windows? They're full of dust and I want to put them outside. I'll have to see if they can be salvaged. If they can, I want to wash them and the widows before they are put back up."

"I'll get them in a minute." He walked up to his wife and put his arm around her shoulder. "I hope I made the right decision by coming here, Gloria. At the time I didn't think I had any other choice."

She leaned into his arm. "I know you didn't, darling. Whether you knew it or not, I realized things were going from bad to worse in Tennessee."

"Thank you for being so understanding."

"Of course, I understand. Now you just wait and see. Everything is going to be fine. By the time we go to bed tonight, you won't recognize this place."

He leaned down and kissed her. "I love you."

"I love you, too, George. I always have and I always will."

He looked into her soft brown eyes and his heart swelled. Though they'd been married almost twenty years, he loved her even more than he did the day they said their wedding vows. He was a lucky man. Not every man could say that about his wife, but he knew without a doubt there were no problems they couldn't overcome as long as they faced them together.

He kissed her again then turned to remove the curtains from the windows.

## *Two*

Jace Renwick paid the watching eyes no attention as he reined his horse up to the hitching rail that ran in front of the Cactus Saloon in Wildweed. He continued to ignore the curious bystanders as they watched him slide his six-foot-two frame out of the saddle, throw the reins around the hitching rail, adjust his gun belt and glance down the dusty main street.

Wildweed was much like most of the small towns he'd seen in his search through the territories. Of the people residing in and around here, he figured there were the good citizens of the town as well as a few bad. Probably a town drunk and a couple of men whose wives tried to run all the social events as well as running their husbands; the hardworking shop keepers and their families; maybe a doctor who also served as the barber and of course the saloon owner with his bevy of girls who were there to entertain the single as well as some of the more adventurous married men.

But Jace wasn't interested in any of that at the moment. He was hungry and he knew that usually a saloon served the best food in town. And after going for almost two days without eating, a hot meal was what he wanted.

It wasn't that Jace didn't have food in his saddle bag, such as it was, but he hadn't taken the time to stop and fix anything to eat. It was as if some unforeseen force was at his back pushing him toward his goal and his goal had been the same as it had been for the last eight years: locate the man who was behind the brutal killing of his father in the Colorado gold field and then claimed to the law they'd been attacked, thus escaping arrest.

Since Jace was in school in Baltimore, where he lived with his mother when the murder happened, his father's partners had filed for the claim and were granted sole ownership. Though he heard the mine produced a few thousand dollars of gold, it was some consolation to him that it didn't turn out to be the rich strike the partners had thought it would be. It wasn't long until the partners of the murdered man sold what was left of the dwindling mine and went in different directions.

Jace figured there was nothing he could do to establish his legal claim on his father's share of the mine and, since there was little profit anyway, he didn't even try. The fact that he would inherit nothing from his father didn't bother him. He knew if there came a time when he needed more than the money he brought west with him, he could work it out on a ranch where they were often looking for an extra hand. What actually made him furious about the whole situation was the fact that at least one of the men his father had trusted was getting away with murder. Though he hadn't seen his father since he was seven years old, Jace vowed he'd not rest until he got even with the scoundrel who had killed the man. Even if the killer or killers didn't get rich from the mine, someone had profited from David Renwick's death and Jace knew he was close to finally discovering the truth.

When at the age of nineteen, Jace had arrived in Colorado to begin his investigation into his father's death, he found it wasn't going to be as easy as he first thought. Though for nine years he'd been following one dead lead after another, he felt sure things were finally going to pan out. Two days earlier, he learned the man who had committed the actual murder was living in or near Wildweed with or close to some of his relatives—a sister or a daughter and maybe a brother. Since so much time had passed, there could also be a wife and several children for all he knew. But none of that mattered. The man who he was after still needed to pay for his crimes.

With the knowledge of the man's location, Jace felt he couldn't reach the town fast enough. He plodded forward for those two days without any thought to his own well- being. He survived on chewing a few sticks of jerky, munching on hardtack and drinking from the canteen whenever he knew he had to stop to rest his horse.

Now he was in Wildweed and he realized he had to play it smart. He couldn't come right out and accuse the man without solid proof. This, he figured, probably would have to be a confession from the perpetrator, and to get the man to confess was going to take a while. In the meantime, he figured it would be best if nobody in town knew why he was there. He would take it slow and make sure there was no slip up. He'd waited all these years for his revenge. He could wait a little longer.

As he shoved open the bat-doors and entered the Cactus Saloon, he hoped they'd serve good food like many of the saloons he'd frequented through the years. He had a hankering for a big steak and a mound of potatoes along with a huge pot of strong black coffee.

Several of the patrons turned to look at him as he strode to the bar. Again, this was nothing unusual. His height, his dark features and the way he carried himself let everyone know he was a man who knew who he was and where he was going. Adding to the mystique was the fact that these small towns didn't get a lot of visitors unless they were gun slingers, outlaws on the run or strangers only passing through. Jace was none of those things, but he had no intention of enlightening the town folk. They could think what they wanted as far as he was concerned.

"What can I do for you, big fellow?" The bartender eyed him.

"I'll have a beer, then a steak if you have it."

The bartender filled a mug with the cheap beer. "Go through the double doors on the left. We keep the eating area away from the men who are seriously drinking and looking for more exciting entertainment than food."

"Thanks." Jace laid money on the bar, picked up his beer and ambled toward the doors. "I'll eat my fill, go to the bathhouse then I'll come back for a room and that exciting entertainment you mentioned."

The bartender nodded and gave Jace a knowing look.

The smell of cooking beef filled his nostrils as he entered the eating area. His dark eyes widened and he did something he seldom ever did. He grinned. It was going to be a good night.

~ * ~

The first rays of sun were beginning to creep through the window when Jace opened his eyes. Glancing at the other side of the bed he'd rented in the saloon's upstairs, he was glad to see he was alone. Though the buxom female had been comforting last night, he wasn't interested in a woman at the moment. He had things to do that morning. He was ready to pursue his quest for revenge for his father's death and forget about anything else. He would get out of there and ask questions to put his plan into motion, but he realized those questions had to be discreet. He figured he'd start at the general store. Since everyone in the area eventually had to deal with them, usually the proprietors of such an establishment were up on whatever was happening in town.

Swinging his long legs off the bed, he moved to the small dresser. Of course the water in the pitcher was cold, but he didn't mind. He often bathed and shaved in cold water on the trail. After finishing those tasks, he dressed, put on his hat and gun belt and headed downstairs to the eating room. He couldn't help hoping the breakfast food would be as good as the supper had been.

~ * ~

The smell of frying bacon woke Opal. She nudged Ruby. "Wake up, sister. Mama is cooking already. We should be helping her."

"Oh, dear." Ruby sat up and yawned. "I think I could sleep until noon."

"So could I, but we can't let the folks down. As the oldest two, we have to help out all we can."

"I know."

Opal reached for her dress and looked around at the cot on the wall next to the door. "Pearl, wake up," she said. "We need to get busy."

Pearl turned over and her voice was weak when she said, "All right. I'm getting up."

"I know it's hard, honey, but we promised each other before we went to sleep last night that we'd do everything we could to make things easier for Mama while we were here." Opal picked up her hairbrush and began brushing her long auburn hair. "Let's hurry and take care of our personal needs so we can get busy."

"If you insist. I'll race you two to the privy," Pearl said and reached for her dress as Opal handed Ruby the brush.

In a matter of minutes, the three of them rushed through the kitchen and out the back door. Re-entering they saw their mama at the stove and Sapphire sitting at their papa's feet playing with the rag doll she often carried. Their father was bent over a piece of paper on the table. He had a pencil in his hand and Opal wondered what he was writing.

Glancing up, he grinned at them and answered her question without knowing she'd wanted to ask it. "I'm making a list of supplies your mama says I have to go into town and pick up today. Is there anything either of you needs?"

"I don't know of anything, Papa," Ruby said through a yawn.

"Neither do I," Opal added.

Pearl bit her lip. "I'd sure like to have a peppermint stick."

George grinned and winked at her. "I think I used the word 'need' when I asked the question."

They all laughed and Pearl turned pink.

"If you're about through with the list, George, I'm ready to put breakfast on the table." Gloria turned with a plate full of bacon.

"I guess I have everything down." George folded the paper and put it in his shirt pocket. "If we think of anything else, we can add it."

"Are you going to town alone, Papa?" Ruby asked.

"I planned to, but your mother thinks you or Opal should come with me."

"I'll go," They both said almost in unison.

George laughed. "We'll decide after breakfast who'll accompany me."

They said nothing more because they both knew he'd make his own decision. Opal had enough faith in her father to know he'd make the right one.

Gloria put the plate of bacon on the table and turned to get the pan bread she'd fried. "You know your father is no good at getting the kinds of groceries we need. He's likely to come back with a hand full of potatoes and a small sack of flour. He has no idea what it takes to feed this family."

George chuckled. "Am I really that bad?"

"Yes, dear, you are. You know I love you dearly, but I'm the one who has always gone to the market. Opal and Ruby are almost as good as I am at shopping."

"Then it's settled." George took a drink of the coffee Gloria poured for him. "As soon as we finish eating, one of the girls and I will head for town."

Gloria took her seat at the table and the family said grace. Since there were only three good chairs, Pearl sat with the parents. Opal and Ruby make plates and went to sit on the couch. The room was so small, Opal still felt as if they were eating with the family.

"It would sure be nice to have some eggs to go with this meat," George said as he took a bite

"Just be thankful we had enough bacon left from our trip out here to cook this morning." Gloria smiled at him. "

"I'm not complaining, dear." He grinned back at her. She cocked an eye at him and he added, "Well, maybe just a little."

They all laughed and were soon discussing which daughter would accompany him to town. No decision had been made when there was the sound of approaching horses outside.

"I'll see who that can be." George stood, put his napkin down and headed for the front door.

"I want to see who it is." Ruby got up.

Opal also stood. "We probably should stay in the house and look out the window."

Gloria wrinkled her forehead. "I guess that'll be all right."

Ruby nodded and the two girls eased to the front window, but tried to stay out of sight. Two riders on horseback reined up near the porch. One was a middle-aged, overweight man. The other, a young boy who looked about Pearl's age.

"Hello, gentlemen," George said.

"Howdy," the man said. "Name's Cletus Finch. I'm assuming yours is Barnett." He didn't introduce the boy.

Opal noticed, from her place at the window, there was no problem hearing and understanding the entire conversation or seeing the man and the boy. She wondered if he was the man's son.

"That's right. George Barnett." Her father nodded to the men.

"Well, Barnett, I was surprised to learn you were here. My partner and me own the ranch that joins yours on the left just over the creek and we'd planned on buying this one to add to our spread. Since you own the creek, we could use the water as well as the grazing land for our herd."

"Had you made arrangements with my brother?"

Cletus shook his head. "I heard about his death and we were going to have the bank get in touch with his heir and make an offer. I didn't know you'd already pulled up stakes and moved here and neither did my partner."

"News must travel fast in Wildweed. We only arrived yesterday."

"Since you're here, maybe we can take care of the business in person. The bank is out of it now." Finch pushed his hat back.

"What business is that, Mr. Finch?"

Cletus Finch frowned. "Why, my buying this ranch, of course and don't think I don't have the authority to speak for my partner, 'cause I do."

"Oh, Opal," Ruby whispered. "If Papa sells this place, we can take the money and go home to Tennessee."

"That'd be wonderful." When she said it, Opal knew it would never happen. She knew her father's heart was set on making this their home. She had an inkling why, but she wasn't positive so she didn't tell Ruby her suspicions.

Their father shook his head. "I don't plan to sell this ranch, Mr. Finch. Not to you and your partner nor anyone else."

"Why not? You don't look like much of a rancher."

"I'm not a rancher, sir, but I have a strong back and I'm willing to learn."

"Takes more than that to be a rancher, Barnett." Cletus had a sneer in his voice.

"It probably does, but I plan to give it a try. My family and I came out here for a new start and that's what we're going to attempt to achieve."

Finch looked disgusted. "Then give it a try, greenhorn. I'd planned to give you a fair price for this sorry piece of land, but after you fail in a few months, we'll be able to pick this place up from the bank for almost nothing."

Before George could answer, Finch swung his horse's head around, spurred him and headed out of the yard. The boy, who hadn't spoken a word, turned and followed him.

As soon as George came inside, Ruby blurted, "Why didn't you sell this place to him, Papa?"

Opal watched as her father gave Ruby a sad look. "Because this is now our home, honey."

Ruby started to say something else, but Opal took her arm to stop her. "Let's go finish our breakfast."

~ * ~

An hour later, Opal walked over to the well in the backyard to draw another bucket of water. She'd already filled the water trough in the corral so her father's tired horses would have a drink when they returned. Now she drew her sixth bucket and began filling the big black wash pot sitting on the fire. At this moment, she wished she'd been the one to go into town with Papa, but Ruby had wanted to go and Opal had seen no reason not to let her. Of course, she hadn't known at the time that her mother intended to wash everything they found in the house plus many of the things they'd brought from Tennessee. If she had known, she may not have been as ready to let her sister leave.

"Mama, where are we going to hang all these clothes?"

"Don't worry, honey. I put clothes line down on your father's list. He'll string us up something when he gets back. In the meantime, we'll put them on the larger bushes and over the porch rail. I scrubbed it this morning so the clothes should be fine."

Opal shrugged and continued carrying buckets of water.

By the time they had boiled the clothes, rinsed them in another tub of cold water and spread them out on the bushes and the porch rail, it was just past noon. Sapphire came running up to the porch with Pearl on her heels.

"Hungry." Everyone in the family knew what the baby meant, even when she talked in one-word sentences.

"I'm hungry, too, baby." Gloria reached down and took Sapphire's hand. She looked around at Opal and Pearl. "Let's all go inside and eat something. The stew I put on this morning should be ready."

As they started into the house, Opal paused. "I think I hear a horse coming."

Gloria frowned. "It's too early for your father and Ruby. I'm sure they haven't had time to go to town and back."

"Maybe it's that man who came earlier." Opal peered into the distance and saw a lone rider headed toward the house. "If it is, he's alone this time."

"What should we do?" Gloria looked confused. "I wish I hadn't sent George to town."

"It'll be fine, Mama. Take Pearl and Sapphire inside. I'll find out what he wants." Opal kept her voice confident and calm. She didn't want her mother to know how scared she was or how she wished her father were here to take care of this stranger.

### *Three*

When George pulled the wagon to a stop in front of the general store, he wrapped the reins around the brake stick then came around to help Ruby down. She climbed the one step to the plank walkway running the length of the building and paused at the door to wait for her father. When he was at her side, they went into the store together.

"Well, howdy, Mr. Barnett," the plump woman behind the counter said. "My husband said you come by yesterday to get directions to Horace's ranch. Sorry I weren't here to meet you."

"Yes, ma'am, I did come by and I'm sorry we didn't meet, too." He removed his hat and added, "I'd like to introduce you to one of my daughters, Ruby."

"Howdy, Ruby, I'm Hilda Mayfield."

"Hello, Mrs. Mayfield." Ruby smiled at her.

"Well, Mr. Barnett, if Ruby is one of your daughters, just how many do you have?"

"I have four. Opal is my oldest. Ruby comes next, then there are Pearl and Sapphire. I call them my four jewels."

"If they're all as pretty as this one, I can sure understand why you feel they're jewels. I bet the young men in town are going to think so, too." Hilda laughed and Ruby turned pink.

George ignored the remark and said, "My wife gave me a list of supplies to get and I need to pick up a couple of tools and some horse feed."

"I probably have the tools you want, but you'll have to go to the feed store to get what you need for your horse."

He looked puzzled and she added, "It's down the street and to the left behind the livery. Matter of fact, my husband Floyd is down there getting some feed for our horse. We have to keep him fed so he'll be able to pull the wagon to make our deliveries."

"Thank, you." He smiled at her. "Also, my wife wanted to have eggs for breakfast and for baking. We'll buy a couple of dozen here, but we need to get some chickens of our own. You wouldn't happen to know where we could buy some laying hens, would you?"

"You might be able to get a few from the Neelys. They supply the café with chickens, but I bet they'd be willing to sell a few live ones." She laughed out loud. "I don't think old man Neely would ever turn down a quick dollar."

"Could you tell me how to get to his place?"

She gave him directions to a place only a mile out of town.

"If I'm not being too presumptuous, do you know where I might buy a milk cow?"

She laughed. "Try the Anderson Farm. It's right next to the Neelys. Fact is their wives are sisters. They'll probably be able to fix you up."

He thanked her and turned to Ruby. "Why don't I go get the feed while you gather the supplies? I won't be gone long and I'll get my tools when I get back. Then we'll see if we can find the Neely and the Anderson places."

Ruby nodded and began to look around. She hoped she'd be able to find what her mother needed here. This general store certainly was no comparison to the one they frequented in Memphis. She almost wished she hadn't come to town with her father. This place only made her more homesick for Tennessee.

~ * ~

Opal watched closely as the beautiful red horse with the black tail and mane approached the house. The rider sat tall in the saddle and looked as if he knew exactly where he was headed. The closer he came, the more her heart pounded. He had his black hat pulled down almost covering his eyes and there was a gun hanging from his right side. There was little else she could distinguish about him at the distance and her thoughts ran wild. What if he were here to cause the family harm? What could she do to protect her mother and sisters? Her father had the shotgun in the wagon and there were no other weapons in the house.

The stranger brought the horse to a stop about fifteen feet from her. He touched the brim of his hat. "Howdy, ma'am. It's mighty hot today. I was wondering if I might get some water for my horse and maybe a drink for myself."

She had a feeling this was a request travelers in the West often made when they spotted a ranch or a farm. She also knew that good manners wouldn't let her refuse, so she nodded and wondered why her heart seemed to flip over in her chest. "There's a trough down by the corral. That's where Papa waters his horses."

"Is your pa around? I'd like to have a few words with him."

She bit her lip. Did she dare tell him Papa was in town? Finally she said, "He's not here at the moment, but I expect him back at any time."

"Good. Then I'll wait for him"

Now what was she going to do or say to him? Finally she stammered, "Would you like that drink of water for yourself now? I have a fresh bucket sitting on the well."

"Thank you. That would be nice." He climbed down from the horse and dropped its reins to the ground.

It was then she noticed how tall and muscular he was. His tight-fitting blue chambray shirt showed wide shoulders tapering down to a trim waist. The denims he wore looked as if they were his second skin. Opal was shocked to realize she felt warm just looking at him.

Then he removed his hat and she almost gasped. Though he was very good looking, he certainly wasn't the most handsome man she'd ever seen. Yet, there was something about his dark features that made her get even warmer inside. She'd never felt this way about a strange man and she didn't understand it.

Looking away, she muttered, "There's a dipper hanging on the side of the well."

"Thank you, again." He gave her a smile and his dark eyes seemed to linger on her body. "By the way, my name's Jace Renwick."

"I'm Opal Barnett." Why was he looking at her so hard? She wasn't used to being looked over in such a manner.

"Pleased to meet you, Miss Barnett." He raised an eyebrow and his dark eyes locked with her deep blue ones. "It is Miss, isn't it?"

"Yes," was all she managed to say.

He nodded, gave her another half grin and walked toward the well. "I'll get my water then I'll take care of my horse and if it's all right, I'll wait at the barn for your father."

"That'll be fine." Her heart pounded as she watched him drink deeply from the well water then amble toward the barn leading his horse. Though it crossed her mind, she didn't tell him that he might have a long wait.

She was glad she'd filled the horse trough that morning before drawing water for the laundry. She'd realized her father's horses would need a drink when they arrived back, but she hadn't counted on sharing the water with this handsome stranger.

Knowing she couldn't stand there and watch him, she turned and went into the house.

"Who is that man, Opal?" Her mother asked as soon as she was in the door.

"He said his name was Jace Renwick, not that that means anything to us. He wanted to water his horse and get a drink for himself."

Her mother frowned. "Is he going to leave as soon as he waters his horse?"

"He said he wanted to talk to Papa."

"Papa's in town," Pearl butted in.

"I know. Mr. Renwick said he'd wait for him at the barn. I didn't tell him that it would be a while before Papa came home."

Gloria glanced out the door. "It kind of makes me nervous with a strange man being here and your father gone."

"Maybe he'll get tired of waiting and leave, Mama." Opal hoped those words would waylay her mother's fears, but she didn't believe them as she said them. From her first impression of the man, she got the feeling that once Mr. Renwick set his mind to something, he'd see it through. She wasn't sure how she got this feeling. It was just there.

Though neither he nor his horse needed water, Jace had a drink, then led China to the trough for a few sips. Afterward he moved him to the corral and looped the reins over one of the standing posts. He removed the saddle and hung it over the fence where the rails weren't broken. He couldn't help noticing how rundown the place looked. He'd learned in town this morning that the owner had recently died and his greenhorn brother and his family had not only inherited the place, but had moved in the day before. He wasn't sure the family's trip from the east was worth the trouble to claim the inheritance. It would take a lot of backbreaking work to make this ranch turn a profit. Work he was sure a tenderfoot wasn't able to put in, even if he were willing.

But the people on this ranch weren't his problem. He had his own objective and these naïve people were unwittingly going to help him achieve it, though they didn't or wouldn't realize they were doing it.

Stepping inside the barn, not only to escape the extra warm spring day, but to look around, he was pleased to find the structure solid, with no signs of leakage from the roof or the walls. There were four stalls and the back doors would give access from both directions. He climbed the attached ladder to the loft and walked around. The boards were fine with the exception of one or two that needed nailing down.

Returning to the main floor, he went to the room which interested him the most. It was built on the right side of the barn before the stalls began. He pushed the door open and entered. He was surprised to find the room larger than he'd thought it would be.

As he did in other areas of the barn, he tested the walls for stability. They were as strong as the rest of the building. He walked to the window and looked out. There was an unobstructed view of the house and the approaching road.

Finding this to his liking, he muttered, "With a little cleaning and a bed built in the back wall, this will be ideal. Yep, for the next few months this will be my bedroom."

~ * ~

Gloria turned from the stove and frowned. "What's that noise I keep hearing?"

Opal glanced outside. "Oh, my goodness."

"What?" Her mother looked frightened.

"It's that Mr. Renwick. He's nailing the boards back to the posts at the corral."

Her mother hurried to the door. "I wonder why in the world he's doing that."

"Can I go help him?" Pearl rushed to the door.

Putting her hand on Pearl's shoulder to keep her from going outside, her mother said, "Absolutely not. What in the world gave you such an idea?"

"All I ever get to do is look after Sapphire. I'd like to do some work for a change." A pouty look crossed her face.

"Looking after your little sister is an important job, honey."

She sighed. "I know, but I'd still like to do something else sometime."

Opal ignored her sister. "Since Mr. Renwick has elected to work on the fence while he waits for Papa, it seems we can relax. He must not be here to cause us trouble, so why don't I go clean the windows in the bedrooms? We didn't get around to them yesterday."

"Can I help?" Pearl asked.

"Go ahead." Gloria glanced at the baby. "Sapphire will be fine in here with me while I'm cooking."

"Cookie," Sapphire blurted and tugged her mother's skirt.

"No, sweetheart, I said cooking, not cookie. You play."

Laughing, Opal and Pearl left the kitchen.

~ * ~

Jace was hot and sweat was running down his chest and back. He knew he'd be cooler with his shirt off, but decided against removing it. He knew to stay on this ranch he had to earn the good will of the family living here. He wasn't sure if the women in the house would appreciate him exposing his upper body if they happened to look out and saw him naked to the waist. Though he'd found the chestnut-haired young woman who had given him water extremely attractive, he knew he could never act on those thoughts. Anyway, she seemed to be pretty uptight and the last thing he needed was to have a family member thinking he was a womanizer. He'd continue to find his women in town and keep his thoughts and actions at bay while here.

Besides, what he'd learned about the family in town this morning was sketchy. The woman in the general store told him the father's brother had died and left the ranch to the man and his family, but she didn't know where they were from except that it was somewhere back east. She only knew their name was Barnett.

He couldn't help wondering why the Barnetts thought coming here would be a better choice for a place to live than staying back east. This rundown ranch certainly wouldn't be his first choice of a place to settle down. That was, if he ever had a chance to settle down, which right then didn't seem like much of a possibility. He had too much to accomplish at this point in his twenty-eight years.

Shaking those thoughts away, he picked up another board and held it against the fence post. At least they'd have a corral when he finished. And it looked to him like he'd get the job done today. He wondered why the man of the house was staying so long in town, but he knew he'd get his answer soon enough. There was a wagon coming up the road.

Glancing at it, he knew he had time to nail one more board to the post before the wagon arrived in the yard. He only hoped his hard work would be appreciated enough to convince the new ranch owner to welcome him as a hand to work on the place, at least until he managed to deal with the man who killed his father. He figured he could talk Barrett into it, because from the looks of things, he sure needed somebody around here who knew what had to be done.

~ * ~

George pulled the horses to a stop in the side yard near the back porch. There was a milk cow tied to the back of the wagon. He frowned when he watched the stranger at the corral put his hammer down and head toward them.

"Who is that man, Papa?"

"I don't know, Ruby, but you go on in the house and I'll find out."

"He's handsome. Why can't I stay and meet him?" She eyed the stranger.

"Do as I say, daughter."

"Oh, all right." She shrugged, climbed down and headed toward the door, but she didn't seem happy about it.

"Mr. Barnett," Jace removed his hat and held out his hand as he reached George. "Name's Jace Renwick. I heard you could use someone to help you around here."

George took his hand. "I don't know who told you that, Mr. Renwick, but I'm in no position to hire anyone."

"I understand you moved from the East and wasn't familiar with ranching."

"That's true, but as I said, I'm not financially able to hire help at this time."

"I'm not looking for pay, sir. All I want is a place to sleep and a decent meal a couple of times a day."

"As you can see, the cabin is small. It only has two bedrooms. My wife and I and the baby sleep in one of them. My three older daughters sleep in the other one. There's no place to put you up, Mr. Renwick."

"I wasn't expecting to sleep in the house, sir. The barn will be fine. I don't even have to eat in the house. I can take my meals outside on the porch."

George frowned again. "You don't look like a man who is down and out, but I guess I could be wrong."

"I'm not exactly down and out. I'm more tired. I've been hunting a lost person for a long time and I need to rest. I figured your place would be a good place to do that." When George said nothing, he went on, "In fact, I think it would work out well for both of us. I don't mind hard work, and I know what it takes to put a ranch on its feet. I would be glad to show you what you need to do."

"You're right about me not knowing what needs doing around here. I was a bank accountant in Memphis. This is my first experience with living on a ranch."

"Then, Mr. Barnett, it looks like we need each other." Again Jace reached out his hand. "Do we have a deal?"

George hesitated. "Do you have any references, Mr. Renwick?"

Jace dropped his hand and shook his head. "No. You'll just have to take my word that I'm who I say I am. Of course, if you stay in the West you'll soon learn that a man's word and a handshake is all that's needed to make a deal."

George thought a minute. He remembered the people in Memphis who he'd checked on and thought were honest and how they turned out to be only interested in how they could use the bank's money for their personal pleasure.

He had a good feeling about this Renwick fellow, even if there were no paper references. He offered his hand. "Then Mr. Renwick, I'll trust that you're a man of your word unless you prove otherwise."

Jace grinned and took the hand. "You won't be sorry, Mr. Barnett."

"There's one condition. My name is George and I prefer you use it when you talk to me."

Jace's eyebrow went up and he nodded. "And you'll call me Jace."

"Now that that's settled, help me put these boxes of kitchen supplies on the porch and then we'll pull the wagon down to the barn, find a stall for the cow and unload the feed."

"You don't want me to carry the supplies inside?"

"No. The women will see to them."

"What about that crate? I see you have some chickens."

"I guess we better leave them crated until I check the coop. It may need some work before I turn them loose."

## *Four*

As soon as George entered the house, the women began asking questions. He laughed. "Please, one at a time. I can't understand when you all talk at once. First, let your mother have her say."

"We're all curious, dear. Who is that man and what does he want?"

"His name is Jace Renwick and he's our new hired hand."

"Hired for what, Papa?" Opal blurted as an unusual shiver ran down her spine.

"He's working for room and board and he's going to help us get this ranch up and running as it should be."

"Does he know how to run a ranch?" Gloria asked.

"He says he does."

"Opal gave him water," Pearl said.

"I know. He told me that while we were unloading the wagon in the barn."

"When are we going to get to meet him?" Ruby asked. "He's awfully good looking."

Her father frowned at her. "He'll be in for supper, but you keep thoughts like that to yourself. He's much too old for you."

"He'll be eating with us?" Gloria's eyes got big.

"Yes, honey. His meals are included and though he offered to eat on the porch, I didn't figure you wanted to have him eat out there. Besides, if he eats with us, we can get to know him and him us."

"Why doesn't he come in now and meet us?" Pearl frowned.

"Because he's working on the chicken coop." George looked at Gloria. "Mrs. Mayfield at the general store told me about a man who sold chickens. Ruby and I went by his place and we bought a half dozen hens and a rooster. We also bought a milk cow. As soon as we get them settled, we should be having milk and eggs for breakfast."

"Eggs," Sapphire muttered.

George reached down, picked her up and swung her in the air. "Yes, eggs, my pretty little one. How do you like that?"

Sapphire giggled.

He put her down. "Now, ladies, I think I should get back out there and help Jace finish that chicken coop before supper."

"What do you think the man will want to eat, George?" Gloria looked worried. "I cooked beans with ham today. Reckon he'll like that?"

He leaned over and kissed her forehead. "My dear wife, he'll be like the rest of us. He'll like anything you cook."

"But…"

"No buts, honey. Just fix whatever you want to." He looked at the rest of them. "Now, girls, I hope I only have to tell you one time that Jace Renwick is working here and he's not husband material for any of you."

"Papa!" Opal looked shocked. "How could you suggest such a thing?"

"Didn't you look at the man when you gave him water, Opal?" Ruby stared at her sister. "I could tell all the way across the yard that he's very handsome."

"Your papa told you that that'd be enough of that kind of talk, Ruby." Her mother gave her a hard look. "Now get Mr. Jace Renwick's looks off your mind and let's finish cooking supper."

Neva Greenwood came through the door of the general store and glanced around. With the exception of the young man behind the counter, it was as deserted as she expected it to be this time of day.

"Hello, Neva." The guy gave her a lopsided grin. "What are you doing here?"

"That's a fine way to greet a lady who came in just to say hello to you." She pursed her lips and tilted her head toward him.

"You know I'm always glad to see you, Neva, but your father made it clear I was never to talk to you again. If he knew you'd been sneaking in here to see me, he'd have a fit."

"I know, Marty, but it's hard not seeing you sometimes."

"It's hard for me, too. But you know how my aunt and uncle are. They want me to stay away from you almost as bad as you father does. I guess it's because your pa is a good customer and they're afraid he'd shop somewhere else if he got mad at them."

"My father thinks he can rule everyone in town since he's such an important businessman, but sometimes I wonder if he's as important as he thinks."

"He does throw his weight around, but as we found out, there's nothing we can do about it."

"I wish we'd made it out of town and got married that night, Marty. I really wanted to be your wife. To keep Daddy from guessing that I love you, I try to pretend I'm interested in other men, but I'm not."

"I know it's not easy for you, but your father is right about one thing. I'm not good enough for you."

"I don't understand my father, Marty. Ever since I came here last fall, he insists I act like I'm above everybody in town. He has no idea how it hurts my feelings when I'm looked at as if I'm poison." She bit her lip. "I don't have any friends and nobody likes me."

"Why don't you treat people nicer, like you do me? Then you'd make friends."

"You were the only one in Wildweed who was ever nice to me."

He grinned. "I like you, Neva. Oh, I don't care much for that uppity girl that comes around with her nose in the air, but the Neva I spent time with down by the lake is different. She's the one I fell in love with."

She blushed and looked around the store. "When can we meet again, Marty?"

He shook his head. "I don't know, Neva. My aunt and uncle keep a close eye on me. The only time they leave me alone in the store is during supper time and that's because there are never many customers that time a day."

"I know. Daddy watches me like that, too. I'm sure he has the housekeeper, Vinnie, spy on me when he can't. I wish he'd left me with Aunt Melinda in Denver."

"Don't say that, Neva. I'd never have met you if you were in Denver."

She smiled at him. "I don't really mean it."

"I'm glad for that."

She gave him a coy smile. "I need to see you, Marty. Can't you slip out one night and meet me somewhere?"

"You know what happened the last time we did that. Your pa came after me with a gun." He sighed. "I guess he would've killed me if he'd come earlier and caught us with our clothes off."

"Don't mention that, Marty. I still feel strange about it."

"If I could, I'd get out of here and we'd run away, but you know I don't have any money and there's no way we could survive on our own."

"I know, but…"

"I'd try running away with you again, if I could, Neva. But that doesn't seem possible as long as I have to work here. You know how much I hate this place. It's as bad as my pa's butcher shop back in Chicago. I just hope someday I'll find something else to do. I hate being cooped up all the time. I want to work out in the open air."

A noise came from the back room and Neva said, as if she'd already practiced the line, "Give me a tin of tea, Marty. It makes me furious when Miss Kingsley lets our pantry run out of it. I think she does it just to irritate me. She knows I hate coffee."

Floyd came into the store from the back. "Hello, Miss Greenwood."

"Hello, Floyd." She raised her voice an octave to let him know she thought she was too important to call him Mr. Mayfield.

Floyd turned to Marty. "Go on to the house, nephew. Hilda has your supper ready. I'll ring Miss Greenwood up and close the store."

"Yes, Uncle Floyd." Marty looked at Neva as if he wanted to say something else, but he knew he'd get them both in trouble if he did.

~ * ~

"Are you sure you did the right thing by hiring Mr. Renwick, George?" Gloria whispered to her husband after they went to bed.

Pulling her close to him, he whispered back, "Didn't you like him, honey?"

"He was fine. Very polite and thanked me generously for supper. It's just that I can't understand why a man like him would work for only a place to sleep and food to eat."

"He said he needed somewhere to rest for a while and from what I can tell, he's a hard worker."

"I know we need someone like him who knows what he's doing on a ranch, but I can't help wondering about him."

When George didn't answer, Gloria went on, "Did you notice how the girls hung on his every word at supper?"

"Of course I did. I told Ruby to forget trying to attract him. He's much too old for her, but it looks like I'm going to have to remind her again. Opal is more sensible about it."

Gloria chuckled. "And what about Sapphire? I've never seen my baby take to somebody like she did him. She's usually shy around strangers."

"I know." George laughed, too. "She climbed right up on his knee just as if she'd known him all her life."

"And he didn't seem to mind."

"He must have been around children sometime in his life."

"I hope you thanked him for finishing the repairs on the chicken coop. I'm sure we'll be gathering eggs soon."

"Of course I thanked him, dear. I even offered to pay him a little for the work, but he wouldn't take anything. He said we had a deal and he had no intention of breaking it."

"I hope he's comfortable out there in the barn."

"Honey, you gave him enough bed linens to furnish two bedrooms. I'm sure he'll be fine."

"I didn't give him that much. Just a couple of sheets, a blanket and a quilt."

"And a pillow and a pillowcase and I don't know how many towels," George finished for her.

"Well, I figured he'd need them."

George chuckled and pulled his wife close to him. "And I figure it's time to go to sleep. I don't mind Mr. Jace Renwick living in the barn, but I refuse to let him to visit us in our bedroom any longer tonight."

Gloria snuggled against his chest. "Oh, George. You say the craziest things, sometimes."

~ * ~

"Opal, didn't you think Jace is one of the most handsome men you've ever seen?" Ruby whispered.

Opal turned over in bed and faced her sister, but she wasn't about to tell her what she really thought of the man. "He looked fine, Ruby, but you know what Papa said. You better listen to him and get your mind off Mr. Renwick."

"Jace told us to call him by his first name, not Mr. Renwick."

"I know, but I feel better using the formal name for him."

"I bet I know why, too."

Opal stiffened. "What do you mean?"

"I saw the way you kept looking at him when you didn't think anyone was noticing. I bet you're hoping he'll notice you and not me."

"You're crazy, Ruby. I was doing no such thing. All I expect from Mr. Renwick is that he does the job Papa wants him to do on this ranch."

"Why?"

"What do you mean, why?"

"I thought you hoped Papa would fail and we'd have to go back to Memphis."

"What gave you that idea? I never said I wanted Papa to fail." Opal frowned into the darkness of the room. "I have faith in Papa. He'll succeed in making this ranch a home for us if that is what he wants to do."

"I know you didn't say you wanted him to fail, but I was sure you were hoping he would give up and sell."

"That's not so."

"Then you'll never get back to Memphis."

"Maybe if Papa makes a success of this place, he can sell it for a big profit and we can go home." Opal's voice was a little sharp, though she didn't mean it to be.

"You're dreaming, Opal. While I was going to town with Papa, he told me how he planned to build this ranch into such a fine place that none of us would ever want to leave. I didn't believe he could do it at the time, but with Jace's help, he might succeed. And that means we'll never get to leave."

"Ruby, don't you think…"

Ruby interrupted her sister. "I can see it now. Papa will make this become a fine place and Jace will fall in love with me and we'll get married and live here all our life."

"You're talking foolishness. What would Jace want with a seventeen year old? I bet he's at least twenty-nine or thirty."

"A lot of girls get married at seventeen." Ruby's voice became stubborn.

"Maybe a lot of girls do, but Papa would never allow one of his daughters to get married so young. He wants us to be grown when we get married."

"I bet Jace could change Papa's mind."

"I doubt that. Once Papa decides on something, it's pretty much settled."

"Will you two stop arguing about Papa and Jace Renwick? You're keeping me awake." Pearl's voice came from her cot on the other side of the room. Opal heard her flop over in her bed. "Besides," she added. "From what I saw at supper, if Jace is going to fall in love with any of the Barnett girls it'll be Sapphire. He took to her right away."

"I bet you're right, Pearl. He doesn't want either of us. He'll wait for Sapphire to grow up, then fall in love and marry her," Opal said and giggled.

"You two are crazy." Ruby couldn't hide the laughter in her voice.

Opal laughed out loud. "Now that we have Mr. Jace Renwick's future settled, let's get some sleep. We've got a lot of work to do tomorrow."

Jace wasn't sure what woke him just before dawn, but he sat straight up from his bed in the hayloft. He'd decided to sleep there in his bedroll until he had the tack room clean and his bed built. He couldn't see putting the nice bed linens Mrs. Barnett had given him in the dirty, musty room. In fact, he wasn't going to use them until he got the place ready.

Without making a sound, he slipped on his boots and moved to the window on the end of the loft. There was a shadow moving toward the chicken coop. The stranger opened the door to the coop. There was a flash of light as he lit the torch he had in his hand.

Jace didn't hesitate. He ran to his bed, grabbed his gun, returned to the window and fired.

The man screamed and the lighted torch fell to the ground. Holding his arm, he turned and ran toward the horse he'd left waiting in the edge of the yard.

Jace scrambled down the ladder and ran into the yard as a light appeared in the house. He fired at the retreating figure then turned toward the chicken coop. The chickens squawked and flew about, but it didn't look as if any had escaped. The torch was on the ground near one of the walls which was ready to go up in a blaze.

Stomping out the fire, he shut the door, ran to the water trough and filled a bucket. He hurried back and dashed it on the wall.

George came out the back door with his shotgun in his hand. "I heard shooting. What's going on?"

"Somebody tried to burn the hen house."

"Did you see who it was?"

"No. I could only tell he was a heavyset man, but he could move fast."

"What do you mean?"

"I think I nicked his arm, but he dashed to his horse and rode off before I could get out here to stop him."

"George, are you all right?" Gloria's voice came from the porch.

"I'm fine, dear. Jace just ran off whoever it was trying to set fire to the chicken coop."

"Oh, my goodness. Is Jace all right?"

"I'm fine, Miz Barnett."

"Go back to bed, dear. I'll be in in a minute," George said when she started down the steps into the yard.

"If you're sure." She paused, but did turn back.

"I'm positive, honey." As soon as she was inside, George turned back to Jace. "Do you think he'll come back tonight?"

"Not tonight and you didn't lose any chickens, but who knows what can happen in the future?" Jace changed the subject. "Is there any reason someone would want to do other damage to your property?"

"I have no idea who would want to do such a thing. Nobody around here knows me well enough to have a grudge against me and nobody in Memphis knew we were coming west."

"Has anyone come around since you've been here?"

"Only you and a man who wanted to buy the place. I told him it wasn't for sale."

"Oh?" Jace's eyes widened. "Who was that?"

"His name was Cletus Finch. Said he was a neighbor."

"I see." To cover his surprise at the name, Jace yawned and added, "I think we'll be fine for tonight. Why don't we try to get a little more sleep?"

"I agree. In the morning I want to go with you to start looking for those cows you mentioned might be on the range."

Without more words, the two men nodded at each other. George went inside and Jace headed back to the barn, though he doubted there'd be any more sleep for him tonight. His mind was working too hard trying to figure out why Finch would choose the chicken coop to burn instead of the house or the barn. If he were trying to get rid of the family, that would surely hurt Barnett more than losing a few chickens.

## *Five*

"Jace!" Sapphire squealed and held her arms toward the tall cowboy as he came in the back door for breakfast.

"Hello, little darling." Jace grinned and reached down for her. "How's pretty Sapphire this morning?"

Opal watched her little sister and wished she could run and greet the handsome man in such an easy way. She quickly turned around, berating herself for having such a thought.

Sapphire hugged the big man's neck and muttered something to him that nobody understood.

He laughed and chucked her under her chin.

"Come on to the table, Jace," George said. "Gloria has made a big stack of flapjacks."

"I hope you like them," Gloria said shyly.

"I love them, ma'am." Sapphire wiggled and he put her down. She ran to the sitting area and grabbed her rag doll.

Jace took one of the chairs at the table and smiled at Opal when she poured him coffee.

She felt herself turn a little pink, but she couldn't help smiling back. To keep anyone from seeing, she turned quickly to the stove and said, "Why don't you sit down and join Papa for breakfast, Mama?"

"I have a few more flapjacks to cook."

"Come on, Gloria, let the girls finish them. I like looking at my beautiful wife over breakfast." George winked at her.

"George, behave yourself," she teased as she took the chair beside him. "We need to get more seating for this big table so everyone can eat at the same time."

"I saw some study wood out back of the barn, Miz Barnett. If you like, I can build a couple of benches that would fit on each side of this table then you could use the chairs on the ends. It would give your family a lot more sitting room."

"Oh, Mr. Renwick, that would be wonderful. I wasn't sure if we could afford more chairs at this time."

"Ma'am, if you don't mind, I'd appreciate it if you'd call me Jace."

"If you insist, but if I do, you must call me Gloria."

"I'll try, but it won't be easy. My mother insisted I call all the women around Miz or Miss."

As Opal turned the pancakes in the big iron frying pan, it pleased her to hear her mother and Jace getting along so well. She wasn't sure why. Before she could figure it out, Ruby came bouncing into the room.

"Well, I got all the beds made. What's next?" She stopped short when she saw Jace at the table. Automatically she smoothed back her cornfield yellow hair and said in a coy voice, "Good morning, Jace."

He had his mouthful of food and nodded at her with a smile.

Ruby smiled back at him and glanced at the table. Seeing no more seats, she joined her sister at the stove. "Where are we supposed to sit?"

"We'll eat when they get through. Why don't you go tell Pearl to come in? I saw her head out the front door a few minutes ago."

George frowned. "I wish you girls would stay close to the house until we get to know our way around this place."

"Oh, I don't think there's any danger for us, Papa." Ruby offered him more coffee.

"I'm not saying there is, but we don't want to take any chances. Do like your sister said, and go get Pearl."

"Oh, all right." Ruby poured coffee for her mother and turned to Jace. "Would you like some, too?"

"Please." He held up his cup.

She poured his coffee and gave him a big smile. "There you go."

"Thank you."

"Now put that pot down, Ruby, and go find Pearl, please." Her mother demanded.

Ruby sat the pot on the stove, but before she could leave the room, Pearl came bounding in the front door. "I saw a pretty dog out there, but I couldn't catch him."

Gloria frowned. "What dog, honey?"

"It was a pretty gray dog. I saw it run around the side of the house when I went outside, but by the time I got out there, it was gone."

"I don't think it's wise to be chasing strange dogs, Pearl." Her mother gave her a hard look.

"Why not?"

"It might be dangerous."

"Besides being gray, what did it look like, Pearl?" Jace looked at her.

"It had a fluffy tail and its hair was kind of long. It was real pretty. Do you know whose it might be?"

"No, but you mother is right. It's best not to mess with animals you aren't familiar with."

She frowned at him. "I don't think it would hurt me because it looked friendly. It was just sitting in the grass beside the porch, then you came out of the barn. I think you scared it when you came to the house."

"Then it may have been a wild dog, Pearl. As Jace said, you have to be careful," George said.

Opal noticed the concerned look on Jace's face. She couldn't help asking, "You know what kind of dog it was, don't you, Jace?"

He looked up at her, but she couldn't read his eyes when he said, "I'm not sure it was a dog."

"What do you mean?" George asked.

Jace took a breath before answering. "I don't want to frighten anyone, but it could have been a fox or even a wolf. If it was, you don't want to mess with it. They're dangerous."

Gloria gasped.

Opal sat the plate of pancakes she was holding down on the table and waited for him to explain.

When Jace said nothing else, George broke the silence. "Why would a wolf or a fox be coming around here? I thought they were wild and kept to the woods."

"Normally they do, but nobody has lived in this place for a while. Since there was a coop, we don't know but what there were chickens here when your brother died. They could have been feeding on them. That could be the reason it came here today and was scared off when he saw me." When nobody said anything, he went on. "After breakfast, I'll ride out in the direction Pearl saw him go and see if I can pick up his trail."

"I'll go with you, Jace," George said quietly. "I don't want any wild animals hanging around here that might hurt my family."

Nobody said anything else and Opal waited until the men finished eating and left. She then turned to her sister. "Pearl, if you happen to see that animal again, please tell someone right away."

"Yes, darling, do. And don't go outside chasing it." Gloria got up from the table. "Now it's time for you girls to eat. Help me put these dishes in the dishpan and then sit."

"Isn't Jace just the smartest man you've ever seen? Nobody else would have thought that animal could be wild."

"Ruby, forget about Jace and sit down." Opal gently pushed her toward the table, though she actually wanted to shove her sister. To cover up, she asked, "How many flapjacks do you want?"

~ * ~

"Jace do you really think that was a wolf or a fox Pearl saw this morning?" George asked as they rode toward the creek. George was riding one of the work horses.

"I'm sure it was. I don't think a wild dog or one from a neighboring ranch would show up here this time of day. Most of the dogs that ranchers own are either hunting dogs or are used to round up cows."

George shook his head. "I've sure got a lot to learn, haven't I?"

"You can do it. Just let a little sink in at a time."

"I don't know. With somebody trying to burn me out and wild animals threatening my children, I wonder if I wouldn't be better off selling this place and moving on with my family."

"Give yourself a while to get used to the way things are in the West, George. I know you were determined to make a go of it yesterday."

"I was, but now…"

"Your wife and your girls are certainly behind you. It didn't take me long to realize that. Of course it's your decision, but I don't think you should give up when you've not really seen what a good life living on a ranch can be."

"I know you're right. It's just that if anything happened to one of them, I'd never forgive myself for bringing them here."

"Bad things happen everywhere, George. Not just in the West." Jace suddenly reined his horse up and peered into a thicket near the creek. "Well, I'll be damned."

"Is it a wild animal?" George stopped beside him.

"It's probably wild, but not by birth. It looks like it we might have found the first cow of your herd. Stay back. I'm going to run it out." With that, Jace grabbed the rope from his saddle and heading into the thicket, yelling and slapping the rope in the air.

George had no idea what to do, so he just sat on his horse and watched.

~ * ~

"Where's Jace? Isn't he coming in for supper?"

"He'll be here shortly. He's taking care of something in the barn."

"Good. I combed my hair and put on this dress especially for him." Ruby looked at her father and smiled.

"Now, Ruby, I've already told you, we'll have none of you girls trying to attract Jace's attention. He's a good man, but the word 'man' is what you must listen to. He's too old for you." He hugged Ruby. "There'll be a man for you when the right time comes, but now is not the time. I don't mind you liking Jace as a friend, but that's all he can be to any of you."

"But, Papa…"

"I mean it, Ruby. I'm your father and I only have your interest at heart."

She shrugged. "I know, Papa. It's just that Jace is so good looking with those steel gray eyes that go dark at times and that black hair."

"Maybe so, but you listen to what I'm saying." George took a seat at the table and turned to Gloria. "Jace said I needed a cow pony if I plan to round up my herd and be a rancher. He said we'd go to town this afternoon and pick me out one. I told him I didn't know a thing about a cattle working horse and I trusted him to buy me one, but he insisted I go along."

"Can I go to town with you and Jace, Papa?" Ruby's eyes got big.

"Not this time. If anyone goes with us, it'll be Opal. It's her turn."

Before Opal could say anything, Gloria asked, "Can we afford another horse, dear?"

"It's a necessity, Gloria. Jace convinced me I couldn't do the jobs that have to be done on a ranch with the work horses I have."

"What are we going to do with the work horses?"

"We'll keep them because we'll use them for plowing your garden, clearing some more land and for taking the wagon into town for supplies. Things like that. They're just no good at rounding up cattle or other range work."

"Do we have any cattle to round up?" Opal asked.

"We found a dozen today. Jace ran them into a canyon where there was plenty of grass. He said once we had them all rounded up, they'd stay pretty close together on the open range."

"Did you find my dog today?" Pearl interrupted the conversation about horses and cows.

George laughed. "No, sweetie. We didn't find anything except cows, but Jace is still convinced it was a wild animal you saw. Not a dog."

"I don't care if it was wild. It was pretty and I bet it would've liked me."

George reached for her arm. "Come here, honey." When Pearl was on his knee, he said, "Sweetheart, there are lots of wild animals in Arizona. Some of them may be pretty, but they can be deadly. If you must have an animal, why I don't ask in town about getting a dog or maybe a cat?"

"Oh, Papa. I love you." She threw her arms around her father's neck.

"And I love you, too. You know you're one of my jewels and I can't have anything happening to you, so I want you to be careful. Now promise me you won't try to take up with some strange animal."

"I promise, Papa."

There was a shuffling of feet on the porch and George said, "That'll be Jace. Now let's get ready to eat.

# Six

Opal was glad when her father pulled the wagon up in front of Mayfield's General Store. She hoped Papa would take a long time picking out a horse because she wanted to be away from Jace Renwick for a while. It wasn't that he had been unkind or said anything out of the way to her, but it was the fact that, in spite of everything she tried to think of, her thoughts kept coming back to the man. She had ridden on the seat between the two men into town. Though they occasionally said something to her, they mainly talked about cows and what kind of horse was needed to work with them on a ranch. Opal had tried her best to listen to them and not be aware of the man beside her, but she couldn't help being mindful that he'd washed up and changed his shirt since going out on the range that morning. And when the wagon bounced and her leg happened to touch his or his arm accidently brushed hers, she felt like flames were running through her body. Oh, what would Papa say if he had any inkling she was having these thoughts and feelings? At least now that they had reached town, she could go in the store and concentrate on gathering the short list of items her mother had asked her to purchase.

As soon as the wagon stopped, her father set the brake and wrapped the reins around the brake stick. She turned to climb out and saw that Jace was standing on the ground reaching up to help her down. There was nothing she could do but reach out to take his hand. She was startled when he ignored her hand and put his large hands around her tiny waist. He lifted her from the wagon and set her on the boardwalk as if she weighed nothing.

He must have noticed her surprised expression because he chuckled and said, "It must have rained earlier today. The street is muddy and I didn't think you'd want to get your boots dirty."

"Thank you," she managed to mutter.

"That was thoughtful of you, Jace," George said.

Opal heard Jace say something back, but she didn't understand what it was because he'd already climbed back into the wagon beside her father.

"We'll be back soon, honey," her father said. "Stay close to this store so I won't have to search all over town for you."

"I will, Papa." She turned, pushed open the door and went inside.

"Well, well, what have we here?" Mrs. Mayfield said with a laugh. "You must be another one of those beautiful Barnett girls. Now let me see if I remember how your father named his jewels. I know you're not Ruby. I done met her and I think he said the little one was Sapphire.

Opal blushed. "I'm Opal, ma'am."

"Of course. I remember now. You're the oldest, and I might add the prettiest so far. Ruby was a beauty, but I swear you've got her beat." She shook her head. "I know the single men in town and on the ranches around are going to be beating paths to your door soon."

Opal was flabbergasted at this friendly woman's words and couldn't think of an appropriate answer. She just rushed to the counter and handed the woman the list of the needed supplies.

"Boy, your mama has a neat handwriting. I sure wish our other customers would make it this easy for me to gather up what they want."

"Mama was a school teacher before she married," Opal blurted.

"She must have been a good one." The clerk changed the subject. "I'm Hilda Mayfield, by the way."

"I'm glad to meet you, Mrs. Mayfield."

"Oh, honey, call me Hilda. Everybody does. You'll have to call my husband Floyd, whenever you meet him. Our nephew, Marty, works here, too, but he mostly delivers and works out back." She looked down at the list. "I see she wants some green thread. I think I'm out of green, but I should have some in a couple of weeks. I'm expecting a shipment of stock from Phoenix. Hope she don't mind waiting that long."

"I'm sure she won't mind."

"If you think there's another color she might be happy with, you can check out the display of what I have over there."

"Thank you." Opal moved to where Hilda had set up her sewing needs section of the general store.

The bell over the door jangled as two young women came in.

"Hello Riley twins," Hilda said.

Opal looked around and was surprised when she looked at the teenage girls. To be twins, they looked nothing alike. One girl had brown hair and the other had black.

"Hi, Hilda," the one with black hair said.

"Did that good looking man come in here, Hilda?" The brown-headed one asked.

"What good looking man?"

"You know. The handsome one who came into town a few days ago. He has black hair and a perfectly built body. I thought I saw him in a wagon going down the street with an old man."

"I have no idea who you're talking about, but I want to introduce you to one of the new residents." The girls walked forward and Hilda motioned for Opal to join them. "Opal this is Peg and Meg Riley. I never can remember which is which, so I just call them the Riley twins. Girls, this is Opal Barnett. She has three sisters and they all have names of precious stones. Their father calls them his jewels."

"I'm Meg," the black-haired one said.

"And I'm Peg," the girl with brown hair added.

Opal nodded and wondered if she'd be able to keep their names straight. "Nice to meet both of you."

"Maybe you saw that handsome man," Meg said. "As I said, he was riding down the street in a wagon with an old man."

Peg giggled. "Yes. I hope they come back here. I want to meet that man before Neva Greenwood sees him. You know her. She'll have her hooks in him before any of us have a chance at him."

"You know what Momma said, Peg. He's probably just a drifter." Meg looked at Opal. "Do you know him?"

"I'd have to see him to tell if I know him or not." Opal shrugged, though she figured they were talking about Jace, since they saw the man in a wagon with an older man, who would be her father.

"We can only hope he'll come in here." Peg turned to her sister. "What was it Momma wanted us to buy for her?"

"I think it was green thread."

"What's going on with green thread?" Hilda frowned. "It took me six months to sell the half dozen spools I had, now I've had a call for two spools in one day."

"Maybe people are making a lot of green things." Peg giggled again. "Momma is sewing a green checked dress for our little sister."

"Maybe she could use white on that. I have plenty of white."

"I'm not sure." Peg frowned. "We better ask her before we get any."

"You do that. Now, I'm going to fill Opal's order." She turned to the shelves and began taking down the things on Gloria's list.

"So, you just moved to town?" Meg turned to Opal, but without giving her time to answer, she asked another question. "Where did you come from?"

"Memphis, Tennessee."

"My, goodness. That's a long way from here." Peg's eyes got big. "Why did you move so far?"

"My father decided to come and live on the ranch his brother left him."

"Who was his brother?" Meg asked.

Before she could answer, Peg interrupted. "Look who's coming, Meg."

"Who?"

"That sassy Neva Greenwood."

"Oh no. If she comes in here, she'll be the first to meet the handsome stranger. "

"Maybe the man you're talking about won't come in here," Opal volunteered.

"If he does, we won't have a chance."

"Why's that?" Opal asked.

Meg shook her head. "I see you don't know Neva Greenwood. She's ruthless where good looking men are concerned. I guess the other men in town decided she was too citified for them, so when Marty Mayfield came to work here in his uncle's store a few months ago, she had him swooning over her in no time."

"She probably thought she could get Marty away from his aunt," Meg whispered.

Peg giggled and added, "And she seems to always know when a new man's going to show up. She beats all of us in making his acquaintance."

It amused Opal to see the jealously in the twins' eyes. They reminded her of Ruby. It seemed a lot of teenage girls often had dreams about a handsome man even if the man was too old for them, and she knew Jace was too old for these girls. But at the moment, it didn't matter. She decided she'd help the twins out. After all, in this small town she was sure there weren't many opportunities to meet new unmarried men.

As the pretty blonde opened the door and stepped inside the store, she glanced at them, but didn't speak. Opal made a quick decision. "Come here, girls," she whispered. "I think I can help you."

They gave her a strange look, but walked over to where Opal stood beside a table of cloth. "What is it?" They asked almost in unison.

"I think I know the man you're talking about. Just wait here with me and together we'll find out if I'm right."

Their eyes got big and a smile turned up the corners of their lips, but they moved a little closer to her without saying anything.

"Hello, Neva," Hilda said, in a lackluster tone. "What can I do for you?"

Neva tipped her chin a little higher. "Not a thing, Hilda. I only stepped in to get out of the sun for a minute."

Hilda didn't answer, but began adding up the prices of the supplies she'd put on the counter for Opal.

Opal couldn't help wondering if the storekeeper felt the same way about Neva as the twins did. Hilda hadn't been very friendly to the girl, but Opal didn't have time to dwell on it. At that moment she glanced out the window and saw her father's wagon pull up in front of the store. Jace was climbing out of it.

"Come with me," she whispered and moved near the door. "I want you to be the first to meet a friend of mine."

"Why…?"

"Meg and Peg. I didn't see you when I came in. The bright sun must have affected my eyes. Daddy says they're delicate, you know." Without taking a breath, Neva looked at Opal and continued. "Is this someone I should know?"

Neva started toward them just as Jace entered the store. She stopped and stared at him for a few seconds. It gave Opal enough time to spring into action.

"Jace," Opal took his arm. Though he gave her a surprised look, he didn't pull away. "I want to introduce you to two of my new friends, the Riley twins. Meg is the beauty with black hair and Peg has the lovely brown hair."

She knew by his eyes he didn't understand what she was doing, but he tipped his hat and smiled at each girl. "Hello, ladies. I'm delighted to meet you."

They both nodded, but seemed too stunned to answer.

Jace went on. "I hope I have the pleasure of seeing you when you visit Opal at the ranch."

"You will." Meg finally managed to say.

"Oh, my. Here's someone I haven't met." Neva batted her eyes at Jace, hurried up beside them and reached for Jace's arm. "Neva Greenwood is my name."

But Opal didn't let go of Jace. She put slight pressure on his arm, hoping he'd not succumb to Neva's attempt at flirting, though the girl's eyes didn't look as if she really meant what she was saying.

Opal thought he might have caught on when he didn't pull away from her. "Nice to meet you, Miss Greenwood. I'm a friend of Opal's."

"I'm sorry. I would have introduced you to Jace, but I didn't know you and didn't want to be presumptuous." Opal gave the girl a sweet, but insincere smile.

"Well, you know who I am now," Neva said as she stared at Opal with hazel eyes.

Again, Opal didn't think the woman's eyes showed any animosity, but she'd started this game and she had to see it through.

Jace covered Opal's hand, which was still on his arm, with his free hand. "I think we better get the supplies and get going. Your father's waiting for us in the wagon and I don't want the horses to get restless."

She nodded, let go of his arm and walked to the counter with him. He paid for the supplies, picked them up and headed out the door.

"Thank you, Hilda. It was nice meeting you and the twins." Opal gave her a smile and followed him toward the entrance.

"I'm glad we met, Jace," Neva called brightly.

"Nice to meet all you young ladies," Jace said as he paused at the door. He then turned to the twins. "As I said, I hope to see you at the ranch soon." With that he stepped out on the boardwalk and headed to the back of the wagon where he deposited the supplies.

Opal said a quick good-bye to Hilda and the twins then went out. She knew it was rude, but she only gave Neva a quick nod. By the time she reached the wagon, Jace was waiting for her. Without a word, he took her by her waist and lifted her to the seat next to her father then climbed in and sat beside her.

There was no way she could know that Neva was thinking she'd met a woman who could either be her worst enemy or the first person she'd met who might make a good friend as she watched them drive off in the wagon. Neither did she know the twins were standing there staring at her back in awe.

~ * ~

Jace notice nobody talked much as they drove out of town. George seemed content to concentrate on his driving. Opal had lost the bravado she'd shown when she was holding his arm in the store.

Now she had reverted to her shy, subdued self and Jace was trying to figure out what Opal's actions had been about. He was also wondering why the feel of her hand on his arm had made him want to take her in his arms and kiss her right there in front of everyone in the general store.

Before he came up with any explanations for his feelings, George broke the silence. "I guess you noticed we bought two horses." He looked at Opal and grinned.

"Yes. Did you need two, Papa?"

Jace didn't give him a chance to answer her. "They were such good horses I encouraged your father to buy them. If he finds he doesn't need them both, I agreed to buy one to take with me when I leave the ranch."

"Do you plan to leave soon?" Opal shot a glance at him and he could see the concern in her eyes.

"Not real soon. I want to help George get his ranch on its feet first."

"I'm sure once Papa learns what he has to do, he'll be able to run the place alone."

Jace shook his head. "To run the place right, he's going to always need a hand or two. Possibly more to work there. The place is bigger than you might think."

"Jace suggested we buy the horse so maybe one of you girls might learn to ride and help us out on the ranch until we get on our feet financially." George gave her a tentative smile.

"You know Ruby would never want to work out on the range and Pearl and Sapphire are much too little." She grinned back at her father. "I suppose you had me in mind all along."

"At first I had thought it would be you or Ruby, but you're right. She'd never agree to ride around on a horse and count cows."

"I think it might be fun. I've never ridden a horse, though. Will you teach me?"

"You know I could give you simple riding lessons, but to ride the range I guess I'm going to have to depend on Jace to teach you what you need to know."

"I'm not sure you're going to think it's fun when we get started, but to get you to help was one reason I picked out the pinto pony. I thought it would be the right match for you." He didn't add that he had known from the beginning that if George couldn't hire another hand, Opal would be the one to help.

Opal blushed. "How did you guess I'd be the one to have to help?"

"When George said it would be either you or Ruby, there was no question in my mind. No better than I know her, I don't think Ruby would be willing to ride a horse and get as dirty and dusty as we do on the range."

Opal frowned. "So you thought I'd be more prone to dust and dirt?"

He chuckled and Opal blushed, but said nothing else.

He was suddenly picturing her with dirt all over her face and clothes. Surprisingly he thought the picture exciting. He didn't know why.

To get his mind off the thought, he said, "There was one thing I couldn't convince your father to do."

"What was that?"

"I said it would be much easier on you if he'd allow you to wear britches while you're working on the range."

"I don't think I'd be comfortable in britches. Besides, Mama would never allow it even if Papa would." Opal couldn't believe he'd suggested such a thing.

"They both may change their minds after they see how hard it will be on you with all the petticoats and skirts."

"I doubt that, Jace," George said. "I may have to let Opal work on the range, but she's a lady and I want her to remain one."

"There's not a doubt in my mind that all your daughters are ladies, George. I was only suggesting the britches because I thought it would make the work safer and easier for Opal, but we'll do it your way and see what happens."

Jace didn't say anything else, but it crossed his mind that Opal would be wearing britches before the week was out. He couldn't wait to see her in them.

A bullet whizzed through the air interrupting their conversation. It kicked up dirt on George's side of the wagon, and the horses reared. George had to strain to calm them down. When they were stopped, Jace jumped off his side of the wagon, pulling Opal with him. "Get down, George," he ordered and took his gun from the holster.

George quickly wrapped the reins around the brake stick and jumped down beside them. He reached up and took his shotgun from under the seat. "What in the world is happening?"

"The shot came from that rise to your left. I don't know yet if it was somebody shooting at us or if it was a hunter's stray bullet."

After waiting several minutes and there were no more shots, Jace said, "It must have been hunters."

"If so, why are you still scanning that ridge with that frown on your face?" Opal's voice shook.

Jace put his hand on her shoulder. "I want to be sure."

"Should we go on?" George looked at him.

"Yes, but if you don't mind, I'll drive the team the rest of the way." When it looked as if George were going to argue with him, he added, "You need to watch out for Opal."

George nodded.

As soon as they were on their way again, George said, "I don't think we should mention this to Gloria. She worries too much as it is."

~ * ~

"Mama," Ruby came running in from the front yard. She had Sapphire on her hip. "I see somebody coming up the road."

"It's probably your father." Gloria turned from the stove and Sapphire reached for her. "It's about time he got back."

"It's not him. It's two people riding on horses." Ruby handed the baby to her mother.

"Horsie," Sapphire babbled.

"Maybe it's the man who came to see Papa the other day." Pearl looked up from the potato she was peeling.

"I hope not." Gloria frowned. "That man wasn't very nice."

"What are we going to do if it's him?" Ruby asked.

"We'll have to go out on the porch and speak to him."

"Why can't we just stay in the house?" Pearl asked.

"I'm sure they know we're here. There's smoke coming out of the chimney and they may have seen Ruby and Sapphire in the yard."

The sound of horses arriving in the front yard came into the cabin. "Hello the house," a man's voice called.

"Come on, girls, but stay close to me. I'll do the talking." Gloria pushed the pot of green beans to the back of the stove so they wouldn't burn and shifted Sapphire higher on her hip.

They all stepped out on the porch as the horses came to a stop near the steps. Gloria waited for one of the two men to speak before she said anything.

The older of the two cowboys removed his hat and revealed sun-streaked brown hair which matched his brown mustache. "Howdy, ma'am. My name's Sam Norton and this young fellow here is my son, Doyle. I own the spread next to yours and thought I'd come by and meet you folks."

Though Gloria was nervous, she managed to say, "I'm Mrs. Barnett and these are three of my four daughters, Ruby, Pearl and Sapphire."

"I must say, you have beautiful children. They all favor their mother."

Doyle didn't say anything, but he removed his hat and glanced at her. His eyes then turned back to Ruby where they'd been since they pulled up.

"Is Mr. Barnett out on the range?" Sam asked.

"No, sir. He went into town, but he should be coming home soon." She wondered if she should invite him in, but decided against it. If George were home, it would be different.

Sam nodded. "I must say I was surprised when I learned you folks had moved into this place."

"My husband's brother left us this ranch." She gave him no further explanation.

"I knew he'd left the place to some family member, but everyone expected it to be sold."

"My husband wanted to move here." She saw him lift an eyebrow, but he didn't indicate what it meant.

"Well, if he decides he doesn't want to stay, I'd be willing to make him an offer."

"Someone has already offered to buy it." After it was out of her mouth, she wondered if she should have told Sam Norton this information.

"It doesn't surprise me. I expect it was Cletus Finch. He's always trying to add to the ranch he owns with his partner, though he's one of the worst ranchers in the area. Nobody knows who his partner is, but there's speculation it's some businessman who doesn't want to get his hands dirty."

Gloria didn't answer because Ruby butted in. "He was an awfully rude man."

"That doesn't surprise me either, young lady. Everybody in town talks about how crude he is."

"Cletus is rude to everyone," Doyle added and smiled at Ruby.

"Ma'am, please excuse us for talking bad about a neighbor, but I don't like to see someone trying to take advantage of anyone."

"I understand."

He tipped his hat at her. "Please tell your husband that I came by and I'll be back to meet him soon." Sam smiled at her and added, "I'm sure my missus and the younger children will be over to meet you in a few days. I know how lonely ranch wives get out here, so it's always exciting for them when a new woman moves in."

"I'd like very much to meet some women around here. It'd be nice for my children to meet some playmates, too."

"As you probably have guessed, there aren't too many around, but as I said, the ones who are will be happy to welcome another family. My wife and I have three children. Doyle here, a boy ten and a little girl three."

"Little Sapphire will be three in six months," Ruby said. "And Pearl is ten."

"I'll tell my wife. She'll be pleased because there aren't many kids around that age."

"I'll look forward to meeting your wife, Mr. Norton."

He tipped his hat. "I'm sure she'll be around soon. It was nice meeting you and your daughters, Mrs. Barnett." He turned to ride away.

Doyle nodded to her, then gave Ruby a big smile. Without speaking, he followed his father out of the yard.

Ruby returned his smile and watched them leave.

Gloria glanced at her and said, "All right, girls. Let's get back in the house and finish up supper. Your papa will be coming along soon." She didn't know why she felt happy about Sam Norton's visit, but for some reason it did. Maybe it was the things he said about Cletus Finch. She didn't like the idea of living so near someone who might be trying to cheat her husband. Knowing there was nothing she could do about it for the time being, she shook the feeling aside and stepped inside.

*Seven*

"Opal, I can't believe you're going to ride this ugly horse." Ruby stood beside the corral fence and watched the pinto move around in the area.

"This horse is not ugly, Ruby. I think he's pretty." Pearl put her hands on her hips and glared at her sister.

"You would."

"Stop arguing, you two." Opal shook her head at them and went on, "Somebody has to help out on the range and Papa doesn't have the money to hire another man. I guess I was the logical choice."

Opal had come to the corral to look over the horse her father had bought her. It had helped her to get over the ordeal she'd been through, which she and her papa and Jace had agreed would be better not to tell the rest of the family. She hadn't expected Ruby and Pearl to follow her, but they did. Now she had to act as normal as possible.

"I could have helped," Ruby said in an emphatic voice.

"You know good and well that you wouldn't want to climb on a horse and go looking for stray cattle." Opal laughed.

"I would have." Pearl sat on the top rail of the fence.

"Papa considered you, but he decided you could help him and Mama more by taking care of Sapphire. Our little sister likes being with you."

Pearl shrugged. "What are you going to name the horse?"

"I haven't thought of a name. Do you have any idea?"

Pearl looked thoughtful. "It has patches of brown and white all over it. What about just calling it Patch?"

"That's a great idea, Pearl." Opal smiled at her little sister. "Patch fits it well."

Pearl grinned, but Ruby turned up her nose. "I don't see why a horse has to have a name. Just call it horse. That's what it is."

Pearl glared at her. "So we should we just call you girl because that's what you are?"

"Don't be silly." Ruby threw back her hair. "I've seen all of this animal I want to see. I'm going in the house." With that, she stalked toward the back porch.

"Pearl, why do you like to tease Ruby?"

Pearl sighed. "I know I shouldn't, but sometimes I get irritated with her. All she wants to do is act fancy. I think she's waiting for some rich handsome man to come along and carry her away to his castle or something. Trouble is, she thinks every new man she meets is the one who'll do it. She thought that about Jace until Papa put his foot down about her flirting with him. Today she changed to that man who came by today."

Opal looked at her younger sister. "Is that so?"

"It sure is."

Opal smiled. "Was he as handsome as Ruby said?"

"He looked all right, but he didn't say much. I guess because he kept smiling at Ruby, she thought he was the handsome man she dreams about."

"I guess all girls hope to meet a handsome prince someday."

"Not me. I'm going to be a ranch hand and ride horses and help Papa. I don't want no old man coming to take me off." She eyed her sister. "I bet you don't either."

Opal avoided the statement by saying, "Ruby is probably still upset with me because I told her she was silly when she kept going on and on about the young man that came here with his father this afternoon."

"I bet you're right. It was silly of her, though. She acted like he'd proposed to her or something. And all he did was grin at her. I bet he's the type to do that to all the girls he meets."

"You may be right."

Jace came out of the barn and walked toward them. "Looking over the new horses?"

Before Opal could answer, Pearl said, "We're looking at Patch. How do you like that name? Opal let me name her."

"Sounds like a good name to me."

Pearl grinned. "When are you going to teach Opal to ride?"

"Thought we might get in a lesson tonight."

"Great. Can I watch?"

"Sure. I'll go get a saddle and we'll get started."

"Are you sure you want to start tonight?" Opal looked at him.

"I don't see why not. There's still plenty of daylight." He headed into the barn.

"This is exciting. I'm going to ask Jace to teach me to ride after he teaches you."

"I'm sure he will, but you need to…"

"Pearl," her mother's voice came across the back yard. "Come in the house. I need you to watch Sapphire."

"Oh phooey, I won't get to watch you ride."

"Pearl!" Her mother called again.

"Coming, Mama." Pearl slid off the fence. "I'll see you later and you can tell me about it."

"I will, honey." Opal watched as her little sister ran toward the cabin.

"I thought she was going to be our audience." Jace returned with a saddle and some things she didn't recognize.

"Mama called her inside to help watch Sapphire. Ruby must be busy."

"In that case, come with me. Since you said you knew nothing about horses, the first thing I'm going to show you is how to get your horse ready to ride." He placed the saddle on the top fence and picked up the bridle. Explaining to her the purpose of a bridle and bit, he took hold of Patch's mane. "When we get the bit in his mouth, we'll lead him over to the fence and saddle him."

"Oh, my. I thought I'd only be riding."

"There's a lot more to it than just climbing on the horse's back, Opal. You need to learn all the basic things. You never know what you'll have to use when you're on the range. First of all, you want to make friends with your horse. Let her get to know your voice and your smell."

"What do you mean?"

"Here," he took her hand and placed it on the horse's neck. "Now rub her and talk to her gently. She needs to know who his owner is."

"What do I say?"

"It doesn't matter as long as she knows you're being nice to her."

Opal rubbed the horse's neck. "Hello, Patch. I sure hope you like your new name. My sister, Pearl, picked it out especially for you."

"That's good." Jace winked at her and patted the horse's neck. "There now, Patch. Let's show this lady what a fine horse you're going to make."

Jace had her lead Patch to the fence where he picked up a blanket. "This goes under the saddle. It protects the horse's back because a saddle tends to rub and make her sore." He then swung the saddle onto Patch's back.

"So, my horse is a girl."

"Yep. She's a mare."

Taking hold of the cinch, he told her what it was and added, "The cinch must be tightened because it keeps the saddle from sliding around. If it's too loose, it can actually fall off and so can you."

"Make sure it's tight. I don't want to fall."

He chuckled. "I will." He turned to her. "Now let me get you on her back, then I'll adjust the stirrups to fit your legs."

"I never dreamed it was so complicated to ride a horse."

"You'll be doing it automatically in no time." After he had everything adjusted, he said, "Now to go to the left, you pull that side of the reins. To go right, pull that side and to bring Patch to a stop, you pull back on both at the same time."

She nodded. "What next?"

"That's about it for your first lesson. I'm going to lead you around the corral a time or two, then you're going to ride around by yourself."

"Do you think I'll be ready?"

He nodded and took hold of the horse's bridle. "Let's go, Patch."

After several turns around the corral, first with Jace leading her then riding on her own, Opal decided she was going to like riding Patch. She even told her so.

~ * ~

After all the lights went out in the cabin, Jace stood in the barn door looking at the house and smoking a cheroot. He couldn't understand why watching Opal ride around in the corral had made him feel hot and bothered. Yes, when she relaxed in the saddle and began enjoying the ride, she cut a fine figure on the back of the pinto. But he'd watched many a woman who sat pretty atop a horse. It was nothing unusual. Yet, he couldn't help noticing how her long hair glistened in the setting sun and how the blue checked dress she wore slipped up her leg enough to show her shapely ankle and her leg almost to her knee. Hell, he'd seen ankles and knees before and then some, but there was something about seeing the one attached to Opal's foot that was different.

He thought when he led Patch into the barn and showed Opal how to brush her down, all thoughts of her ride would slip from his mind. In a way it did, but it was only replaced by the sight of her delicate hands as she passed the brush over her horse's back. Her gentle strokes make him think she'd probably be as gentle with the man she loved someday. And then there was her voice. It was almost magic as she talked sweetly to the animal, telling her how beautiful she was and how much she had enjoyed riding her.

Shaking his head, Jace threw the cheroot down and turned back into the barn. "Wonder if it's time to make a trip into town and look up that little redheaded saloon girl? Or was she a blonde? I can't seem to remember," he muttered aloud as he opened the door to his room.

Looking around, he realized he was making good progress though he was only working on it during the afternoons and early morning before Gloria called him to breakfast. He'd finished laying the floor the previous night and had attached an inside sliding board to lock the room when he was there. He didn't know what possessed him to do these things to a room he was only going to be living in for a short time. He chuckled when he realized he'd not only made preparations to put a small stove in one corner, but had started building a full sized bedstead.

*If I'm not careful, the next thing I'll do is put up curtains and order a settee.*

~ * ~

"Did you like riding Patch, Opal?"

"Yes, I did, Pearl. She's such a sweet horse."

"My Lord, Opal. Who ever heard of a horse being sweet?" Ruby tossed the sheet from her legs. "I'm hot."

"I bet he is sweet. I can't wait to get to know him."

"You're right, Pearl, she is sweet and I told her so."

"She's a girl?"

"Yes, Pearl. Jace said she was a mare."

"You're kidding about telling a horse that, aren't you?"

"No, Ruby, I'm not kidding. Jace told me I should talk to her so she'd get to know my voice and my smell. So I talk to Patch a lot. Especially when I'm brushing her."

"Well, I'd rather Jace got to know my voice and my smell." Ruby laughed and again kicked at the cover.

"Are you planning on brushing Jace, Ruby?"

"Don't be silly, Pearl."

"Well, I thought you might like him to be close enough to see you smell like onions." Pearl giggled.

"Don't smart mouth me, little sister. Besides, Mama made me chop the onions for the stew. I couldn't help getting the smell on me."

"You could have washed yourself or changed your dress."

"Oh, Pearl, you're such a nuisance."

"I am not, am I, Opal?"

"I'm not letting either of you bother me. I'm trying to go to sleep because I have to get up early to go out on the range with Papa and Jace tomorrow."

"I still think Jace would rather have me go with him," Ruby said.

"It's too late to change now." Opal turned over.

"Besides, you can't ride a horse. Opal can," Pearl said. "Jace is going to teach me how to ride next." Pearl sat up in bed.

There was enough moonlight coming through the one window that Ruby asked, "Where do you think you're going?"

"I'm going to look out the window. I think I heard something outside."

"I didn't hear anything."

Opal yawned. "What did you hear, Pearl?"

"I don't know, but I thought it might be that dog I saw." She walked to the window.

As soon as she peered outside, she jumped back with a little scream.

"What is it?" Ruby sat up. "Do you see something?"

"It's a man," Pearl whispered. "He's running away."

Opal jumped from the bed and rushed to join her sister. Ruby was right behind her.

Looking outside, Opal said, "I don't see anyone, honey."

"He ran around the corner of the house." Pearl's voice was shaky.

"Probably just your imagination." Ruby looked out the window again, then turned back to the bed, shaking her head. "Pearl, sometimes I wonder if you're not adopted."

"I am not, am I, Opal?"

"Of course not. I remember well when you were born." She frowned into the night. "Maybe Ruby is right. You do have a vivid imagination."

"I'll say she does." Ruby fluffed her pillow. "Anybody who thinks a wolf is a dog can see things that aren't there."

"You're mean, Ruby. I hope someday you see something and nobody will believe you."

"I believe you, Pearl." Opal put her arm around her sister's shoulder. "Can you tell me what the man looked like?"

"No. He ran away too quickly."

Though she was sure the whole incident was a figment of her sister's imagination, Opal whispered, "Well, why don't we stand here and watch for a while. He may try to look in our window again."

Pearl leaned against her sister. "Okay."

After about fifteen minutes, Pearl began to yawn. "I guess I scared him away. We might as well go to bed, too. Sounds like Ruby is already snoring."

Opal chuckled. "I think that's a good idea. I want to get to sleep before she begins to snore any louder and keeps me awake."

Pearl turned and hugged her sister. "I love you, Opal. You're my favorite sister." She then moved to her bed and got into it.

Opal pulled the sheet up to Pearl's neck and kissed her forehead. "I love you, too."

Within another fifteen minutes, Pearl was breathing deeply. Opal wasn't as lucky. She was still sure her little sister hadn't seen a man, but she knew the girl had seen something. No matter what Ruby said, Pearl wasn't given to wild imaginations and she didn't lie. Something outside that window scared her. It could have been the wind or even a wild animal, but on the off chance that what Pearl had seen was human, Opal slipped out of bed and looked outside two more times before finally falling asleep.

## *Eight*

At ten o'clock the next morning, Jace pulled his horse up alongside Opal. "How's it going?"

"I feel useless. I don't seem to be doing anything except sitting on Patch and watching you and Papa chase cows out of thickets and bushes."

"That's all I want you to do today. You need to get the lay of the land around here and you're still adjusting your body to being on a horse. When we go in for the mid-day meal, I want you to quit for the day."

"Why? I'm not tired."

"You may not feel it yet, but I'm sure your muscles are going to hurt when you dismount. Not to mention how sore your backside is going to be from sitting in the saddle all morning."

Opal blushed. "I'll be fine."

"Sure you will, but it's going to take some getting used to. There are times when I get tired myself."

"I don't feel sore."

"Wait until you stand up."

She thought he was wrong, but she decided not to argue. Deep down, she wouldn't mind going back to the house at noon. Sitting on the horse and watching the two of them working was beginning to be boring. She hoped this wasn't the only thing Jace would let her do when they were on the range. If it were, she might as well be helping Mama with the cooking.

When he started to ride off, she called to him and he turned and asked, "What is it?"

"It looks like there's a creek over there around those trees. Why don't I ride over that way and see if there are any cows in the stream?"

He looked in the direction she pointed and nodded. "That's fine, but if you see anything, signal us by waving your hat or something. Don't try to run them out yourself."

She didn't see why she couldn't scare the cows out on her own, but she'd promised her papa she'd do everything Jace told her to do. She nodded and kneed Patch lightly.

The horse responded and went at a slow pace in the direction she led her. Even if she didn't see any cows in the creek, she realized the shade of the trees would be a more comfortable place to watch the two men work the cows than sitting here in the sun.

She was disappointed not to see any cattle around the creek, but she did like the area. There was an outcropping of rocks in the middle of the slowly running water causing tiny waterfalls as it drifted along. "This will be a good place to bring Pearl to play," she muttered aloud. "She'll love it."

Opal had almost decided to dismount when she caught a glimpse of something bright red slipping through the weeds on the other side of the water. Her heart beat a little faster, but she wasn't really frightened. She figured it was some pretty bird. Maybe a cardinal. She'd seen plenty of cardinals in Tennessee and the vibrant red color of the male of the species made it one of her favorite birds. She hoped there were cardinals in Arizona, but if they weren't, she figured there were red birds of some kind.

It dawned on her then that there was too much red crouched in those thick weeds to be a bird. It had to be an animal of some kind. But she didn't know of an animal that was such a vivid red. She saw more color as the weeds parted. Immediately she found herself staring into the dark eyes of a young man. He had long straight black hair and there was a band around his forehead. The red shirt he wore was much too big for him, but his buckskin pants seemed to fit.

Opal froze. She wanted to cry out, but her throat went dry and her tongue wouldn't work.

The boy didn't smile, but continued to stare at her. He looked like he wanted to speak, but seemed to be as afraid of her as she was of him.

Finally she found her voice. "Jace!" she screamed as loud as she could.

This must have frightened the boy, because he turned and ran in the opposite direction.

Opal turned Patch and started across the field toward her father and Jace. She was riding the fastest she had ever ridden on her horse and wasn't paying much attention to her surroundings.

A branch from one of the bushes grabbed her skirt as she rode by, ripping a section away and almost jerking her off the horse. She screamed as the reins slipped out of her hand. She did have enough presence of mind to hang on to the saddle horn as tightly as she could.

Jace reached her first and pulled up, stopping both his horse and hers. Her father wasn't far behind him.

"Honey, what's wrong?"

"I thought it was a bird…a boy was there…I almost fell off the horse…" She knew she was babbling, but she couldn't help it.

Jace dismounted and lifted her from the saddle. When her feet touched the ground, she wobbled. He steadied her by keeping his arm around her waist. "Calm down, Opal. Whatever it was, we're here now. You're safe."

She closed her eyes and took a deep breath. Finally she could speak plainly. "I was looking at the water and saw something red on the other side of the stream. At first I thought it was a bird, but then the weeds parted and I saw it was a young fellow with a red shirt on. It frightened me and I called for you." She looked up at Jace. "It scared him and he ran in the other direction."

"Honey, are you sure you saw someone?"

"Yes, Papa. He stared at me and I did the same to him. Neither of us spoke."

"I'm glad you screamed for us. He could have hurt you."

Jace shook his head. "Probably a neighbor kid. I don't think she was in as much danger from the boy as she was this damn dress."

"What do you mean?" George looked at Jace.

"Look at it, George. If the side hadn't ripped away, it could have jerked her off the horse and could have broken her neck when she fell." His voice showed his irritation. "Now do you see why I said she should wear pants when she works out here with us? She was lucky this time, but next time she could be killed."

"Yes, but..." George frowned. "You may be right. I sure don't want her to get hurt."

"Then it's settled. I don't want her back out here until she has the appropriate clothes. I want her to be safe."

"You're right, Jace. I should have listened to you in the first place."

Opal put her hands on her hips. "If you two are finished discussing my wardrobe, I think somebody should see if they can find that boy I saw."

"Honey, as Jace said, he was probably a neighbor kid. I don't think you have anything to worry about." Her father looked at Jace again. "It's a little past noon. Why don't we go on in and eat dinner? I'll see if Gloria can cut down a pair of my britches for Opal so she can come back with us tomorrow or next day."

"That's a good idea, George. I'd offer a pair of mine, but I'm a lot taller than you. I'm sure yours would be easier to make fit."

Opal shook her head and climbed back on Patch. When she sat in the saddle, she realized Jace had been right about her being sore. She thought she was going to cry out from the soreness she felt, but she didn't want either of them to know how much she ached and that everywhere her body touched the saddle she felt as if she were being beat with a stick of stove wood.

Without saying anything else to her, they mounted their horses and the three of them rode toward the house. Jace and George were still discussing what Opal should wear. She only shook her head and said nothing. She was concentrating on staying in the saddle without screaming.

~ * ~

"So you actually saw someone?" Gloria turned from putting the last dish in the cupboard.

"Yes, Mama. He scared me, but I think I scared him more. He ran off." Opal stood at the back door. She was watching Jace and her father riding out toward the range. She felt a little envious, but she knew her backside wouldn't allow her to get back on Patch.

"Maybe you're like Pearl. You're imagining seeing somebody." Ruby folded the dish towel and hung it on the small rod beside the sink.

"I didn't imagine anything." Pearl spoke up from the floor where she was stacking blocks with Sapphire. "Opal and I could have seen the same person."

Gloria frowned. "What are you girls talking about?"

"Oh, Mama. You know how Pearl is. She thought she saw somebody at our window last night. If you ask me, it was probably a shadow."

"It was not. I saw somebody."

"Why didn't you call your father?" Gloria looked concerned.

"We all got up and looked out the window. There wasn't anybody there. I went back to bed and left the two of them standing there." Ruby shook her head. "I'm sure she didn't see a thing."

"Opal?" Gloria looked at her.

"Ruby's right. We all did get up and look, but if anyone had been there, they were gone."

"I still think you should have called your father."

"We would have, but we watched for a long time and nobody appeared." Opal didn't want her little sister to think she didn't believe her, but she wanted to reassure her mother that there was no danger.

"Of course, there wasn't anyone. It was just Pearl's imagination. She can think up more things than anyone else in the family."

"What do you mean?" Pearl glared at Ruby.

"Well, you said you saw a fox or a wolf or something and thought it was a dog. Now you say you've seen a face in the window when there was nobody there. I'd call that an imagination."

"I did so see somebody and I saw a dog or something." Pearl stuck out her lip and looked as if she might cry.

"Ruby, I think you've said enough. If Pearl says she saw something, I'm sure she thinks she did. Now, stop arguing with her."

Ruby looked as if she might say something else, but she only muttered, "Yes, Mama."

"Now that the dishes are done, I'm going to start on those pants for Opal. Ruby, I want you to be in charge of checking out the garden. I think some wild greens have grown up and we can make a nice meal of them."

"Oh, Mama, why can't Opal be in charge of the garden? I had to milk this morning and help you get the wash started."

"Opal is working with Jace and your father. We can't expect her to work around the house, too."

"I don't mind helping out," Opal put in.

"I know you don't, honey, but you need to come with me so I can measure you."

Opal followed her mother to the room she shared with her husband. "I hope you don't mind me wearing pants, Mama."

"I don't like it much, but when Jace explained how you were almost pulled off your horse by your dress, I understand you must wear them. I want you to be safe while you're out there with the men." She went to the wardrobe. "Your father has an old pair he doesn't wear much anymore. I think those are the ones I'll cut down for you."

Opal sat carefully on the bed and let out a little grunt.

"Are you all right, Opal?"

She nodded. "I'm a little sore from being in the saddle all morning. Jace warned me that I would be."

"Maybe you should stay home for a few days. At least until the soreness is gone."

"No, I don't think so. Jace said it would get worse if I didn't get right back on the horse tomorrow. He did want me to rest some this afternoon."

"And that you'll do." Gloria pulled a pair of brown pants from the wardrobe and sighed. "I never dreamed when we left Tennessee that my oldest daughter was going to have to do a man's work."

"Somebody has to help them, Mama, and it looks like I'm the only one who can do it."

"I guess you're right, but there's still something about it that I don't think is right." She shook her head and handed Opal the pants. "Slip these on and I'll see what I can do to make them fit you better."

## *Nine*

Jace was glad he decided to take up the rear this morning because he liked the view. He couldn't help smiling as he watched Opal ride her horse out across the meadow behind her father. He had to admit to himself that she cut a fine figure in those pants. Her mother had done a good job of making them hug her curves, though he figured that wasn't Gloria's intention. He could tell the woman wasn't pleased to see her daughter dressed this way, but it couldn't be helped. If Opal was going to learn to work on the range, he figured there were several things she'd have to do that wouldn't exactly please her mother—or her father, either, for that matter. That was just the way it was in the West.

Without warning, he yawned, then chuckled. *Shouldn't have stayed up so late working on my room in the barn, but it's beginning to take shape. It's going to make a right cozy place for as long as I'm here. Then they can use it for a bunkhouse until one is built. Of course, that's got to wait until they're able to hire someone to help work this ranch.*

Though he knew he shouldn't boast, Jace couldn't help being proud of his handiwork . He had all the walls sealed so little to no air could come in. He knew this would be a good thing this winter, but he couldn't figure out why he'd decided to put a floor in the room. The dirt was well packed and would be easy to cover with some sort of rug, but for some reason he hadn't wanted that. The wood floor would be much nicer. And he still planned to put a small stove in the corner. It wasn't that he needed it to cook on because Gloria kept him well fed. But, besides for the heat it'd provide this winter, it would be nice to have a cup of coffee anytime he wanted it without disturbing the family in the house. All he had to do for the stove to work was cut out a spot for the flue so he wouldn't choke himself to death on smoke.

His bed was almost finished and he planned to start sleeping in it soon. He could have probably had it done already if for some reason he hadn't decided he needed a big bed. Of course, a bunk type would have been fine, but it was too late to change now. Besides, the sheets and blanket Gloria had given him fit a bigger bed. "Room for another person if the opportunity ever arises," he muttered to himself. Then he chuckled.

What was he thinking? The Barnetts would run him off if he ever brought a woman to his room. Besides, what woman would agree to visit him in a barn anyway? He didn't know anyone in town to invite except that little redhead or blonde or whatever at the saloon. He wondered why he couldn't remember which color of hair she had. He knew it didn't matter because he wasn't going to ask a woman of her morals to join him here and upset the family anyway. He had too much respect for them. Besides he had to keep a sharp lookout for his enemy.

He chuckled again and told himself to get women off his mind and think about why he'd come here in the first place and the work he had to get done today. They had cows to round up and that had to be his first priority.

As if on cue, a wild cow came rushing out of the bushes and headed straight for Opal's horse. Jace kneed his mount and rushed up beside her. Grabbing his hat, he yelled at the beast and turned him in the other direction.

Opal pulled back on the reins and stopped Patch. "Thank you," she yelled at Jace.

He nodded and drove the cow to the area where two others were grazing.

Gloria had put a roast in the over and washed the greens Ruby had picked the evening before. Pearl and Ruby had finished making the beds and sweeping the house and they came into the kitchen for a drink of water.

Their mother smiled at them. "I think I'll make a pie from those berries Pearl picked in the woods yesterday."

"That would be good, Mama. Papa loves pie."

"Yes and he's working so hard, he needs a little pampering."

Ruby laughed. "Not that you don't pamper him already."

Gloria smiled. "I guess I do, but he's good to me, too."

Ruby helped her gather the makings of the pie. "How about baking some of those wonderful cookies Sapphire loves so much while you're in a baking mood?"

"I'll do that."

They were taking the bake goods out of the oven when there was the sound of horses arriving in the front of the house. Gloria looked a little scared. "Where are Sapphire and Pearl?"

"I think they're in the back yard. I'll get them."

Gloria went to the front door as Ruby went out the back. Stepping out onto the front porch, Gloria was surprised to see a small ranch wagon pulling up near the steps. She smiled as a woman somewhat younger than she called, "Hello there."

In a matter of minutes, her daughters joined Gloria on the porch. Ruby held Sapphire on her hip and Pearl stared at the buggy.

A boy about ten climbed out and a little girl who looked to be around three followed.

"Hello, Mrs. Barnett. I'm Aloma Norton. My husband, Sam, told me you had moved in and I couldn't wait to meet you since there aren't many women to be friends with out here on the prairie." The woman got out of the buggy, shook the dirt off her blue skirt and pushed back her blue checked bonnet which was tied under her chin. This motion revealed sandy colored hair. Aloma's eyes sparkled when she said, "These are my children. The boy is Heath and the little girl is Daphne."

"I'm so glad you came, Mrs. Norton. I'm Gloria Barnett and these are three of my four daughters. Ruby, Pearl and Sapphire." She pointed to each one. "My eldest daughter, Opal, is helping her father out on the range." She indicated the door. "Please come inside. I've just taken a pan of cookies out of the oven and I bet your children would like one."

"Thank you. I'm sure they will and I think you should call me Aloma. It's easier to be less formal when you know you're going to end up as friends."

"I agree; therefore, I'm Gloria."

"Good." Aloma tied the reins to the hitching post and climbed up the steps. "Come, children, and be sure to mind your manners."

When they entered the combination kitchen and sitting room, Gloria put the platter of cookies on the table. "Would you children like to sit on the rug to eat your cookies?"

"Cookie." Sapphire squealed and plopped down on the floor.

Aloma laughed. "I see your little one knows what to do when she has a cookie."

"Yes, I think she knows if she doesn't go outside to eat it, the floor is her only option. Opal taught her that and Ruby here has reinforced it."

"I think it was because Opal and I got tired of sweeping up her crumbs. She had a habit of walking all over the room dribbling everywhere she went." Ruby turned to her mother. "I'll get milk for the children."

"Thank you, dear." Gloria turned to Aloma. "Would you like tea or coffee with your cookies?"

"Oh, my, I haven't had tea in a while. I'd love a cup." She glanced at the platter of cookies. "Your sweets look wonderful, Gloria. For some reason I can't ever get mine all to come out the same size."

Gloria smiled. "You happened to get here on a day mine came out better than usual. I've had my share of different sizes, too."

"Daphne, come sit with Sapphire," Pearl coaxed her.

Daphne stared at her and looked as if she might cry.

"Maybe you better sit with them, Heath. That way Daphne will feel comfortable," his mother said.

The boy nodded at his mother and took his little sister by her hand. "Come on, so we can get a cookie, too."

Aloma moved to the table and took a seat. "If you don't mind, I'll sit here. I like to have conversations with my friends at their kitchen tables."

"I like that, too."

"Why don't you sit and talk with Mrs. Norton, Mama? I'll make the tea."

"Thank you, Ruby." Gloria took a seat. "Now, Aloma, tell me about yourself."

"There's not a lot to tell. You met my husband and my oldest son a day or so ago. Well, Doyle is actually my stepson, but I think of his as my own. I married his father when he was six years old. Our ranch borders yours on the right. My husband inherited the place from his father and we've lived there ever since we were married and that was almost twelve years ago."

"Then you must have known my brother-in-law, Horace Barnett."

"Slightly. My husband knew him better than I did. Horace didn't do so well taking care of his place after his wife died."

"I didn't know he was married."

"Oh, yes, but they didn't have much to do with folks around here. With her being an Indian, most folks were just as pleased to leave them alone."

Gloria raised a surprised eyebrow. "Did you know her?"

"Somewhat. I tried to be friendly, but she was so shy. I think she thought I'd treat her like most of the folks in town did."

"Did they have any children?"

"Yes. They had a son, but after his mother died, the boy tended to run rather wild. I know he went to live with his mother's people when his father died. I heard it was because he was afraid they'd put him in a home or even make a slave of him. I guess he's still there."

Heath broke into the conversation. "I liked Daniel. He'd take me fishing sometimes at the creek."

"So he was about your age?" Gloria looked at the little boy.

"No, ma'am. He was older than me, but he showed me how to fish and how to shoot a bow and arrow. He also showed me how to clean the fish so Ma could cook 'em."

She glanced back at Aloma. "This comes as a big surprise to me. I never dreamed there was a child. I'll tell George that we have a nephew we knew nothing about. I'm sure my husband will want to check up on him."

"That would be kind of him."

Ruby set the tea cups on the table for the two women.

"This smells wonderful. I bet you didn't get it at Mayfield's store."

Gloria shook her head. "I brought it from Memphis, but I'm running low. I'm sure I'll have to buy whatever they have at the general store from now on."

The conversation turned to the merits of the store and what could and could not be purchased there. It then changed to cooking and by the time Aloma said she had to head home to start her husband's supper, she had a fist full of recipes she'd written down and, on the table, Gloria had just as many she'd gotten from her new friend.

## *Ten*

The next week things didn't change much. Opal continued to work on the range with her father and Jace. Her soreness had subsided somewhat and she was getting more proficient on the horse. Jace and her father decided it was time to let her help run the cows out to join the herd when she found them. They had rounded up a good number of cows and had managed to put together a pretty nice herd. Jace said they would need to start branding the calves they had found soon.

Gloria and her other daughters had worked in the house, the garden and the yard. The place took on a neat lived-in look and the entire family began to like living in Arizona more than they thought they ever would.

Jace's room was near completion and Gloria and all her daughters had stuffed a mattress with straw for him. On Wednesday afternoon, after they had come in from the range, George went on to the house when Opal and Jace offered to cool down his horse and turn him into the corral. Opal was concentrating on Patch and wasn't paying much attention to what was going on, but she glanced up when she heard her mother's voice.

"Jace, I know you have your new bed finished and I wanted to give you something the girls and I made for it."

He put down his brush and looked around.

George and Gloria were carrying a stuffed mattress between them.

Jace shook his head. "You folks are awfully good to me."

"There's no way we can ever pay you what you're worth around here," George said. "But Gloria and the girls stuffed this for your new bed."

"We didn't go into your room to measure because we didn't want to intrude, so we hope it fits."

"It looks perfect." He walked toward them. "Come in and see what I've done in here." He saw Opal looking at him and he added, "Why don't you come, too? Maybe you and your mother can tell me what else I'll need this winter."

Opal couldn't help it, her heart jumped a little. From his statement she surmised that Jace would be there through the winter. This pleased her.

He opened the door and stood back for George and Gloria to enter. They went to the large bed and put the mattress on the frame.

"It's a perfect fit." Gloria grinned. "I'm so pleased."

Opal was looking at the things Jace had done in the room. "This looks wonderful," she muttered.

"It sure does. I'm afraid my girls are going to be jealous. Their room isn't nearly as nice."

"When we get things together on the ranch, Gloria, I'd be happy to help George build another room on your cabin."

"Oh, Jace, that would be wonderful. Right now, Opal, Ruby and Pearl are sharing a room. They'd love to have more space." She looked around. "I see you plan to put a stove in here. I hope it isn't because you don't like my cooking."

He chuckled. "Your cooking is great. I just thought I might need it for warmth this winter, but I might get a coffee pot."

George laughed. "Shoot, Jace, you've got things set up so well in here, you look like you're ready to settle down and maybe look for a wife or something."

"It'll be a long time before I start thinking like that, George. Besides, what woman would want to live with a man in a barn?"

Opal shocked herself when she thought, I would. She shook her head and walked to the window. "Maybe you should make him some curtains when you and Ruby have time, Mama."

"That's a good idea, honey. Would you like that, Jace?"

"I hadn't thought about curtains."

"Well, if you're going to be living in here, you certainly don't want some stranger peeping in on you."

He raised an eyebrow. "I hadn't thought about that either."

"Then we'll make you some curtains. I probably won't get around to it this week, but in a couple of weeks, I will."

"Please don't go to so much trouble, Gloria."

"Relax, Jace," George butted in. "You might as well give in. If the women want to sew you up some curtains, they're going to, whether you like it or not."

"Well...I..."

"Don't worry, Jace." Gloria laughed. "I promise I won't make anything pink or with flowers. I don't think that'd suit you."

He chuckled. "You're right about that."

After her parents left, Opal and Jace went back to finish brushing their horses. After a minute of silence, she said, "You really do have a nice place, Jace. I'm surprised you went to all the trouble to put in a floor and everything."

"I guess I did get carried away a little, but I like building things. I'm sure it comes from helping my uncle in his woodworking shop back in Baltimore."

She glanced at him. "I didn't know you were from Baltimore. I thought you were born and raised in the West."

"I was born here and lived here until I was about seven. Then I moved East with my mother."

"How long have you been back?"

"Almost ten years."

"Are you going back East someday?"

"Not to live. I've always felt the West was my home. I plan to spend the rest of my life here." He put down his brush. "All right, China, you look ready to go roll in the dirt and undo all my work."

"I've wondered why you named your horse, China, Jace. Do you mind telling me?"

"Not at all. I bought him from a Chinese man I met about four years ago. I figured the name was as good as any."

"That makes sense." She put her brush on the shelf beside the stall. "Patch is ready, too. Let's get them in the corral and go see what Mama has on the table tonight. I'm a little hungry."

~ * ~

Jace lay on his back with his hands behind his head in his new bed. The ladies had done a great job with the stuffing. He didn't think he'd slept on such a comfortable mattress since the last time he'd splurged and spent a night in a hotel, and that had been a couple of years ago. In fact he was so comfortable he was having trouble going to sleep.

Or maybe it wasn't the comfort of the bed that was keeping him awake. It could be the fact that he was here with this wonderful family that was causing him to fight falling to sleep. A family with a father that was hell bent on making this a good home for his family and a mother that was caring and thoughtful. Not like the mother he'd been raised by.

Jace had loved his mother, but they'd never had the closeness that Gloria had with her children and certainly Aster Renwick had never shown the compassion Gloria Barnett showed a stranger. He couldn't remember seeing his mother showing compassion to anyone. She certainly didn't have any when it came to her husband.

The day his mother whisked him away from his father floated across his mind. Jace knew he'd never been able to get the memory of the day he'd been dragged away from his father out of his mind. He remembered vividly how he, as a young boy, kept trying to get free of her firm lock on his arm as she pushed him into the stagecoach without looking back. As she was settling herself inside, Jace managed to look out the window and see the tall miner with tears in his eyes whispering, "I'll see you again someday, son."

But it was not to be. His father had written several times through the years asking his estranged wife to please let Jace visit him, or let him come to Baltimore and spend some time with his son. She never failed to come up with an excuse of why it wasn't possible at the time.

When Jace was fifteen, he found one of these letters by accident and had angry words with his mother. After this confrontation, her unhealthy heart put her in bed for two months. After that, Jace never mentioned his father to his mother again, but he did write to his dad and tell him he would come to Colorado as soon as he could. His father wrote back that he was excited about the impending visit and couldn't wait. This letter was the only thing Jace had left of his father. It was seldom very far away from the shirt pocket closest to his heart.

The sound of someone trying to open his door interrupted his thoughts. He frowned and waited.

There was a jerk on the door.

Without making a sound, Jace stepped from the bed, picked up his gun and eased across the room. He lifted the bar and jerked open the door.

For an instant, wide brown eyes stared up at him then the young man turned around and started to sprint away. He wasn't fast enough. Jace's hand reached out and gripped his shoulder and stopped him.

"Who're you and what do you want here?"

The boy glared at him, but didn't answer.

Jace pulled him into the room and put his gun back in the holster hanging on the nail he'd put in the wall beside the bed. "Now tell me…." Before he could finish his sentence, the young man collapsed at his feet.

"What the…?" Jace knelt down and looked at the boy. His eyes landed on the red shirt. It was plastered to the young man's back by dark wet spots and there were several rips. Lifting it as carefully as he could, Jace frowned. The boy's back was covered in slashes. Somebody had beaten him mercilessly with a whip.

Jace knew he didn't have anything to use to help him. He grabbed his pants and slipped on his boots. Though he hated to wake the Barnetts, he had no choice. This young man needed attention. He scooped the boy up in his arms and headed toward the house. As soon as he reached the back door, he kicked on it as a knock and yelled for George.

In a minute George came to the door with a lit lamp in his hand. "What's the matter, Jace?"

"This boy's hurt."

George stood aside. "Bring him in. I'll get Gloria."

"I'm here, George." She saw the boy in Jace's arms. "Bring him over here." She indicated the couch. "What's wrong with him?"

"Somebody's beat the he…I mean somebody's beat him with a whip or something." Jace put him face down on the couch.

"Oh, my goodness. He's hurt badly. Bring the lamp over here, George, so I can see better."

Opal came into the room. "Is something wrong?"

"Yes. This boy is hurt and Jace brought him to us," her father said.

Gloria glanced up. "You can help me, Opal. I need some warm water and a clean wash cloth."

Without speaking, Opal rushed to the stove and poured some of the still warm water from the kettle into a pan. Grabbing a clean dishtowel, she took them to her mother.

Gloria shook her head. "I can't believe anyone would do this to another human being."

"How did you find him, Jace?" George looked at him.

"I hadn't gone to sleep and I heard somebody trying to open my door. When I went out, I found this Indian."

"Did he say anything?"

"No. When he saw me, he turned to run, but collapsed before he could get away."

Opal came back with a pan in her hand. "Here's the water, Mama."

"Thank you, Opal."

"Is he going to be all right?"

"I don't know, honey. He's hurt badly." Gloria dipped the rag in the water.

Opal looked at Jace. "Do you know who he is?"

He shook his head. "Never saw him before in my life."

"I wonder what he wanted."

"It looks to me as if he was running away from whoever hurt him. I think he was trying to hide in your barn."

Her mother's voice broke in the conversation. "I have some of the ointment I keep to use on the children when they get scrapes and cuts. It's on the shelf in our room, George. Will you get it?"

"I'll be right back."

Opal glanced at the red shirt in the floor where her mother had dropped it after taking it off the boy. She reached down and picked it up. "This looks like the shirt the boy I saw near the creek the other day was wearing."

Jace lifted an eyebrow. "It could've been him."

George returned with the ointment and handed it to his wife.

"Opal, I think I hear your sisters getting up. Maybe it would be best if you kept them in the bedroom. Your mother will call you if she needs you."

Opal nodded and left the room.

Jace turned to George. "I'm going to look around outside and see if I can find anything to give us a clue as to why he came here. Of course, I really don't expect to find anything. Indians don't leave trails unless they want to."

"You never know. There's a lantern hanging on the porch. Might better take it."

Jace knew he was right and he wouldn't find anything when he went outside, but he knew he had to get out of that house. It wasn't because of the hurt stranger or to go looking for clues. It was because the sight of Opal in her nightclothes had stirred him more than he ever thought a woman could. He was afraid George was going to see the evidence of his desire if he didn't hurry.

Rushing out the back door, he lit the lantern and made a sweep around the barn, trying to get Opal's slim shapely body in her light blue robe off his mind. It wasn't working and he didn't know why.

He kept telling himself, yes, Opal is a pretty young woman, but she certainly isn't the most beautiful female I've ever seen. She's smart and kind, but there are a lot of kind woman, smart and otherwise. What was it about this particular young woman that intrigues me so? I've got to get over these feelings about her. Maybe I need to get back to the saloon in Wildweed and find that blonde. Or was she a redhead?

~ * ~

"Do you want me to find some bandages, Gloria?"

She looked up at her husband. "I think it would be best to leave his wounds open to the air for the time being."

"I suppose you're right."

She sighed. "That's all I can do for him, George. I hope it's enough."

"I hope so, too, dear." He shook his head. "I agree with Jace. What kind of evil person could be cruel enough to do this to someone?"

"Maybe the boy will rouse up soon and tell us what happened to him."

"Maybe so." He helped his wife from her kneeling position beside the couch. "Do you want me to go ask Jace to take him to the barn to sleep?"

She shook her head. "Let him sleep here. That way I'll be close if he needs something. I'll sit with him for a while. Why don't you go back to bed? You have to work on the range tomorrow."

"No. I'll stay here. You go back to bed."

"Don't argue with me, George. I'm staying with him. I can rest tomorrow and Ruby can do what needs doing in the house. You don't have anyone to take your place out there."

"But…" He closed his mouth when he saw the determined look on his wife's face. "I'll go sleep a bit, but I think I should go tell Jace we're keeping him in the house."

She nodded and he added, "I'm doing this only if you promise to call me if the boy wakes up and tries to get up or something."

She smiled at him. "I promise."

George leaned down and kissed his wife's forehead. "I'll be right back."

True to his word, he was back by the time Gloria emptied the pan of water and returned to the boy.

George glanced at her. "Don't forget your promise."

"I won't." She watched her husband as he disappeared into their bedroom.

## *Eleven*

It was almost dawn when Opel awoke. Ruby and Pearl were still sleeping. Trying not to wake them, she slid out of bed, put on her work pants and the shirt her mother hadn't yet had time to cut down for her. It didn't matter. She tucked it in the pants and slipped on her boots.

In the main room she heard her mother talking, but nobody was answering her. Frowning, she came into the room.

In her kindly voice, Gloria was saying, "Can you tell me what happened to you?"

The fellow lying face down on the sofa didn't answer.

"Won't he say anything, Mama?"

She shook her head. "He just stares at me with those big brown eyes. I think he might be afraid of me."

"He's hurt pretty bad, isn't he?"

"Yes. I don't see how he's stood the horrible pain. It looked like somebody was trying to kill him."

"That's awful."

Gloria looked down on the sleeping boy. Or at least she thought he was sleeping. "You're right. I can't imagine anyone doing what's been done to this young man."

"Has he tried to get up?"

"Yes, but I put my hand on his shoulder and told him he needed to rest. He got quiet after that, but still wouldn't talk."

"Did he sleep well?"

"Off and on. He's still awfully weak and I want him to get all the rest he can."

Opal patted her mother's shoulder. "Look, Mama. He's opening his eyes. Do you want me to try to see if I can get something out of him before he goes back to sleep?"

"If you will. Your father built a fire and made the coffee before going out to check with Jace. I'll go start breakfast."

She took her mother's vacated chair and looked down at the patient. There was something familiar about him, but it took her a while to realize it was his eyes. She knew now he was the person she'd spied when she was at the creek.

Forcing a smile, she said in a soft voice, "We met down by the creek a few days ago. Do you remember?"

He didn't say anything, but she was sure he lifted an eyebrow slightly. She couldn't tell if he was afraid of her or if he was remembering seeing her that day.

She went on. "You probably know you scared me half to death because I wasn't expecting to see you. I hope I didn't scare you when I screamed."

There was a slight shake of his head.

"Good. I was afraid I did and that was why you ran off."

He shook his head again.

"As I said, I'm glad I didn't frighten you. If I hadn't been so startled, I would've stopped and talked to you, but it all happened fast. The next thing I knew, you were gone. You must be a fast runner."

His mouth moved and she was sure he said, "I am."

Good. He could speak English. She didn't let him know she was surprised. "What's your name?"

He didn't answer.

"I just want to know what to call you. I don't think you'd like me always saying, boy or young man, would you?"

His eyes closed, then opened and she thought she saw him shake his head.

"My name's Opal. Opal Barnett."

He stared at her for several minutes. She could barely hear him when he said, "Daniel."

She kept her voice low, too. "Hello, Daniel. Do you have a last name?"

He didn't answer and his eyes closed.

"If you don't want to tell me your last name, could you tell me who hurt you?"

He shook his head.

"Why not? Did they threaten you?"

Before he could answer, Pearl and Ruby came into the room. "Who in the world is that?" Ruby looked at the sofa.

Her mother turned from the stove. "He's a young man who somebody has hurt. We're trying to help him."

"Why? We don't know him."

Opal glared at her sister. "For heaven's sake, Ruby, don't be so selfish. If you were hurt, wouldn't you want somebody to help you?"

Ruby dropped her head. "I'm sorry. You know I'm grumpy in the morning."

Gloria shook her head. "Well, come over here and help me finish up breakfast, Grumpy. Opal is taking care of our patient."

Ruby didn't say anything, but she stalked over to the kitchen area.

Pearl moved up close to Opal's shoulder. She whispered, "Is he an Indian?"

"Jace said he was." Opal turned back to Daniel. When she saw his eyes had opened again, she said, "This is my sister, Pearl. She wants to know if you're an Indian."

He nodded, but kept quiet.

Pearl looked back at him. "I've never met an Indian before. Have you ever met a white person?"

He nodded again.

The back door opened and George came in. "I see you're cooking. How's the young man?"

"Opal's looking after him."

"Has he said anything?"

"I've heard him mumble to Opal, but I don't know what he's said."

George moved over to where the boy lay.

Daniel's eyes grew big and he looked as if he might try to run.

Opal said, "Don't be afraid, Daniel. This is my papa. He's not going to hurt you."

"Of course I won't, son. I want to find out what happened so whoever did this to you pays for his crime."

Daniel glanced at Opal as if he was asking her if he could believe her father. She smiled at him.

"He's telling the truth, Daniel. The Barnetts don't believe in hurting innocent people."

"Barnett."

"Yes, that's our name. We're the Barnett family."

He nodded and pointed to himself. "Daniel Barnett."

Opal looked at her father. He shrugged, but her mother rushed over to them. "Did this child say his name was Daniel Barnett?"

"Yes, Mama."

She walked over and looked down at Daniel. "George, we've been so busy I forgot to tell you what Aloma Norton told me the other day. She said your brother was married to an Indian woman and they had a son named Daniel."

George frowned. "If Horace was married, why didn't he leave this ranch to his wife and son?"

"She said his wife died before her husband. When Horace died, the boy went to live with his mother's people."

Ruby came over to them. "I know Mrs. Norton said there was a child, but I don't believe this is it."

"Why not, Ruby?" Pearl glared at her.

"Don't you realize that if he's Uncle Horace's son, that'd make him our cousin and I don't know if I want an Indian for a cousin."

"That's enough of that talk, Ruby." Her father's voice was firm.

"But, Papa..." She didn't finish her sentence when her father gave her one of those looks that everyone in the family knew meant that as far as he was concerned, the matter was closed and there would be no more discussion.

His next words sealed his position on the subject. "If we find out this child is family, we will treat him as family. Now let's move to the table and have breakfast. I saw Jace headed for the house when I came in."

Opal was sure Daniel didn't hear the discussion. He'd gone back to sleep. "At least we know his name is Daniel. Maybe when he wakes up we can find out more about him."

Cletus Finch came into the barn to untie the half-breed and was shocked to see the ropes he'd been tied with lying on the straw at the foot of the post where he'd been secured. Confused, he knelt down and muttered, "What the hell?"

He grabbed the ropes and looked closer at them. He then frowned. "Looks like the devil gnawed through them with his teeth.

I might've knowed he'd act like a wild animal when left in here alone. I don't care how much white blood's in a person, it can't wash out the dirty Injun part that's there."

Standing, he yelled as loud as he could, "Billy, get yourself in here."

Instantly a scrawny boy of around seven came running into the barn. "Yes, sir, Mr. Finch."

"Where did that damn half-breed go?"

Billy looked stunned. "I don't know, sir."

"What do you mean you don't know where he went?" Cletus snarled at the shaking boy. "You slept in the barn loft, didn't you?"

Billy backed up a little and his voice shook when he muttered, "He must've slipped out when we was working or after we went to bed."

"That ain't no excuse. Was he here when you come in and went to bed or not?"

"I don't know. I was tired and didn't pay no attention."

"Well, you lazy varmint, you should've paid attention." He reached out to slap the boy, but Billy backed up a little more and he missed. "I bet you know exactly where he is and you're covering for him."

"No, sir, I ain't."

"Where's Glen and Ivan?"

"They rode out with Duff. I don't know where they went."

"Damn, you don't know much, do you, you stupid kid?"

"No, sir."

Cletus squinted his eyes and sneered. "You do know I'll have to tell Mr. GW you let him the Injun get away, don't you?"

"I didn't let him get away. I swear I didn't." Again his voice shook.

"Well, somebody has to take the blame and I guarantee it ain't gonna be me."

"But…"

"Don't argue with me, you little snot. And if you want anything to eat today, get back out there and finish slopping them hogs, then get on with cleaning out the stables."

Billy didn't tarry. He left the barn as quickly as his scrawny legs could carry him.

Cletus watched him leave and muttered, "Won't be nothing for you to fill your gut today, you little bastard. I know good and well you know where that redskin is. If you get hungry enough, you'll tell me, too." He grinned a sinister grin. "Of course, a few licks with my whip will make you talk faster."

He bent down and picked up another of the scattered pieces of the rope. "You'll be sorry you did this, you stinking half-breed animal. I'll find you and when I do, I'll make you eat the rest of this rope then I'll see that you don't become a full grown Indian. We got enough of the likes of you in this world already."

## *Twelve*

After breakfast, Jace and George headed out to the range. They
insisted Opal stay at the house to help her mother, since Gloria had
spent most of the night beside Daniel's bedside.

Opal, who had eaten with the men, cleaned the table and made
places for the rest of them to eat and her mother filled the kettle to
heat water to wash the dishes. Ruby cooked more eggs and Pearl
poured herself a glass of milk.

Sapphire came toddling into the room. Her eyes got big and she
stopped the instant she saw Daniel lying on the sofa. Starring at him, she
muttered, "Who?"

"It's Daniel," Pearl explained as she motioned to her little sister.
"He's asleep and we have to stay quiet."

Sapphire moved closer to the sofa. "No."

Ruby walked over and reached for her little sister's hand.
"Come on, honey. Let's get you some breakfast."

Sapphire pulled her hand away. She was still looking at Daniel.
"Eat?"

Daniel didn't say anything and Ruby grabbed her hand. "I said,
come with me."

"Eat." Again she pulled her hand away.

"Sapphire, for heaven's sake. Come over here and eat your breakfast."

Opal put the last plate on the table and moved over to them. "I'm through, Ruby. You can have my place."

"But ..."

"Go on. I'll take care of Sapphire." Opal bent down beside her little sister. "Sapphire, this is Daniel. He's been hurt and we're trying to help him."

"Help?"

She nodded and looked at Daniel with a smile. "Are you feeling better, Daniel?"

He nodded.

"Eat?"

"Sapphire wants to know if you want to eat."

He nodded.

"Come on, Sapphire. You go let Mama feed you some eggs and I'll get Daniel something to eat."

She nodded, took Opal's hand and waved at Daniel with the other. "Bye."

"I'll be right back, Daniel. Would you like some eggs?"

His eyes got big and he nodded.

"Mama, after you feed Sapphire, why don't you lie down and take a little nap?" Ruby asked.

"I might rest in a little while." She held out her arms. "Come on, baby. Let's get you fed before your sisters eat all the food."

Sapphire giggled and climbed on her mother's lap.

Opal picked up a plate and dipped some eggs, took two slices of bacon and a spoon full of potatoes on it. She moved beside Daniel and pulled up a chair. "I know you're weak, but would you like to try to sit up? I'm afraid you might choke if you attempt to eat lying on your stomach."

He sat, but she could tell he was in pain though he was careful not to hurt his back. His feet moved to the floor beside the sofa and she couldn't help noticing the ragged moccasins he wore.

Glaring at the plate in her hand, he muttered, "For me?"

"Of course. When was the last time you ate?"

He shrugged.

"Well, you looked like you might be hungry."

He nodded.

"Do you think you can feed yourself?"

"Yes."

She pulled the small table beside the sofa in front of him. "I'll put your food here. It'll make it easier for you to eat." She handed him a fork and sat the milk beside the plate. "If you'd rather have it, I'll get you some coffee."

"Milk is good." He looked at her for a moment, then dived into the food as if he thought he'd never get another meal.

"Slow down, Daniel. Nobody's going to take it away. You'll get sick if you eat too fast."

He slowed, but continued to eat in silence.

Opal knew everyone at the table was waiting for her to start asking him questions, but she wanted to see if she could win his trust. When she realized he wasn't going to talk, she said in a soft voice, "Why did someone do this to you, Daniel?"

He took a drink of milk and looked at her. When she didn't say anything else, he mumbled, "I stole something."

Opal tried not to look shocked. "What did you steal?"

It took a minute for him to answer. Finally he said, "An egg."

Stunned, Opal gasped. "They beat you like this because you took an egg?"

He nodded. "I didn't think they'd miss one egg. I was hungry 'cause they don't feed us."

"Who did it?"

He shook his head. "He'll kill me."

"Surely not."

"He would. So I run away as soon as I could."

"Why did you come here, Daniel?"

"It's home."

"What do you mean?"

He didn't answer and she added, "You don't have to tell me now, but let me assure you, nobody is going to kill you as long as you're here with us. My father won't let them."

He shook his head. "He's mean. He'll find me."

"Do you have any family around here, Daniel?"

He looked down at his empty plate. "My dad is dead."

"I'm sorry. How about your mama?"

"She's dead, too."

He looked as if he were getting tired. Opal wanted to know one more thing. "Tell me your last name."

"I told you. Barnett." He kept looking at his plate. "I feel better. Do I have to do some work now?"

She was puzzled. "Of course not. You're in no shape to work. Why don't you lie down and rest. We'll talk again later."

He looked at her as if he didn't believe her. "Are you sure?"

"I'm sure."

He still looked as if he didn't believe her, but she could tell he was too weak to argue. He laid again on his stomach. Though she knew he was fighting it, he soon fell asleep.

"Looks like you and the Indian have a nice relationship," Ruby whispered to Opal when her older sister came back to the table carrying the empty glass and plate.

"Why are you being so catty, Ruby? That young man is hurt and we're only trying to help him."

Ruby flung back her hair. "I don't like him being here."

"Why not?"

Pearl butted in. "Because Ruby thinks she's better than anybody else, that's why."

"I do not?"

Opal ignored their argument. "Did Mama go lie down?"

"Yes. She said to start a stew for dinner."

"Did Sapphire go with her?"

Ruby nodded and headed to the door. "I've finished washing the dishes and I'm going to gather the eggs."

"Want me to do it?" Pearl asked.

Opal and Ruby both raised an eyebrow. Ruby asked, "Why would you volunteer? You never want to get the eggs."

"I don't like those old chickens flying in my face, but I don't want to start peeling vegetables for a stew."

Opal chuckled. "Then you go get the eggs, Pearl. Ruby and I will chop the vegetables."

As soon as the door closed, Ruby turned to Opal. "Why did you send her? You know she hates the chickens."

"I want to tell you something."

"What?"

"How much did you hear of my conversation with Daniel?"

"I heard you talking, but you kept your voice so low I couldn't understand what you said."

"You're going to have to change your attitude about Daniel, Ruby."

"Why?"

"Because I think that young man is our cousin."

Ruby looked stricken. "He can't be."

"Of course he can. You said yourself that Mrs. Norton told Mama that Uncle Horace was married to an Indian woman and they had a son."

"Yes, but…"

"Don't fight with me, Ruby. Think about what you're saying about another human—one that could be a relative."

Ruby bit her lip. "But what will Doyle think of me if I tell him I'm related to an Indian?"

Opal looked at Ruby in disgust. "If Doyle doesn't want to be your friend because we have an Indian cousin, I'd say you're better off without him."

Ruby didn't say anything else. She went to table and began peeling potatoes.

Opal only hoped Daniel was asleep and didn't hear what they were saying.

The men came in for the mid-day meal. Gloria was up and rested, so Opal went back with them to work on the range.

By mid-afternoon, Gloria had finished the supper stew and Pearl and Sapphire had made friends with Daniel. He didn't talk much, but seemed to enjoy having them talk to him. Ruby didn't say much to anyone. She was trying to digest what Opal had said to her.

As she let the bucket down into the well, she let her mind linger over the idea of having an Indian for a cousin. Was she wrong not to want to be related to him? Her sister seemed to think so. But what if people talked about her because she had an Indian cousin? Did the people in Wildweed think it was all right to have a wild person as kin? And weren't all Indians wild? Of course Daniel seemed to be awfully educated for a wild Indian. He spoke English as perfectly as anyone she'd ever heard. Especially for a teenager, which she was sure he was. Even with their mother's strict teaching of the English language, the Barnett girls said things wrong sometimes.

Coming in from the back yard with a fresh bucket of water she'd drawn, Ruby looked down the road. A horse and rider were headed in the direction of the house. He looked as if he was in a hurry.

She rushed inside. "Mama, there's a rider coming up fast."

Gloria turned from the table where she was preparing the makings of a pie. "Where are Sapphire and Pearl?"

"I thought they were entertaining the Indian."

"They went outside a few minutes ago. Call them in."

They didn't have to call. Pearl came through the door leading Sapphire. "Somebody's coming."

"I know. You girls stay inside." Gloria rubbed the flour off her hands and headed to the front door as the rider came into the yard.

Ruby didn't know why a sudden rush of fear ran through her. She turned to Pearl. "Why don't you take Sapphire into the bedroom? Make a game of it so she'll be quiet."

After a look at her sister's face, Pearl didn't argue. "Come on, Sapphire. I want to show you something in Mama's room."

Without argument, Sapphire followed Pearl into the bedroom.

Ruby glanced at the sleeping boy on the sofa. She bit her lip, but ignored the feeling that she should hide him. She eased up to the door where she could hear her mother talk to the stranger.

"Howdy, ma'am. My name's Cletus Finch," the man said and Ruby's heart lurched. This was the man who came on the first day they were here and tried to buy the ranch from her father.

"Yes, sir. I'm Mrs. Barnett. What can I do for you?"

"I'm looking for a runaway and I thought he might have come here." His voice wasn't very friendly, and Ruby could tell he was trying to control his anger.

"There's nobody here but my family, Mr. Finch."

"Maybe he's hidin' and you just ain't seen him."

"I don't think so, sir?"

"Mind if I take a look around in your barn? That's probably where he'd hide."

"If he was there, my husband would've seen him when he saddled his horse this morning."

"I don't know about that. Indians have a way of making themselves invisible."

"Well, Mr. Finch, I guess it would be all right for you to look in the barn, but I'm sure you won't find anyone."

"If he's not in the barn, maybe you've got him in the house."

Gloria put her hands on her hips. "Don't be ridiculous. As I said, you may look in the barn, but if you don't find him there, I suggest you leave our ranch."

"How's the ranching business treatin' you? You 'bout ready to give up on the foolish notion of living here and sell out to me?"

"My husband is not selling this ranch."

"Oh, he'll eventually give in. You'll see."

"Sir, why are you getting off that horse?"

"I think I better check your house before I go to the barn."

"You will not check my house." Gloria moved to the door and started inside.

He bounded to the porch and grabbed her arm. "Do you think you're big enough to stop me?"

"Nobody is allowed to come into our home without an invitation."

"Then I suggest you invite me in."

"I will not. Now climb back on your horse and get off our property."

"I'm not going anywhere until I see if that Injun is inside." He shoved Gloria away from the door, but she grabbed the back of his shirt.

He turned and raised his hand. "I said I was going inside. Now if you don't want me to knock some sense into you, you'll get out of my way. You won't be the first woman I've knocked down.

Ruby didn't wait to hear any more. She turned to the sofa and shook Daniel. "Wake up. I've got to hide you."

He was startled. "What?"

"There's a man here looking for you."

He sprang up. "I've got to get out of here."

"No." Ruby took his arm. "Come with me. I'll hide you."

He started to protest then he must have heard the voices outside. When he stood, his legs wobbled. Ruby put her arm around his waist, being careful not to touch his raw back. "This way."

As they came into the bedroom she saw Pearl and Sapphire playing with a rag doll on the bed. "There's a bad man here. He wants to hurt Daniel, so we have to hide him."

Pearl whirled around. "What can I do to help?"

"We'll see in a minute." She turned to Daniel. "Do you think you can crawl under the bed?"

He nodded and dropped to his stomach. In an instant he slid under the bed.

"Grab the sheets off, Pearl. I'll pretend I'm changing them. You see if you can keep Sapphire interested in playing so she won't say anything,"

"Play." Sapphire held her doll toward Ruby.

"Yes, we'll play later, baby. You play with Pearl now."

Sapphire turned to Pearl. "Play."

Ruby heard heavy footsteps in the house and heard her mother say, "I told you I don't want you in here."

"Well I'm in and I plan to look in every room until I find what you're hidin'.

Ruby turned to her sister. "Mama can't stop him. He's coming. Be careful what you say. When he comes in here, I'm going to pretend he frightened me."

Pearl nodded.

"Well, he ain't in here." His voice sounded disappointed.

"I told you he wasn't. Now, leave this instant." Gloria's voice was sharper than any other time they'd heard her. Even when she was upset with someone.

"What them blankets doing on the couch?"

"I don't think that's any of your business."

"Look, lady, if you're hidin' that Injun..."

"Are you threatening me again, Mr. Finch?"

He ignored her and headed to the bedrooms. When he came to the door where the girls were, Ruby whirled around and let out a little scream.

It scared Sapphire. She dropped her doll and ran to her mama crying.

"I was looking for somebody…"

"Mama, don't let him come in here." Pearl moved beside Ruby and grabbed her arm.

"You're scaring my children." Gloria's voice was shaking with fear and anger. "Now, I'm going to tell you one more time to get out of my house."

He swung around and stomped toward the door. "I guess you was telling the truth." He slammed the door when he went outside.

Gloria reached down and picked up Sapphire. "Don't cry, baby. The bad man has gone." Her voice took on its usual calm gentle tone.

"Has he gone, Mama?"

"He'll probably check the barn before he leaves. Where's Daniel?"

"Bed," Sapphire said as she clung to her mother.

"Honey, you don't have to go to bed."

Ruby and Pearl both laughed a nervous laugh. "I don't think she wants to go to bed, Mama," Ruby said. "She's telling you Daniel is under the bed."

Gloria smiled and knelt down. "Are you all right, Daniel?"

He nodded.

"I'm sorry, but you better stay there until Mr. Finch is gone. He won't stay long after he doesn't find you in the barn."

"Thank you." His voice was a whisper.

"We'll let you know when it's safe to come out." She stood. "Come with me, girls. I need one of you to watch the front door and the other to watch the back. We want to be sure he leaves before Daniel joins us."

## *Thirteen*

They were around the supper table and Gloria was telling them what had happened earlier. Jace wanted to interrupt, but forced himself to listen without speaking. There would be time for questions later.

"So he just came in the house?" George stared at his wife.

"I told him he couldn't come in, but he didn't listen to me."

"But you said he didn't see the boy."

"Ruby heard him say he was coming in to look and she hid Daniel under the bed in our room."

"I helped," Pearl said from her seat on the floor beside the sofa where Daniel sat eating his supper as he had his breakfast.

"Lord, I wish I'd been here. I can't stand the thoughts of someone coming in on my family without an invitation." He looked at her closely. "And you're sure he didn't hurt anyone?"

"No, George. We were scared, but we weren't hurt."

"Me and Ruby watched until he checked the barn and then left."

"Ruby and I, Pearl, dear," her mother said.

"Yes, ma'am."

George looked at Ruby. "I didn't think you liked the boy. What possessed you to hide him?"

Ruby shrugged. "I might not like it, but he may be our cousin. Just in case he is, I couldn't let an evil man like that Mr. Finch get hold of him."

Jace couldn't help smiling to himself. Maybe Ruby was the self-centered young woman he thought she was, but deep down she was a caring person. Not as caring as Opal, but caring nonetheless.

George glanced at Jace. "I'm not sure I should go out on the range and leave the women here alone."

"If you want to be the rancher you say, you don't have a choice, George. Women have stayed alone at the homestead for years, because the men have to do the range work." When George looked uncertain, Jace went on. "We do need to work out a signal so the women can let us know if we're needed at the house."

"What kind of signal?"

"For years it's been gunshots."

Gloria stared at him. "I don't know anything about a gun, Jace."

"You don't have to know much, Gloria. Just how to point a gun in the air and pull the trigger a couple of times. I could teach you and Ruby in no time."

"I can't have my daughter firing a gun, Jace."

Jace took a deep breath. "I hate to say this, George, but if you're going to make a home here in the West for your family, you're going to have to accept and do things that you would have never done in Tennessee."

Gloria said, "Jace is right, George. Before she was almost jerked off her horse by her dress, you'd have never considered letting Opal wear pants. Though we're not pleased about it, we have no choice but to accept it as a necessity. If it means keeping our children safe, I will learn to shoot a gun."

"I guess you're right. I can accept you can learn, but I'm not sure it's something Ruby should do."

Before Jace could say anything, Ruby said, "I need to learn, too, Papa. Mama might not be able to signal you, so it would be important that I could do it."

"She's right, George."

"Then I guess I don't have a choice but permit you to learn about guns."

Jace took a drink of his coffee. "Then after I pay Mr. Cletus Finch a visit, I'll give you both shooting lessons. I might as well teach Opal, too. She might need to know about guns while we're on the range."

"Why are you going over to Finch's place?" It was the first time Opal had spoken.

Jace smiled at her. "If we don't go and confront him, he'll think he has our permission to come around here and bother your family anytime he wants to."

"Jace is right. We'll go as soon as we finish eating."

Jace didn't say he hadn't planned on George going, but now that the man had volunteered, he thought it wasn't a bad idea. It would be good for Finch to see that George Barnett had no fear of meeting him face to face.

~ * ~

George couldn't help but be impressed when they pulled up in front of the Finch ranch. Though the house was a log cabin, he could tell it had at least three bedrooms. Maybe more. The yard was neat with flowers growing beside the steps to the long front porch. Smoke came from the chimney. The out buildings seemed to all be in good shape and there were several strong-looking horses in the corral. Smoke also rose from another building. He wondered if this was the bunkhouse, but didn't let his thoughts tarry on it because a tall woman with a gray ball of hair on the top of her head came out the door and watched them rein up their horses.

"Howdy, Ma'am. We're here from the Barnett ranch next door. This gentleman is Mr. Barnett and I'm his foreman, Jace. We'd like to speak to Mr. Finch, please."

"He's eatin' his supper right now and he don't like to be bothered when he eats."

Before Jace could say anything, George got off his horse and headed toward the house. "Then I'll come inside and talk to him."

The woman looked scared. "No, sir. You can't do that. He'll be angry and…"

"Since he had the audacity to walk into my house without an invitation, I feel I have the right to walk into his."

"Cletus!" The woman yelled.

The burly man stomped out the door. "What the hell's going on, Inez?"

"These men are coming in…."

He whirled around and saw George at the bottom of the steps. Jace was right behind him. "We need to talk to you," George said.

"Well, Barnett, unless you've come here to sell your ranch to me, we've got nothing to talk about." He started to turn back into the house.

"I came to tell you if you ever come to my place again and force your way into my house, I won't be responsible for what happens to you."

Cletus sneered. "What can you do about it, tenderfoot? I bet you can't even fire a gun."

"I hope it won't come to that, but I will not allow you to frighten my wife and children."

When Cletus continued toward the door, Jace butted in. "You're right about Mr. Barnett being a nonviolent man, but you'll find that I'm not so peaceful. I've lived in the West long enough to know if a man is shot for bothering a lady, there is no consequence except maybe a few handshakes. You were just lucky we were on the range today. If not, you'd be a dead man right now."

Cletus Finch glared at him.

George didn't know what to say. He hadn't been prepared for Jace to speak so violently to the man. He didn't understand this land or how things were done, but maybe Jace was right. Maybe a gun was all some men understood and he wasn't sure he could ever live that way.

Finch broke the silence. "Inez, get in there and fix my dessert." Turning back to the men, he said, "You two get on your horses and get out of here, but if I learn you're hiding that bastard half-breed somewhere, I'll come visiting and next time I'll have a gun of my own."

"Let's go, Jace. You can't reason with an irrational man." George started toward his horse, but turned. "You've been warned, Finch. If you ever bother my wife and daughters again, it'll be the last time you bother anybody."

Anger welled up in Cletus. He grabbed the gun in his holster and pointed it at George's back.

Jace was quicker. He drew his gun and fired.

Finch let out a yell and grabbed his wrist as his gun tumbled to the floor. He glared at Jace. "I'll kill you for that."

"You should thank me. I saved you from hanging for shooting a man in the back, you coward." Jace holstered his gun. "Next time I won't aim for the gun, I'll go for the heart.

~ * ~

"What the hell were you thinking, Cletus Finch? Why did you walk into Barrett's house without being asked in?" GW pounded his fist down on the table. "You're going to screw up the whole thing."

"I had a feeling they were hiding the breed, but they wouldn't tell me."

"And did you find him when you barged into their house?"

"He weren't there, but I have a feeling he was around somewhere."

"Did you search the outbuildings?"

"He weren't in none of them. I even checked the outhouse."

"Then, Mr. Finch, I'd say he wasn't on Barnett's property."

"But he had to be somewhere." Cletus looked frustrated.

"Forget him. He could've been anywhere. A cave, in the woods, in the next town. He could've even gone back to his people."

"I don't like the idea of a half-breed getting away from me like that, GW. If we don't catch him, he'll end up making trouble for us."

"I said forget him for now. If you want to look for him later, fine, but now you need to concentrate on how you're going to get the Barnetts off that ranch. I want that place and I want it before the weather starts to turn cold. You've got a couple of months so I want it done right and I want it done as quickly as possible. And you know I don't care what you have to do to get it for me."

"Yes, sir. I won't fail you this time."

"You'd better not, Cletus Finch. You know what will happen if you do."

Cletus nodded. "I shore do."

"Now get out of here. I'm expecting a business associate to come in any moment and the last thing I want is for him to see you here."

"I understand." And he did. He knew GW's family thought they were the epitome of social graces in Wildweed. Of course, everyone else in town seemed to think they belonged in the group, too. They would never understand nor would they ever forgive him if they found out how GW cheated, lied and at times even killed to retain his lofty positon. Well, as long as he was being paid, Cletus would never let them catch on that he even knew the man, much less worked for him. It was better that way.

~ * ~

The next day, Opal came in for the mid-day meal and found her mother bandaging Daniel's back. "Where is everyone?"

"Sapphire is napping and Pearl found some more berry bushes in the woods, so she and Ruby have gone to pick them. I thought I'd make a pie for supper. They should be back anytime." She finished the bandage and stood. "Why don't you sit here and talk with Daniel and I'll get dinner on the table before the men get in?"

Opal nodded and took her chair. "And how are you today, Daniel?"

"Better."

"Good, because I want to ask you some questions." Opal gave him a grin.

"What?"

"After Mama has doctored and fed you and Ruby hid you from that man, don't you realize you can trust us?"

"I guess so."

"Then, don't you think it's about time you told us what happened to you? We all have an idea, but we want to know for sure."

"I told you. I stole an egg."

"I don't mean about that. I mean about you saying you're a Barnett."

"I am."

"Then tell me about your parents. What happened to them?"

He looked at Opal a long minute, then said, "Ma was gonna have a baby. She kept screaming and crying all night long. The next day Pa sent for the doctor, but he didn't help her. Her and the baby both died. After that, Pa didn't seem to care much about nothing. He let the place start to run down. I tried to help him keep things going, but he started drinking and I couldn't keep it running by myself."

"I can sure understand that." She smiled at him. "What happened to him?"

"One day some men came and told him they were going to take the ranch away from him. He laughed at them and they didn't like it. They got off their horses and beat him up. I think they would've beat me, too, but I hid."

"I'm sorry that happened to your father, but I'm glad you were able to hide."

He took a long breath. "After he got better, he told me the law wouldn't let me own the ranch if anything happened to him since I had Indian blood. He said I was to go to Ma's people because he didn't want any of the mean men to get their hands on me."

"What happened to your pa, Daniel?"

"I had been fishing with Heath. I caught four big ones and I knew Pa would clean them and we'd have a nice supper for a change. He wasn't much of a cook, but he could fry good tasking fish. He wasn't at the house when I got home, so I went to the barn to look for him. I found him hanging there from a rafter. He was dead."

Opal was horrified. "Oh, Daniel. I'm so sorry. I didn't know you father killed himself."

Daniel's eyes blazed with sudden anger. "Pa might drink too much and not take care of this place, but he'd never kill himself. I know they said he did, but it's not true. Somebody killed him."

"But if he was hanging…"

"I don't care. He didn't do it!"

"Maybe he…"

"I knew you'd be like everybody else and not believe me, but it's the truth. I tried to tell the sheriff that, but he said I was just a half-breed kid and didn't know anything about it."

Instead of arguing with him, Opal decided to change the subject. "What happened to you after your pa's death?"

"The preacher let me stay at his house till after Pa's funeral. After that, he sent me to live with the man who runs the saloon. I stayed a little while, but he decided he didn't need me. He sent me to work on Mr. GW's ranch. It wasn't long until Mr. Finch was beating me because I didn't work as hard as he thought I should. I run away and found my ma's people."

"Who is Mr. GW?" Gloria looked at him.

He shook his head. "Mr. Finch says he owns the ranch, but we've never met him. Mr. Finch runs things there, but he sometimes tells us what Mr. GW wants him to do to us."

"Who are your mother's people, Daniel?" Opal asked.

"She was a Ute princess, but when she ran away with my pa, they disowned her."

"What did they think of you?"

"Some of them were pretty nice, but her brother didn't want a half-white boy in the family. He sent me away." He sighed. "I didn't know where to go, so I came back here. I did all right looking after myself. I hid when anybody came around and I hunted and fished for food. Then you folks showed up, but I still managed to keep hidden for a while." He looked away. "I'd been stealing some things from gardens. That's how I got caught."

"Oh?"

"GW's ranch had the best garden that was nearby and I slipped in one night to get some things. Miss Inez had been missing some vegetables and had told Mr. Finch about it. He was watching for me the next night. I'd been there for three weeks 'til I ran away and came here again. You know what happened after that."

"Yes, Daniel. I know." Opal patted his shoulder. "I don't think you have to run anymore. We are your family."

He stared at her. "You'd want a half-breed in your family?"

She laughed. "I don't think there's anything we can do about it. Uncle Horace was your father, so that makes you our cousin, so it doesn't matter what we like. As I said, the truth is, you're family."

## *Fourteen*

Jace reined his horse up in front of the Cactus Saloon. He hoped he could get a lead on some hands who would work for the Barnetts for room and board. If not, he had a little money and he could pay them until the cattle were branded. There weren't enough to go to market this year, but by next year he felt there would be. Of course, he wouldn't be around to see them to the rail yard.

The bartender looked up when Jace came through the bar doors and walked up to the bar. "Howdy, again. Hadn't seen you in a few weeks. Thought you'd moved on."

"Picked up a cow-punching job. Been busy." He put a coin on the smooth wood. "How about a beer?"

"Sure." He filled a mug and sat it in front of Jace. "Gonna need anything else?"

"I'm looking for a couple of hands. Got some branding to do. Know of anybody looking for a job?"

"You might check with Floyd Mayfield. Heard their nephew's gettin' on their nerves somethin' fierce. He don't like working in the store and they don't like having him there."

"He ever cowboyed?"

"Don't know about that, but he's always saying he wants a job where he can be outside. Said he had to leave his pa's butcher shop in Chicago only to land in a general store and he wants to move on to something else."

The bar doors swung open again and a man only a couple of inches shorter than Jace came through. He wore a black suit and there was a gold watch chain across the chest of his blue brocade vest. His hat was a Stetson and his boots were of expensive leather. *Wants everyone to know he's one of the moneyed locals*, ran through Jace's mind.

"Hello, Mr. Greenwood," the barkeep greeted him. "Want your usual bourbon?"

"Sure do, Hank. Been a rough morning."

Hank served him the drink without asking about his morning.

Greenwood looked at Jace. "Don't think I know you. You new in town?"

Jace took an instant dislike to the man. He knew the type. They always threw their weight around, most of the time by intimidation. He figured Greenwood wasn't any different. He had to use all his strength to keep his voice calm. "Been here a little while."

"Oh." Greenwood laughed. "Been hiding out here with the whores?"

Hank butted in. "He's working on a ranch. Came in here looking for a couple of hands. You wouldn't happen to know of anybody looking for a job, would you, Mr. Greenwood?"

"Not right off." He looked at Jace again. "What ranch you working on?"

Jace knew better than to make an enemy of the man right away. He decided to be honest. "George Barnett's place."

Greenwood laughed. "I heard the tenderfoot was trying to make a go of that rundown ranch."

"Oh?" Jace turned and looked at the man. "How'd you hear that?"

He shrugged. "I don't know exactly where I heard it, but it's no secret. This is a small town with very few secrets. Lots of folks are talking about it."

"I see." He finished his beer and sat the mug down. He waved the bartender to pour him another one.

"Names Alton Greenwood. I'm a businessman here in town."

"Jace Renwick."

A frown crossed Greenwood's face. "Renwick. Don't think I've ever heard that name around here. Where're you from?"

"Texas." Jace lied.

"What are you doing in these parts?"

"Looked like as good a place as any to light for a spell."

He raised an eyebrow. "There're more interesting places than Wildweed for a young fellow like you."

"San Antonio was an interesting place. So were New Orleans and Phoenix, but sometimes a man gets tired of those *interesting places*. I've found some of these small towns can give a man peace.

"What do you mean by that, Renwick?"

"Nothing in particular."

"Sounded like you meant something."

"If you must know, it sometimes makes one think about life. The roving around life can be interesting, but there comes a time when a man thinks about settling down."

"So you want to settle down in Wildweed?"

Jace glared at the man. "No, Mr. Greenwood. When I decide to settle down, I'll go back to Texas and, as my father puts it, take on my share of his million acre ranch near Amarillo like my brother Warren has done." He sat his mug down and turned. "Now if you'll excuse me, I have to go to the general store."

As he walked out the door, Greenwood turned to Hank. "Think he's telling the truth?"

"I wouldn't doubt it. He's always got plenty of money and I don't think he's getting it from Barnett."

Jace was glad his back was turned. The two men had no idea he'd heard what they said. He couldn't help grinning because he knew they'd swallowed his lie. He just hoped he did the right thing by making up such a fantastic tale, knowing it would soon be spread all over town. That he didn't care about. It was only important that the man he was determined to make pay for his father's death hear and believe the tale because he wasn't ready for him to realize the Renwick boy who was born in Colorado was now in Wildweed and hot on the murderer's trail.

*Guess I better go send a wire to my good Texas friend, Warren Renwick. He likes getting involved in these play-along games and I wouldn't put it past Greenwood to wire Texas to find out all about Jace Renwick's daddy and his million acre ranch.*

~ * ~

"Hello there," the man behind the counter said as Jace entered the general store. "I don't think we've met. Floyd Mayfield here."

"Hello, Floyd. Jace Renwick. I work for George Barnett."

"Oh, yeah. I knew the Barnetts had moved into his brother's old rundown place. Didn't know they're hired a hand though."

"I needed a place to stay put for a while and he was kind enough to give me a job."

"Well, good for you." Floyd chuckled and his big belly shook. "You know you're going to have to work your tail off to make that a fit place to live, don't you?"

"You're right, it's going to take some work. Hard work at that. That's one reason I'm here."

"Oh?"

"I'm looking for some men to help with some branding. The barkeep told me you might know somebody who'd like a job. Your nephew, maybe?"

"He's my nephew, but it pains me to claim the lazy bastard sometimes. He was getting in trouble in Chicago and my brother sent him out here to see if we could straighten him out. Can't get much work out of him, 'cause he'd rather play cards or read his books or disappear on his horse than work. Don't know if you want to fool with him or not."

"Could I talk to him about it?"

"Sure." Floyd turned and yelled toward the stock room, "Marty! Get out here."

In a minute a lanky young man of about twenty or twenty-one came ambling out of the back room. "What you want, Uncle Floyd?"

"This here's Jace Renwick. He's looking for somebody to help with branding cows out on the ranch where he works."

Though he only nodded, Jace saw a flicker of interest in the boy's eyes.

"Can you ride a horse?" Jace asked.

"Yes, sir. I'm good on a horse."

"Have you ever worked on a ranch?"

"No, sir, but I'm willing to learn. I've always wanted to work on a ranch."

Jace swallowed a smile. With his enthusiasm, this man might just be trainable. He decided to lay out the facts of the job, good and bad. "If I decide to hire you, Marty, you're going to work the hardest you've ever worked in your life. You'll get up at dawn and you'll work until dusk and sometimes 'til dark. Most days you'll only eat twice, but you'll have plenty of good food at both times. The bunk house isn't finished, so you'll have to sleep in a bedroll in the hay loft of the barn until it's built. No smoking or drinking in the barn. Could be a fire and it's too dangerous for the animals. Pay is twenty dollars a month until you learn the job, then it'll go to thirty if you do well. You'll have to supply your own horse and saddle, but we'll furnish the feed. If the week's work goes well, we might knock off early on some Saturdays, but Sunday is the one day of the week you'll most likely have off and that only if some emergency doesn't come up, which often happens on a ranch. Think you might be interested?"

Marty didn't hesitate. "Yes, sir, I'm interested."

"Then get your gear together and come out to the ranch tonight or early in the morning. You might want to eat supper before you come if you decide to come this evening. I told Mrs. Barnett I'd eat in town tonight. If I'm not there, go ahead and make your bed in the loft and I'll wake you for breakfast."

"Thank you, Mr. Renwick. I won't let you down."

"I'm counting on that, and call me Jace." He handed Floyd a list. "Have Marty bring this with him when he comes to the ranch."

"Yes, sir."

Jace paid the shopkeeper, put on his hat and headed out the door.

On the walk, he glanced up when a buggy pulled up to the sidewalk. "Hello there, Mr. Renwick," the driver called in a lilting voice.

He looked up and tipped his hat to the pretty blonde. "Miss."

"I hope you remember me. I'm Neva Greenwood. We met in the general store the other day. You were with that Barnett woman."

"I remember."

"I see you're alone today. Where are you headed, Mr. Renwick?"

"I have some business to take care of, then I'm going to the café down the street for supper." He wondered why this pretty young girl was interested in his plans.

"I see. I hope you enjoy your meal."

"Thank you."

She turned her head sideways and a lock of her blond hair fell out the side of her fancy blue bonnet. "Don't you think you'd enjoy it more if you shared your meal with somebody?"

He didn't get a chance to answer because a voice called out to him, "Hey, cowboy. You looking for hands for brandin' cows on your ranch?"

Jace turned to see a slight man in his late forties or early fifties dressed in buckskins hurrying toward him. "I am. You going to recommend somebody or are you applying for the job?"

He caught up to Jace. "Dag-nab-it. Don't you think I can do the job?"

"I have no idea whether you can or not, so you tell me. Can you do it?"

"You dang tootin' I can. I was brandin' calves afore you weren't no more'en a idee in your mama's mind."

"That's good to know."

"Excuse me, Mr. Renwick, I think we were discussing your supper at the café." Neva had her hand on her hip.

"Ah, sister, he don't want to go there. They don't know how to cook for a hungry cowboy. He needs to go eat at the saloon if'en he wants a filling meal."

"Well, I never…"

"No, honey, you probably didn't." The old man glared at her a minute then looked back at Jace with his eyebrow raised as if he were asking if he was hired.

Jace could hardly hold back the grin. To cover he stuck out his hand. "Jace Renwick here."

"Sly Doub, Boss."

"Call me Jace. Mr. Barnett is actually the boss." Before he could go on, he saw Alton Greenwood coming out of the saloon. He must have seen them because he headed their way.

As soon as he reached them, Alton said, "I see Sly found you. I told him you were looking for help at the Barnett place. I hear he's pretty good with cows."

"Daddy, I was talking to Mr. Renwick."

He turned to Neva, "Neva, what are you doing here?"

"I just happened to run into Jace and stopped to speak to him. We were discussing supper when this rude man came bursting down the street and interrupted us."

"I see. Well, dear, Mr. Renwick has some business with this rude man and now I need to speak to Jace myself. Why don't you go on home? Tell Vinnie I'll be along soon."

"But, Daddy…"

"Don't argue with me, sweetheart. Now go along with you."

She had an irritated looking on her face, but she didn't argue with him. Jerking the reins, she said, "I hope I'll see you again, Mr. Renwick."

Jace's nod to her was noncommittal.

"Well, now she's gone, can we get on with our business?" Sly asked.

"Yes, we can. Pay is thirty dollars a month for experienced hands. I'll expect you to help me train a couple of young fellows." Jace went on to tell him more about the job in much the same words he'd told Marty. "Are you interested?"

"I say I am. I'll do you the best damn job of anybody and I'll be out to that there ranch afore you get home to go to bed tonight." He nodded and turned to go. "Now, if'en you want that good supper I told you about, you best come to the saloon. That's where I'm gonna eat my supper tonight."

Jace ignored the remark about the saloon. "One more thing, Sly. Step into the store here and see if Marty Mayfield needs any help with the supplies I ordered for him to take to the ranch. He's one of the young men you'll have to help train."

Sly headed for the general store door.

Jace turned back to Greenwood. "Thanks for sending him to me. He doesn't look like much, but I bet he's strong as an ox."

"I agree. That's why I suggested he see you." He pulled a cigar from his vest pocket. He held one toward Jace, but Jace declined. "Say you hired the Mayfield boy?"

"Yeah. Seems his aunt and uncle agree it's a good thing for him to work away from the store for a while."

"Good."

"Why would you care?"

"Well, he's been a little too informal with my Neva. I don't want her around him anymore." Alton puffed the cigar. "Now, tell me what in the world was Neva saying to you?"

"Nothing important. She simply stopped to say hello. We happened to meet the other day in the general store."

"I see." He started to move away. "Then I hope to see you again, Mr. Renwick."

"I'm sure you will, Mr. Greenwood."

When he was again alone on the street, Jace wondered if Greenwood had only come to speak to him because his daughter was here. He couldn't help thinking this was the case since he'd told the girl he wanted to discuss something with Jace then after she left, he had nothing to discuss. It really didn't matter. He had nothing more to say to Greenwood at this time and he certainly wasn't interested in the man's uppity daughter.

Shaking his head, he wondered if he wanted to go to the saloon to eat as Sly had suggested or did he want to head on to the café as he had planned. He knew the food in the saloon might be better, but he wasn't looking forward to sharing a meal with Sly. But if he went to the saloon, he might be able to seek out that woman he'd met on his first night in town. After a few seconds of thinking, he headed on to the café. If he was still so inclined after he ate, he would return to the saloon and look up that gal. He was still trying to decide if her hair was blond or red or something he'd completely forgotten as he stepped into the door at the Apple Blossom Café.

## *Fifteen*

Daniel always awoke before Gloria came into the kitchen to cook breakfast, but he never let her or anyone know he was listening to them. He was still suspicious of this family and didn't understand this woman at all, so he wanted to find out what he could about them without anyone knowing. So far, the mama had been nice to him, but he wondered when she would decide to beat him like that old witch, Inez, did whenever he didn't get all the morning chores done before he got his breakfast scraps if she decided to feed him.

Though these people said they were his family, he didn't believe it. He'd heard Mr. Finch say too many times that somebody had stolen the Barnett ranch. He wondered what the real name of these people was, but he didn't ask. He might have the devil to pay later, but as long as they let him lie around and do nothing, he was going to do it.

He heard someone walk into the kitchen from outside. He knew it was the hired hand, Jace, because of the sound his boots made on the wooden floor. Daniel had learned how to distinguish a person's walk a long time ago. This had served him well, especially if he or one of the other boys were doing something that would result in a beating if they were caught.

He heard Gloria's surprised voice say, "Jace, you're early."

"I know. I needed to tell you something."

She looked at him. "Is something wrong?"

"I knew George, Opal and I couldn't handle the branding alone so I hired a couple of people while I was in town yesterday."

"I don't know that we have the money to pay them, Jace."

"Don't worry about that. I worked it out with them."

Daniel decided it was time he tested these people for real. He raised up from his place on the sofa. "I can help with the branding. I used to help Pa."

Jace glanced at him. After a minute he said, "Are you sure you're able?"

"I've worked before when I was in worse shape than this."

Nodding, Jace added. "We'll be glad for the help."

Daniel stood and walked over to the table.

Gloria said, "I'm not sure you should get out so soon…"

"I'll be fine, Mrs. Barnett."

"I think I told you to call me Gloria."

"Yes, ma'am."

"Gloria, I know this is going to be an imposition on you, but I told the men that as part of their pay they'd be fed twice a day." When she said nothing, Jace took a deep breath. "It'll be more work for you, but since Opal won't be doing the branding, she can help you with the cooking. I bought some extra supplies. They're in the barn and I'll bring them in later."

"I understand, Jace. How many men are we talking about and when will they be here?"

"There are two and they're here now. They slept in the barn last night."

"Oh, my. I better put more on to cook. I'll need more eggs and I'll have to slice up more bacon."

"I'm sorry to do this to you, but…"

"Would you like me to go gather the eggs?" Daniel asked.

"Oh, Daniel, would you?"

"Yes, ma'am." He picked up the basket and went out the door. Now, he'd see if she got angry if he didn't bring back as many eggs as she thought he should. The witch, as the boys had called Miss Inez behind her back, often accused him of eating a couple of the eggs before he brought the basket in. Then she'd tell Mr. Finch he didn't need any food because he'd already eaten the eggs.

This morning Daniel found five eggs in the chicken coop. He wondered if this would be enough to feed the two men, but he didn't think it would.

He came back into the kitchen and held the basket toward Gloria. "This is all I could find."

She looked in the basket, nodded and turned back to the stove. "Then we'll have to stretch them as far as we can. Maybe I could scramble them with chunks of ham or sausage or something. I'll also make pancakes. I hope the new men like them."

"I'll not eat any eggs."

She didn't turn around, but she said, "Don't be silly, Daniel. You've been laid up and you're still weak. You need to eat a lot to make sure you have the strength to help today. I told Jace not to work you too hard. I don't want you having a relapse on us."

Daniel stared at her back. Was this woman really as nice as she seemed to be? It wasn't possible. White people had never been this nice to him. He didn't expect this family to be, even if they really were Barnetts.

Opal came into the room. Gloria seemed to ignore him as she turned to her daughter. "Oh, dear, I'm glad you're up. Jace has hired two more men and we have to make extra food."

"He told me he was going to hire them." Opal looked at Daniel. "Good morning."

He nodded and mumbled, "Morning."

She turned back to her mother. "Where's Daddy?"

"He went outside earlier. I guess he's getting to know the new men." Gloria got out her bread-making bowl. "Now, I want you to be sure Daniel eats well this morning. Jace said he could come out to help them."

"I don't see why he wouldn't let me help today. I could've done something, I'm sure."

"Well, honey, you're going to have to do a lot of work to do just helping me. I've never cooked for this many people."

"Want me to see if we got more eggs this morning?"

"Daniel already did. There were five, but we can make do." Her mother smiled at her. "By the way, it's nice to see you in a dress for a change."

Opal shrugged. "I figured if I wasn't going to be helping on the range today, I'd wear one."

"Please go see that Ruby and Pearl are up. I can use their help, too. If Sapphire is awake, make sure she's looked after."

"Yes, ma'am." Opal left the room.

Daniel moved back to the sofa and sat. He was still trying to figure this family out. It was sure a confusing situation, but one he enjoyed so far. He couldn't help wondering how long was it going to last. Maybe he'd learn more about them by working with the father today. That was if George Barnett didn't make him work so hard he didn't have time to look around.

~ * ~

"Mama, I don't see why we have to cook for those men," Ruby complained as she snapped the beans for supper.

"It was part of the bargain Jace made with them, dear."

"What gave him the right to put this extra work on us?"

"Ruby, just finish snapping the beans and then start peeling the potatoes."

"Why isn't Opal in here helping us?"

"Because she's taking in the wash she did this morning. Do you want to switch jobs with her?"

"No, ma'am." Ruby sat the pan with the beans on the table and picked up the bucket with the potatoes. "I guess since those men showed up, we'll have to do their wash, too."

Gloria laughed. "From the looks of the older one, he won't have that much and not very often."

"But we're already doing Jace's clothes."

"Are you saying we shouldn't do his clothes?" Her mother paused and looked at her. "Look at those benches at the table. He stayed up most of two nights last week making them so we'd have room for all of the family to eat at the same time."

"I know Jace has been a big help to us, but you've got to admit, even he makes more work. Since we've come here, it seems all we ever do is work, work, work."

"For heaven's sake, Ruby, don't you know if we're going to make a go of this ranch that we all have to work? Even Pearl is doing her share by babysitting Sapphire most of the time, and you know the last thing she wants to do is take care of her baby sister. She'd rather be outside."

For a minute Ruby didn't say anything. Finally she muttered, "I don't want us to make a success of this ranch."

Gloria stared at her. "I can't believe you said that, seeing how hard your father is working to make this a good home for us. Why did you?"

Ruby looked at her mother with tears in her eyes. "I hate it here and I want to go home. I thought if we failed here, Papa would have no other choice but to take us back to Tennessee."

Gloria turned from putting the roast in the oven. She moved to Ruby and put her arm around her shoulders. "Sometimes I forget how hard this move has been on you children. Your father and I had hoped you'd look at it as an adventure and maybe Pearl has done that. I think Opal has decided to help make it a good place to live, whether she likes it here or not, and Sapphire is too little to know the difference, but you're different. You don't want to fit in here and I'm sorry for that, because we won't ever be going back to Tennessee."

"Why not, Mama? If this ranch fails…"

"Ruby, there's nothing left for us in Tennessee."

"Of course there is. Papa could go back to work in the bank and we have the house and…"

"No, dear, we don't. You father didn't want you girls to know how bad it was in Memphis, but the bank was doing some underhanded things and your papa tried to make it right. For his effort, he was turned out of the bank and Mr. Dilworth spread the word that he was a thief. No bank in the state would hire him. As for the house, when we couldn't make the payments, the bank took it. I don't know what would have happened to us if Horace hadn't left us this ranch. So you see, if we don't make it here, we have nowhere else to go."

Horror crossed Ruby's face. "Oh, Mama, I didn't know."

"We didn't tell you girls because we were trying to protect you."

"Does Opal know?"

"I haven't told her, but I think she's figured most of it out."

"What about Pearl?"

"I'm sure she doesn't know all the details and I'm glad. I think she's too young to understand it all."

Ruby nodded. "I'm sorry, Mama. I promise I won't complain any more. I don't know if I'll ever like living here, but I'll do my part to help you and Papa make this a good home."

"Thank you, Ruby." Gloria kissed her cheek. "Now, let's see how fast we can get this meal together. I expect to see a bunch of hungry men come through that door at supper time."

Jace knew he had to talk with George alone before he went to bed. He glanced around the table and noticed the men were eating without paying much attention to anything else. This didn't surprise him. He knew they were tired and hungry. He was exhausted himself, but it had been a good day. They got more of the cows branded than he thought they would with inexperienced young men, but Sly had been right. He was extra good at the job. Marty did better than he thought he would. Daniel worked hard and seemed to know his way around a ranch. His help was invaluable, though because of Gloria's insistence, Jace took it easy on him. Marty made some mistakes, but was eager to learn and listened to instructions. Sly took him under his wing and had the patience to show him how something needed doing several times.

Sly caught everyone's attention when he smacked his lips and said, "Miz Barnett, I ain't had a tasty meal like this in many a year. You are a good cook and Mr. George shore is a lucky man."

Gloria blushed. "Why, thank you, Sly. I'm glad you enjoyed it, but I didn't cook it by myself. My daughters helped."

"If they cook as good as their mama, the young men around here'll be lining up at your door for their hands before you know it."

George chuckled. "You're right about me being a lucky man, Sly. I've never had any complaints about my wife's cooking. She's teaching the girls how to do it right, but I hope it'll be a while before the fellows start nosing around."

For some reason, the thought ran through Jace's mind that no man better start coming around to see Opal. Pushing the thought away, he held his coffee cup for Ruby to refill it. "Thanks." He wondered where Opal was, anyway. She usually helped serve the meal, but tonight Ruby was the only one helping.

Ruby smiled at him. "You're welcome, Jace."

He noticed Marty was checking out the pretty young woman. Again a strange thought ran across his mind. He didn't want Marty smiling at Opal in that way. Shaking his head, he said, "Men, I want to tell you I appreciate the job you all did today. I know George does, too."

"I sure do. You're all good hands and I'm glad Jace hired you."

"Well, sirs, if'en we get fed like this every day, I'm glad he did, too. Don't you agree, Marty?"

"I sure do. It may be hard work, but I like it better than working in the store."

"You were a big help, too, Daniel," George said. "I know you're family, but you'll be paid just like the rest of the men."

Daniel stared at him in surprise. "I could've done more, but Mr. Jace wouldn't let me."

Gloria turned from the stove toward him. "That was my fault, Daniel. I wanted to make sure you didn't overdo because you're not yet well."

"Well, folks," Sly said as he pushed back his chair, "I think it's time we headed for the barn. Gotta rest up for tomorrow."

Marty and Daniel both stood.

"Daniel, you need to sleep in the house tonight," Gloria said.

"I don't mind sleeping in the barn."

"You don't have a bedroll, son," George said. "We'll make arrangements to get you one when we go into town. For the time being, it's best if you sleep in here. Besides, I learned a long time ago not to argue with Gloria. Most of the time she's right anyway."

Gloria laughed. "What do you mean, most of the time?"

George shook his head. "Breakfast will be at dawn, fellows."

"Yes, sir." Sly turned to Gloria. "Thank you again, Miz Barnett."

"Thank you, ma'am," Marty said.

"You're both more than welcome."

"Come along, boy." Sly led the way out the door.

Jace stood. "George, if you're through, let's move out to the porch so the ladies can eat. We need to discuss tomorrow's lineup."

As soon as they stepped outside, Jace saw Opal in the front yard with Pearl and Sapphire. He couldn't believe how pretty she looked in the green checked dress. It was nice to see her in something besides pants, though they were attractive on her, too. Especially when he was riding behind her horse and saw her shapely behind in her saddle.

"Jace!" Sapphire came running with her arms held up to him.

Jace scooped her up. "How's my pretty girl today?"

Sapphire babbled something nobody understood and kissed Jace's cheek.

They all laughed.

George shook his head. "Sapphire may be the daughter I need to worry about."

Pearl put her hands on her hips. "I told Ruby and Opal that Jace is going to wait until Sapphire grows up, then he'll marry her."

"Why in the world did you say that, daughter?"

"Don't pay any attention to her, Papa," Opal said. "She's always saying things like that."

"Well, she may be right." Jace chuckled. "I might be ready to settle down when my pretty Sapphire is all grown up."

Opal shook her head and reached for Sapphire. "Come on, honey. Time for us to go eat."

Jace watched Opal disappear into the house with Sapphire in her arms and Pearl on her heels. A strange thought filtered across his mind. *Opal will make a great momma one of these days.*

After they took seats, George asked, "Now, what was this lineup you wanted to talk to me about?"

"That was an excuse to get you alone, George. I need to tell you something."

George frowned. "What?"

"When we were winding up the branding this evening, I saw something that I think you need to be aware of."

"Did we do something wrong?"

"Not at all. I happened to look toward the woods and I saw somebody. They were mounted and I swear I thought they had a spyglass and were watching what we were doing."

George frowned. "Why would anybody be watching us?"

"The only reason I could think of was that they were looking for Daniel."

"Oh, my lord. I hoped they'd given up trying to find the boy."

"Finch didn't impress me at the kind of man to give up."

"You're probably right about that. Maybe we shouldn't let him work with us tomorrow."

"I think we can keep him safe since we're aware of what's going on." Jace sighed. "I don't want to leave him here with the women. They could be in danger if Finch comes around again."

George nodded. "You're right. I sure don't want them to get hurt."

Later that evening, Jace lay on his back with his hands looped behind his head and stared into the darkness. He knew he'd done everything he could to protect Daniel. George agreed they would keep a sharp eye on the young man. For their protection, Jace would wear his guns and they would both keep rifles nearby.

So why was he lying there feeling unsatisfied? It couldn't be because he missed having Opal with them today. Or the fact that he hadn't seen her at supper until he went outside. She looked so pretty in that green checked dress that he'd started to make some excuse to keep her from going inside to eat, but she and her sisters were inside before he could work up his courage to do it.

*Damn, that trip to town last night didn't help a bit. It only made me think about her more. What is the matter with me? I've got a busy day again tomorrow and I've got to get some sleep. I also need to remember why I'm really here. Not that I don't want to help George get his ranch started in the right direction, but that's not the reason for my presence in Wildweed. I've got to keep that foremost in my mind. Next time I go into town, I'll set the plan in motion. I'm sure my friend in Texas will not mind me using him.*

Thinking it might help to shut off the thoughts, he flipped over to his side and raised his fist to give his pillow a good pounding.

It didn't help and he didn't know how much longer his thoughts went on until he finally fell into a restless sleep.

## *Sixteen*

It rained on Saturday so Jace told the men to take the day off. They'd work on Sunday if the weather was better.

"If you insist on moving into the barn, I think today would be a good time to go to town and get the things you need, Daniel," George suggested as he finished helping Daniel and Jace feed the stock.

"The roads could get too muddy for a wagon, George. Why don't I go in on horseback and bring back what I can carry?"

"Can I go?" Daniel asked.

"I don't know about that, son. What do you think, Jace?"

"I think he'd be fine. I'll be with him."

George nodded. "Then, I guess it'll be all right. Let me see if there's anything that Gloria needs before you go."

Thirty minutes later the two were headed to Wildweed. Daniel broke the silence. "I want to ask you something, Jace."

"Go ahead."

"Do you know why the Barnetts are being so nice to me?"

Jace shrugged. "As far as I can tell, the Barnetts are nice to everyone until they're given a reason not to be."

"But people don't usually treat half-breeds the way these strange people do."

"I don't think they care about your heritage, Daniel. They know you're their nephew and they accept you as part of the family."

"I'm not used to people like them."

Jace chuckled. "To tell you the truth, neither am I. They took me in and I was a stranger to them, too. As you can see, they trust me completely."

"It feels strange. Nobody has trusted me since my pa died and I ain't trusted anybody either."

"Maybe it's time you trusted again, Daniel. I know for a fact these people want you as part of their family."

"How do you know?"

"For one thing, they've let you continue to sleep in the house. They'd never let someone they didn't trust stay with the family. For another, I saw you out in the yard alone with Sapphire. If they didn't trust you, they'd never let that little girl anywhere near you. They're very protective of their daughters."

"I like Sapphire. She smiles at me." He almost smiled. "I think I like Pearl. She acts like she might like me a little."

"What about the older girls?"

"Opal is nice to me, but Ruby doesn't like me." He frowned. "I was confused when she hid me from Mr. Finch."

"You don't have to worry about Ruby. She's still trying to grow up. She'll be all right when she gets it straight in her head."

They rode on in silence for a while. "What do you think of Opal?"

Jace glanced over at him in surprise. "What makes you ask that?"

"I thought you might want her as your woman?"

"Why would you say that?"

"I've noticed how you look at her sometimes. You think she's pretty."

"There are a lot of pretty women, Daniel. Doesn't mean I want one of them to be my woman."

Daniel didn't answer, but for the first time his mouth spread in a full grin. It was as if he knew something Jace hadn't yet admitted to himself.

The telegraph office was their first stop when they reached town. Daniel stood by silently while Jace sent his wire. Going outside, they led their horses to the hitching rail in front of Mayfield's General Store.

As they stepped inside, Hilda, called out in her cherry voice, "Hello, Mr. Renwick."

"Hello, Mrs. Mayfield."

"I'm so glad to see you. I wanted to find out how Marty was doing, but I didn't know how to do it."

"He's doing fine. Seems to like the job."

"Glad to hear it. I was afraid he'd not want to do the hard work."

"He's pulling his weight and I think he'll work out."

"Good. Now how can I help you?" All the time she ignored Daniel.

Jace put his hand on Daniel's shoulder. "This young man needs a sleeping bag and a bedroll."

"They're on the left wall." Her voice lost some of its friendliness.

"Why don't you step over there and pick out the one you want, Daniel? I've got a couple of other things to get."

Daniel nodded and walked away.

Hilda leaned across the counter and whispered, "Are you sure you should trust him to go over there alone?"

Jace raised an eyebrow. "Why shouldn't I?"

"Well, you know how Indians are. He could pocket something when we're not looking."

"Mrs. Mayfield, I'm surprised you'd say such a thing. That's Daniel Barnett."

She frowned. "Horace's boy?"

"Yes, ma'am."

"I thought that half-breed went to live with the Indians after his pa died."

"He's now living with his uncle and his family. I'm sure you'll be seeing him in here with them."

"Well…" She sputtered, but still looked unsure. "I guess it's all right, then."

"I should hope so." He turned to the rack of tools near the counter.

The door opened and Aloma Norton and her two children walked in.

"Hello, Mrs. Norton." She looked glad not to have to talk to Jace any longer. "How can I help you?"

"I need a tin of Arbuckle's, a pound of sugar, and if these two mind their manners, I'll get two peppermint sticks."

"I'm sure they'll be good." Hilda smiled at them. "Won't you, Heath and Daphne?"

"Yes ma'am," Heath said, but his little sister only held on to her mother's skirt.

"I'll get your things for you while Mr. Renwick is looking around."

"Mama," Heath's voice was excited. "I see Daniel."

"What?"

"My friend Daniel. Can I to talk to him?"

Aloma looked across the store and smiled when she saw the young man. "Well, Daniel Barnett, when did you get back into town?"

Daniel walked up with the items he wanted in his arm. "I've been here for a little while."

"I'm glad you're back, Daniel." Heath grinned up at his friend. "Can we go fishing one day?"

"Maybe some Sunday, if we don't have to work."

"Do you know this boy, Miz Aloma?"

"Of course. He's Horace Barnett's son." She turned back to Daniel. "I thought you went to live with your mother's people, Daniel."

"Excuse me, ma'am." Jace removed his hat and looked at Aloma. "I'm Jace Renwick, the Barrett's foreman. Daniel is now living with his uncle and his family. We came into town for supplies."

"Hello, Mr. Renwick." She introduced herself and told him that she had visited Gloria Barnett. "I told her about Daniel and she said she and her husband would love to find the boy. I'm so glad they did."

"It'll be a good thing for all of them." He turned to Daniel. "Find what you wanted?"

Daniel nodded. "Good. Let's pay for it and head home."

"Be sure to tell Mrs. Barnett that I'm looking forward to her visiting me soon."

"I'll tell her, Mrs. Norton."

Out on the street, Daniel looked up at Jace. "Why didn't you tell her that I ran away from Mr. Finch?"

"I thought it should be up to you who you tell and what you tell them."

They mounted their horses and started down the street. From the corner of his eye Jace saw Finch come out of the saloon on the other side of Main Street. "Daniel, don't look around, but I think we're about to have a confrontation with your enemy."

Daniel kept his eyes straight ahead. "What do you mean?"

"Finch has seen us, but try not to react."

Fright covered Daniel's face, but he said nothing.

"Hey, you!" The voice was harsh. "Where'd you get that Injun?"

Jace ignored him. "Keep going, Daniel."

"He'll probably pull a gun on you."

"I figured as much."

"I said, where'd you get that Injun?"

Jace looked over at the man. "You yelling at me, Finch?"

"I shore am. That half-breed belongs to me."

"I don't think it's been legal to own another person in this country since the war ended over twenty years ago, Finch."

"You fool, I'll deal with you later." He glared at Daniel. "Get down off that horse and come with me. You ain't got no business being with this man."

Jace spoke before Daniel could. "This young man has nothing to say to you. Now if you'll excuse us, we're on our way home."

"Like hell you are." He reached for his gun.

Before it cleared leather, Jace's gun was in his hand and it was pointing at Finch's head. "This is the second time I've had to stop you from committing murder."

"Who the hell do you think you are?"

"I'm the man who is going to make sure you don't take Daniel away from his family."

"We'll see about that. I'll have him back if I have to kill you to get him."

"If you come around bothering the Barnetts again, you'll see who gets killed." Jace holstered his gun. "Let's go, Daniel."

They turned their horses and headed out of town.

~ * ~

"That bastard. I ought to shoot him in the back right now," Cletus Finch said aloud.

159

"No, Finch. You're not going to shoot him in the back or otherwise. If you do, I'll see that you end up with a noose around your neck." Alton Greenwood stepped out of the saloon.

"You heard what I said, Mr. Greenwood?"

"Yes, I heard."

"Why do you care if I kill him or not?"

"For the very good reason that if he checks out, I intend to get to know that man better. He's rich and he can be of use to me, though he doesn't know it yet." Alton chuckled. "Now go back into the saloon and get yourself a drink. Tell the barkeep it's on me."

Cletus still looked furious, but he didn't argue. He turned back into the saloon as Alton went down the street whistling as he formulated a plan in his head.

~ * ~

Neva opened the door when her father stepped onto the porch. She looked upset. "I'm glad you finally got home, Daddy."

"Well, hello there, little girl. It would a pleasant surprise to have you greet me if you didn't have that terrible frown on your face."

"I was watching for you."

He reached out and put his arm around her shoulder. "Then why the frown?"

"I have good reason to frown." Which was the truth, but a truth she couldn't tell her father.

"What's wrong, sugar pie?"

"Vinnie Kingsley has upset me for the last time. You've got to get another housekeeper, Daddy." It was almost the truth. Vinnie had been watching her with suspicion in her eyes. It was as if she knew the things Neva said weren't the real things she was thinking or feeling. Neva was afraid she'd give herself away to the woman.

"What in the world has Vinnie done now?"

Neva had to think fast. "She had the nerve to tell me I'd eat whatever she cooked or I'd go hungry. Get rid of her immediately. Send her away today."

Alton planted a kiss on the top of her head. "Now, don't fret, child. I'm sure you misunderstood Vinnie. You know she's a wonderful cook and housekeeper and they're not easy to find in a place like Wildweed."

"But she's mean." Of course she knew her daddy never would let the woman go. Not only was she a good housekeeper, she was good at keeping her father happy. He had no idea Neva knew this, but she did. She'd heard her father go into her room on many nights.

"Tell me what happened."

"I told her I wanted chicken for supper, but she said she was cooking beef."

He smiled at her. "You like beef, too, honey."

She crossed her arms across her chest and stomped her foot. "I know I do, but I wanted chicken tonight."

Alton shook his head. "Come, now, sweetheart. Let's forget about what Vinnie is cooking. I have something to tell you. Put thoughts about Vinnie aside for the time being."

Neva pursed her lips. "What are you going to tell me?"

He urged Neva through the door. "Come into my study. I don't want to discuss it standing here on the porch."

In the study, Neva dropped to the chair in front of her father's desk. After straightening her pink flowered skirt, she glanced at him. "Now, tell me what's more important than making Vinnie realize she's our housekeeper. Not the mistress of our house like she seems to think she is. If Aunt Melinda were here, she'd make her step around like a servant should."

"Calm down and forget about Vinnie. When you hear what I have to say, I think you might think it's important."

Puzzled, she cocked her head and looked at him. "What are you talking about?"

"A man recently came to town and has gone to work with the Barnett family."

"So, what does he have to do with us?"

He chuckled. "He's been traveling around hiding his real identity."

"Is he an outlaw?"

"No, child. At first I thought I might know him from a long time ago, but now I'm pretty sure he's from a different family than the one I knew. I'm checking him out to be sure, but from what I've learned so far, he's from one of the wealthiest families in Texas."

"As I already asked, what does that have to do with us?"

"Think about it, Neva. If you could meet a man who could give you everything you've ever wanted…."

Her eyes grew large. What was her father implying? "Are you saying you want me to marry this stranger?"

"Oh, not right away, daughter. If he checks out, I don't see any reason why you shouldn't at least get to know him."

"I bet he's ugly and I'll hate him."

Alton chuckled and shook his head. "Sweetheart, I have a feeling you already think he's rather handsome."

"How could I? I don't know the man."

"Then why were you talking to him as he came out of Mayfield's the other day?"

She lifted an eyebrow. "You don't mean Jace Renwick?"

"None other."

Neva did think Jace was handsome, but he wasn't the man she wanted. She loved somebody else, though she couldn't let her father know this. "Oh, Daddy. He is one of the best looking men I've ever seen. Are you telling me he's rich as well?"

"That's exactly what I'm saying. I've sent some wires to Texas to check him out, but what I've learned so far is promising."

"Oh, how exciting." She tried to sound as if she really felt this way.

"I thought you might like the idea. What we need to do now is invite him to supper so you can get to know him better. I'm sorry your Aunt Miranda wouldn't come from Denver with you. I'm sure she'd approve of this man."

She forced a smile. "Then that Barnett girl wouldn't act so high-handed, would she?"

"What do you mean?"

"When I first met Jace, she rushed him out of Mayfield's before he could talk to me, though I knew he wanted to." She had no idea if the man wanted to talk to her or not, but it sounded good to say.

"Well, you won't have to worry about that here, my dear." He grinned at her. "Well, when he visits, you'll have all of Jace Renwick's attention. I might even find a way to give you a little time alone with him."

She threw her arms around his neck. "Oh, thank you. Thank you. I have the best daddy in the world."

He held her close and patted her back. "Now, let's go see if Vinnie has supper ready. I'm hungry."

"Since you've given me such good news, I don't even mind eating her beef tonight, but she'd *better* cook what I want the night Jace Renwick comes for supper."

"We'll see that she does, sweetheart."

She locked her arm in his and they headed to the dining room. She knew he could never guess his daughter's attitude was all an act. If he knew the turmoil going on inside her head, he'd probably disown her.

## Seventeen

George glanced at Daniel as they walked toward the barn. The young man had his new bedroll under his arm. "Are you sure you want to sleep in the barn, son?"

"Yes sir. I'm used to sleeping in a barn, but I always had to sleep on a burlap bag or sometimes when I could get away with it, I'd slip and sleep on the hay."

"You must have really had it rough at the Finch ranch."

"We all did." Daniel glanced up at him. "I hope my work pleases you and you'll not send me back to that awful place. I'd rather stay here even if you beat me sometimes."

"Don't let such things worry you, Daniel. There's no way I'd ever send you back there, and I've never beaten anyone in my life. I certainly have no intention of starting by beating you."

Daniel looked surprised. "Not even if I don't do something the way you think I should?"

"We all mess up at times. I don't do everything right the first time I try it myself. You should have seen me when I first moved here. I didn't even know the proper way to ride a horse. I've learned a lot from Jace."

"Mr. Finch would knock me across the yard if I messed up on something."

George took a deep breath to control his temper. "Finch is a mean bully, Daniel. I'm surprised somebody hasn't knocked his teeth down his throat before now."

"I sure wish somebody would. He's as evil as the devil. It's no telling what he's done to Glen and Billy and Ivan since I've been gone."

"Are they his children?"

Daniel shook his head. "They're like me. Their parents are dead and they have nowhere else to go. Mr. Finch grabbed them off the orphan train."

"Is that how he got you, Daniel?"

"No, sir. After my pa's funeral, the preacher sent me to live with him. Mr. Finch beat me the first day I got there. He said it was to show me who the boss was. As soon as I got a chance, I ran away and went to find my ma's people. When her brother, who is next in line for chief, didn't want me, I came back here and hid out. Mr. Finch caught me trying to steal vegetables from the garden at his place. He tied me up, beat me and then made me work for him. I thought he'd kill me the next time he whipped me, so I escaped and that's when I came here again. I knew you were here, but I thought I could hide from you. I never dreamed you'd help me like you have."

"I'm glad you came here, Daniel. I want you to know you're home now and you don't have to ever worry about going to Finch's place again."

"Why are you being so nice to me?"

George saw the confusion in the boy's eyes and added, "You're my brother's son, and as I've said before, that makes you family. Family always looks out for one another and since my brother is gone, I feel it's my job to take the best care of you I can."

"Nobody cared before."

"I wasn't here before, but I'm here now. I know if I'd been the one to die, Horace would have done the best he could for my children."

"Pa was a good man, but people didn't like him much."

George frowned. "Why's that?"

"Cause he married an Indian. They said he was a squaw lover."

"I'm sure your mama was a good woman, but there are some people who don't or won't look past somebody's heritage to see the good in them."

"Pa said something like that once when we were in town and some men were yelling at him and calling him squaw man."

They entered the barn and George said, "Now if you decide you don't like sleeping out here, the sofa is always available to you in the house."

"I'll be fine." He scurried toward the ladder leading to the loft.

"Good night, Daniel."

"Good night, sir."

"One more thing, son."

Daniel turned and looked at him. "Yes, sir."

George went on, "I'd appreciate it if you'd call me Uncle George instead of just sir."

Before continuing up the ladder, Daniel smiled a genuine smile and nodded. He disappeared into the loft.

~ * ~

It was the next Saturday evening and Jace cursed himself inwardly for accepting the supper invitation from the Greenwoods. He'd only done it because he thought he might find a way to get more information on the man. Now he wasn't sure he did the right thing. He wasn't even sure he liked the chicken cordon bleu, as Neva had called it when the maid sat it before him. It reminded him too much of the fancy dishes his mother had insisted on when he was living with her back East. He'd have preferred fried chicken with gravy and biscuits the way Gloria cooked it, but maybe he was just being picky. He figured the Greenwoods were trying to impress him because he was sure Alton had wired his friend in Texas and got a glowing report of how wealthy his family was. He couldn't help smiling inside thinking of how Warren had probably laughed when he'd been asked to spread the lie. Of course he never had a doubt his friend would do it, and with relish. Jace had once saved the man's life and Warren had felt beholding to him ever since. He even changed his last name to Renwick. Said it made him feel like Jace's brother. Knowing Warren, when he got Greenwood's wire he probably added a lot of unnecessary details to the report he sent back to Alton. And there was no doubt in Jace's mind that Alton had contacted Warren. Why else would he be stuck here with this overbearing man and his twit of a daughter? They would never invite a working cowboy into their fancy home if they didn't have an ulterior motive.

Alton's voice cut into Jace's thoughts. "Can I ask you something, man to man, Renwick?"

"Sure."

"Why would a man like you, a man who has everything, want to spend his time working with a tenderfoot who is bound to fail as a rancher?"

Jace lifted an eyebrow. "I'm not sure Barnett will fail. He's catching on to what has to be done to make his ranch prosperous and he's not afraid of work."

"You and I both know it takes more than a willingness to work to make a ranch pay. Looks to me like he'd be better off selling the place and going into a business he knows something about."

"I suppose he wants to give ranching a fair try."

"I wonder if he's had any offers to buy the place?"

"He's had some people stop by. I suppose some of them may have offered to buy the ranch."

Alton's eyebrow lifted. "Anybody I know?"

Jace shrugged. "I wouldn't know if you would know them or not."

"I keep forgetting you're not from around here, but I bet Sam Norton has been nosing around the place. Cletus Finch may have been, too."

"Finch had better keep away from the Barnetts if he knows what's good for him."

"Why do you say that?"

"Finch came bursting in on Mrs. Barnett and her daughters when we were out on the range one day. It scared them something awful and when he found out about it, Mr. Barnett was furious."

Jace noticed that Alton acted as if he didn't know what to say, but finally muttered, "I bet he was."

"I went with him to warn Finch that he better never try a stunt like that again."

"I'm sure Finch was surprised the man came to see him."

"Maybe, but as I said, he better not bother them again. Mr. Barnett is protective of his wife and daughters. I'm sure he'd not hesitate to kill to protect them."

Alton changed the subject. "Tell, me, Jace. How many cows has Barnett been able to round up?"

Before Jace could answer, Neva butted in. "Oh, Daddy, do you have to keep talking about ranching and cows and such? I'm sure Jace would rather talk about something more pleasant than his daily chores."

"I'm sorry, dear and you're right." He smiled at his daughter and turned back to Jace. "How about telling us about your Texas ranch?"

"Oh, yes, Jace, please do. I've heard it's a fabulous place." Neva leaned closer to him and batted her eyes.

There was something Jace didn't understand about this dinner. It was obvious Alton was trying to promote something between his guest and his daughter, but according to the hidden message in Neva's eyes, she wasn't on board with her father's plan. For some reason, she only went along with this seduction to please him. Jace stuck a spoonful of green beans with some kind of nuts in them into his mouth to give him time to think of an answer. When he swallowed he said, "It's actually my father's ranch, Miss Neva."

"Daddy said it was a huge place and that you'd be going back there soon. He said you might even take a wife with you." Her voice was flat.

Damn. Could Alton be any more obvious? "I might eventually return, but I'm in no hurry."

Alton chuckled. "I'm sure when you do decide to go, you'll not find many suitable young women to marry around here. Of course there are a few. My Neva included."

Jace only nodded.

Neva blushed and there was a hint of anger in her eyes. "Oh, Daddy, I'm sure Jace could have any girl in town he wanted. Maybe even one of Mr. Barnett's daughters."

"I'm sure he wouldn't be interested in one of them. Before your mother died, she taught you how to be a lady and my sister Miranda has continued with the lessons. You'll make a great wife for some wealthy man someday."

Jace decided he'd made a mistake by accepting their supper invitation. Now he had to figure a way to get out as soon as he could and not be rude. Maybe the best way was to change the subject. "When did you lose your wife, Alton?"

"It's been over eight years now." He glanced at his daughter. "Neva was about twelve. After her mother passed, I sent her to one of the best schools in Denver. She only came to live with me in Wildweed a few months ago. Before that she lived with my sister Miranda in Denver."

Jace looked at the girl. He had to admit she was pretty, but the education her father was bragging about hadn't seemed to help her personality. Though there was something the girl was hiding, she still reminded Jace of the women in the East. The ones who looked at every man they met as husband material. Well, there was no way he was going to let them think he could possibly be interested in Miss Neva Greenwood. If he was interested in any female, it would be Opal Barnett and he'd already decided that beauty was not for him. He was on a mission and until that was completed, there could be no woman in his future. But he wasn't about to let Alton know that. Not yet, anyway.

He picked up his coffee cup. "Denver is a nice city. I spent some time there a couple of years ago."

"I wanted to go to school in New York, but Daddy said he couldn't let me go that far away. He said Denver was a town he could get to every so often."

"That's true. After losing her mother, I didn't want to lose my Neva to any of those fancy dandies in the East."

Neva shook her head. "I think it was more that he had some business in Denver than it was visiting me."

"Now, baby, you know that's not true."

"It is true, too. If I hadn't caught you, you might have married that woman you were slipping to see there." She stuck her nose in the air and gave her father a hard look.

"Now, Neva, let's not say such things in front of our guest. He doesn't care why I went to Denver."

She smiled. "You're right, Daddy." She turned to Jace. "Now tell me more about yourself. I want to hear all about your parents and your brother and about your wonderful ranch in Texas."

Jace felt cornered, but he decided to humor her a bit. After all, he'd learned that Alton had been seeing a woman in Denver. That might be just the thing he needed to know to tie all his suspicions together.

Without making things sound too fantastic so they'd believe his tale, he began talking about Texas and the imaginary ranch his father was supposed to own.

~ * ~

George came in the back door and looked at Gloria. "Has Daniel come in here?"

"No. I haven't seen him since supper." She frowned. "Why?"

"I was just in the barn and he wasn't there."

"He said something about showing Pearl a better patch than the one where she usually picks berries. I think it was down by the creek, Papa," Opal said as she walked into the room after putting Sapphire to bed.

"When did he say this?"

"After we ate. I was sitting on the porch patching a shirt and Pearl was playing with Sapphire when he came walking up. We talked a bit about the good pie Mama made for supper. He said he knew where there was a big berry patch up the creek a ways that would give us plenty of berries to make pies."

"Did they go to the creek then?" Her mama asked.

"I don't think so. He said he'd show her tomorrow when they came in from work because it was too late to go this evening."

"Where's Pearl? Let's ask her." George started toward the bedroom.

"She's not in there, Papa. She said she wanted to go pet Patch and I told her it was okay for her to do so."

George shook his head. "Patch is in his stall and Pearl is not in the barn. I just came from there."

"Oh, my Lord." Gloria put down the beans she was getting ready to soak overnight for tomorrow's meal. "Do you think they went to the creek after all?"

"We'll check around here first." George looked at Opal. You and Ruby check the outhouse and the chicken coop. I'll go back and check to see if Daniel is in the loft with Sly and Marty."

Opal ran down the hall to get Ruby.

Gloria was wringing her hands. "I'll look…"

"No, honey. You stay here. Sapphire might wake up and somebody needs to be in the house."

She looked worried, but nodded. "I guess you're right, but you'll let me know…"

"Yes, dear. As soon as we find her, we'll let you know." He turned to head for the barn. Opal and Ruby followed him out the back door.

Gloria couldn't sit still. She began to pace the floor, praying as she did. "Oh, dear Heavenly Father, don't let my little girl be lost. Watch over her. Protect her and bring her safely home. She's such a special child. I don't think I could stand it if something bad happened to her."

Wandering to the front porch, she scanned the area between the cabin and the trees. She saw nothing.

George rounded the house. Sly and Marty were with him. Opal and Ruby followed. "Marty said Daniel mentioned something about going for a swim at the creek. Maybe he took Pearl with him."

"Oh, George, do you really think he'd do that?"

"I don't know, honey, but we're going to find out."

The group started toward the trees and the creek that was a quarter of a mile away when a shot rang out from that direction.

"Oh, my Lord!" George ran toward the house. "I'll get my gun."

Sly turned and ran back toward the barn yelling, "I'll get mine, too."

For a minute, the women all stood as if they were paralyzed. Ruby broke the silence, "Do you think the Indian would hurt Pearl?"

"No." Opal's voice was sharper than she meant it to be. She softened her tone. "He wouldn't hurt her. He's family."

"But he looks at us strange sometimes. Kind of like he doesn't trust us."

"Be quiet, Ruby," Gloria commanded. "Nobody knows what's going on. We'll have to wait and see."

Ruby dropped her head. "I'm sorry."

George came back through the door and jumped off the edge of the porch. "You women wait here. I'll be right back."

"I'll go with you, George."

"No, Gloria. Stay here."

"But…"

"There's no time to argue." He glanced at Ruby and Opal. "Watch out for your mother."

They nodded.

George went across the yard at the same time Sly came around the house carrying his gun. The two men were almost out of the yard when Gloria screamed.

"Wait!" She pointed toward the edge of the woods.

George whirled around. "What is it?"

She ran off the porch. "Somebody's coming out of the woods. It looks like Pearl."

George grabbed her arm. "Where?"

"There." She pointed with her free hand and tried to pull her away from George's grasp. "Let me go. I've got to get to my little girl. She looks like she's hurt."

George let her arm go and followed as she began running toward the stumbling figure exiting the woods.

"Stay with Sapphire, Ruby. I'll go with mama." Opal ran from the yard before Ruby could protest.

## *Eighteen*

Jace frowned as he turned his horse down the road toward the entrance to the Barnett ranch. The shot that split the quietness of the early night had to be on the ranch. Somewhere near the creek, he'd guess. *But why would George or one of the men be down at the creek at this time of the evening?* It was almost dark. The tired hands were normally in the barn by this time and George was usually tucked in the cabin with his family. If he hadn't been committed to the supper with the Greenwoods, Jace knew he'd either be in his room or sitting somewhere in the area smoking a cheroot and plotting his revenge on the man who killed his father. Until this gunshot interrupted his thought, he'd been looking forward to getting home and relaxing a little while to rid his mind of Neva Greenwood's silly chatter and why he had a feeling she didn't mean half of what she said. It was even nicer to be away from her overbearing father's endless questions about the non-existent Texas ranch.

The shooting had taken care of these thoughts as he reined his horse to a stop and looked around. Though there had been only been one shot, he had a feeling it wasn't something as simple as a rattlesnake that someone came in contact with or a coyote slinking around the chicken coop. George wouldn't hesitate to shoot one if it was after the chickens. But that shot came from the creek area, not anywhere near the chicken coop.

Knowing he'd never be able to relax unless he found out who had discharged that gun and why, Jace turned his horse toward the woods that surrounded the creek.

As he came in sight of the area where the trees grew thick before pouring into the yard, his heart leaped. George and Gloria where racing toward the trees. Not far behind them were Sly, Marty and Opal. He looked to where they were headed and saw Pearl stumbling forward. Something was wrong. Bad wrong. He spurred his horse and reached her before the family got there.

Dismounting almost before the horse stopped, he dropped the reins and raced toward the girl. His breath came fast when he saw the blood on her face and the way she was limping. He swooped the crying child up in his arms and did a quick appraisal of her injuries. Seeing most of the blood came from her nose, his fright turned to instant fury. Who did this terrible thing to a little girl? And why? There was no doubt in Jace's mind that whoever it was, he'd track them down and they would pay— and pay dearly.

"There, there, Pearl. It'll be all right. I'm not going to let anyone hurt you."

"Oh, Jace…" She threw her arms around his neck and continued to sob.

Before he could ask her what happened, Gloria and George were beside him. "Oh my baby, you're bleeding." Gloria reached for her, but Pearl clung to Jace.

"Was she shot?" George glanced at Jace.

"I don't think so. It looks like she's been hit in the nose."

"But we heard a gunshot."

"So did I." He looked down at Pearl. "Honey, let's get you to the house and see how badly you're hurt."

Pearl shook her head. "Get Daniel."

Jace lifted an eyebrow. "Did Daniel hurt you, Pearl?"

"No. Daniel tried to stop him." She began to cry again. "Get Daniel."

"Let's get her to the house, George," Gloria said.

"No!" Pearl cried. "Help Daniel."

Jace said in a calm voice, "All right, Pearl. We'll help Daniel, but can you tell us what happened so we can?"

She nodded and in a stumbling voice she said, "The man grabbed me and Daniel came running up and hit the man. The bad man wouldn't let me go. He knocked Daniel down and was gonna shoot him. I grabbed his arm and he hit me in the nose and I fell. Daniel tried to fight, but he shot Daniel anyway. I ran away to get you and Daddy."

Jace glanced at George and muttered, "Finch."

George nodded. "Let's get Pearl to the house and I'll saddle my horse."

"I'll do that for you Mr. George," Marty said.

"I'll go with him. We'll saddle all the horses."

"Wait, Marty," Jace said. "Somebody has to stay here and protect the women. You're a good shot, so I want you to do it. Sly can go with us."

"Yes, sir, Jace."

Jace looked down at Pearl and winked. "Let's get you to the house. I'm sure your mama wants to get your pretty face cleaned up."

She gave him a sly grin. "Are you and Daddy going to get the man who hit me and took Daniel?"

"We sure are. We'll have Daniel back before you go to sleep tonight."

$$\sim * \sim$$

*It's probably all over now. I should have never stayed with the Barnetts. Then I'd never know how it was to be with a real family.*

Daniel gritted his teeth and refused to cry out as the whip came down on his back and he felt his skin tear again. He'd lost count of how many times he'd been struck, but he was sure it was a lot.

*He'll kill me for sure this time.*

A woman's voice floated to his ears as he felt himself passing out.

"I think you better stop now. It looks like he's gonna die."

"I don't give a damn if he does. He should've never left here."

"Well, he's not gonna do us any good around here if'en you kill him."

"Just one more time." He brought the whip down across Daniel's back with force enough to split the boy's back all the way across.

Somehow Daniel held on to enough consciousness to realize the man was at last cutting him down from the post he'd been tied on. He didn't have the strength to resist as he felt himself being dragged over to a corner of the barn where straw was scattered on the ground. It actually felt good when he was dropped face down on the hard earth.

"Want me to get some salve for his back?" the woman asked.

"Nah. He'll be all right without it. Damn half-breeds are mostly animal. They don't need doctoring." The man took a deep breath, then said, "Now you bastards see what happens when you try to run away from here, don't you?"

When nobody answered, the man yelled, "Don't you?"

"Yes, sir."

Daniel recognized Glen's voice.

"What about the rest of you?"

Two more voices muttered, "Yes, sir."

"Now, get your lazy selves outta here. You've got work to do."

Daniel knew they left in a hurry when he heard them run out of the barn.

"Think they'll come here looking for him, Cletus?"

Daniel recognized Duff's voice. It was the first time he'd known the one adult ranch hand was in the barn.

"Hell, yeah, they'll come. We'll be ready for them, too. Ain't nothing I'd like better than killing that Barnett man."

A chuckle came from Duff. "Guess we could claim his ranch for GW then."

"Damn right. Don't know why the man ever thought he could become a rancher in the first place. Him and his purty wife and daughters should head back East."

"Now, Cletus, I think it'd be right nice if he left them purty women here." He laughed again.

"Shut your mouth, Duff," the woman said. "You know good and well them women wouldn't look twice at either one of you."

"Now you don't know that for shore, Inez," Duff said. "They could very well be lonesome enough to invite me and your brother over."

"You're a fool if you think that would ever happen."

"That's enough, you two," Cletus said. "We gotta git outta here and start watching for Barnett to show up."

"So you really think he will?"

"I shore do. He's probably as stubborn as his brother ever was. Horace warned me that when his brother got here, I'd regret killing him."

Daniel's body jerked. *So Cletus Finch really did kill my pa.*

"Maybe you should've believed him."

"How was I to know he really had a brother back East? A man who'd marry a squaw is likely to say anything."

"Well, he did have a brother."

"Yeah, I know that now, but how was I to know the fool would want to take in his Injun nephew? I figured some fancy tenderfoot wouldn't want anything to do with a half-breed."

"I guess you figured wrong again, brother."

"Yeah, I guess so, Inez."

"Are we gonna kill Barnett?"

"Yeah, Duff, we are. And it'll be a pleasure."

"What if the boys here see what we're doing?"

"They won't say nothing."

"But they might."

"Stop arguing, you two. If the young'uns see the killing, we can always git rid of them and nobody will ever miss them. Them orphan trains come through here regular like and we can always git more." Inez's voice was sharp. "As you said, you need to get yourselves prepared for Barnett to come looking for his nephew."

"You're right," Cletus said. "How about you stake yourself out on the edge of the yard behind that big tree, Duff? Inez can be at the winder in the cabin and I'll be down by the corral."

"Reckon he'll bring his hired hand with him?"

"I'm shore he will and I owe that damn man. Saw him in town with the Injun a few days ago. Looks like the whole crowd sticks purty close together."

"Then, I suggest we do the same," Inez put in. "Maybe you should get the boys in for the night. They could cause trouble if they're on the loose."

"She's right, Duff. Round them up. Just be shore when the shooting starts, you don't hit the hired hand."

"Why not?"

"Cause I want him."

"Why?" Inez asked.

Daniel didn't hear the answer, but he heard footsteps retreating as the threesome left the barn. His mind began to work. Though he could barely move, he knew he had to do something to warn his uncle. He couldn't help smiling to himself. At least Finch had answered his questions about the Barnetts. George was his uncle and all those girls were his cousins. Maybe he'd been wrong to suspect they had an ulterior motive for helping him. Maybe they really did accept him as family. This was a strange thought, but a nice one.

In a matter of minutes, Daniel heard new footsteps enter the barn. He knew by the sound they were created by the young boys that worked the ranch. In another few seconds the barn door slammed shut.

"Think we ought to check on Daniel?" Ivan whispered.

"I'll do it. You two go ahead and settle down." Glen also spoke in a whisper.

Instead of settling down, Ivan and Billy followed him and stood at his back as he knelt down beside Daniel.

Daniel felt Glen's hand on his shoulder. "Are you all right, Daniel?"

"I will be."

"Can I do anything for you?"

Daniel took a breath. "Help me sit up."

"Are you sure?"

"Yes."

It was a struggle, but they finally got Daniel to a sitting position. Though he could hardly keep from passing out, Daniel said, "Listen, fellows. Things are going to get rough around here in a short time and I need you to do something to protect yourselves."

"What can we do?" Glen asked.

"Is that board on the back of the barn still loose enough to move aside?"

"No," Billy said. "When they found out that was the way you slipped out, they nailed it down tight."

"Ever since you left, they shut the barn door and lock us in at night. I guess they're afraid we might try to run away."

Daniel thought a minute. "Is there any other way you can get out?"

They all shook their heads.

"Think a minute. There's got to be something you can do."

"We've tried, Daniel." Glen said. "Ivan even fixed a rope so we could slide down from the window in the loft, but Finch saw it and took it down. He gave us all a few licks of his whip and said if we ever tried anything like that again, he'd kill us next time."

"He would, too," Ivan added.

"If you don't get out of here, he's going to do that anyway."

"What do you mean?" Glen asked.

Though he hated to, Daniel told them about the conversation he'd overheard.

"So, they're going to kill us anyway?" Glen, the oldest of the three at eleven, looked angry.

The other two looked scared.

"Seems that way." Again Daniel thought a minute. Finally he said, "I have an idea."

"What?" It seemed the three of them asked at the same time.

"Get the reins and the head stalls for the horses."

Glen frowned. "Why?"

"Because I'm trying to save your lives."

The boys gathered the equipment and brought it to him.

"Now, take it to the loft. Use the reins to make a kind of rope and lower yourselves out the window on the side of the barn. When you get out, hurry to the woods at the back of the range. Duff is in the front yard so don't go that way and don't go through the corral. Finch is there. Stay clear of the house. The witch is at the front window."

"You're coming with us, ain't you?" Ivan asked.

Daniel ignored him. "Now when you get out of sight, head for my old ranch. When you get there, tell the woman there I sent you. She'll see that the Finches don't get you back."

"Will she be as mean as the witch?" Billy asked.

"No, Billy. She's my Aunt Gloria. She's a good woman and she treats boys nice." He winced as he turned his body. "Now go on before one of them decides to come back in here. Leave the extra bridles and head stalls in the loft. That'll slow them down if they decide to come in here to get their horses."

"Okay, we've got it. Let's go," Glen said.

"I'm not going with you."

"Why not?"

"There's no way I can climb the ladder to the loft. I don't even know how I've been able to keep from passing out to tell you all this. Go on now."

"We don't want to leave you, Daniel."

"Don't argue. My uncle will come for me. He'll get me out of here. Now scoot before Duff or Finch comes back."

Reluctantly, the boys did as he'd instructed.

As he heard the first one go out the feeding window, he almost smiled. He hoped they'd be able to get to the Barnett ranch before either of the Finches caught them. As he was passing out, he wished them God's speed. He didn't hear the other two leave the loft.

~ * ~

Jace reined his horse to a stop in the trees at the side of the yard. "Hold up a minute, men."

George and Sly pulled their horses to a stop. "What is it, Jace?"

"I don't like the looks of this. Something's not right."

"I know it's not right. They've got my nephew here and I intend to get him back."

"We're going to get him back, but I don't want one of us getting killed in the meantime."

"Do you think they know we're coming?"

"I'm sure of it." Jace waved toward the cabin on the horizon. "See how dark it is. I don't think these people go to bed this early. There should be a light burning in the house. I think they might be waiting for us."

Sly broke into the conversation. "Jace, I was a scout for the army a while back. Why don't I work my way off to the left over there and see what I can nose out? I can cover you guys from there."

Jace nodded. "Good idea. I'm sure they're only expecting George and me."

"Don't you think we should move a little farther to the side of the house?" George asked.

"Another good idea. They probably expect us to come up to the front."

When they came to a stop in the thick trees, Sly dismounted.

"Leave your horse hidden here in the trees and walk, Sly. If they happen to have this area covered, they'll never watch for somebody on foot. George and I'll wait here to give you time to work your way around to the back."

Sly nodded.

"By the way, see if you can manage to slip into the barn. Daniel told me that's where they keep the boys they have working here," George said. "They may have Daniel tied up in there."

"I'll do it. Give me at least twenty minutes to get in place, then move in."

After he left, George turned to Jace. "It'll be a long twenty minutes."

"I know you'd like to go rushing in there and shooting everyone in sight until we find Daniel. So would I, George, but I know it's not the smart thing to do in this situation. Not only could one of us get shot, but they could kill Daniel just to keep us from getting to him."

George sighed. "You're right. I guess I'm thinking with my heart, not my head."

"That's what makes you a good father."

"You'll be a good father someday, Jace."

Jace chuckled. "I don't think so. I don't know a thing about kids. I'm not even sure I like them."

"Don't tell me that. I've never seen Sapphire take to anyone the way she has to you. Children can tell when somebody likes them."

"Sapphire's different. She's special."

"Yes, she is, but so are Opal, Ruby and Pearl."

"I can't argue with that."

"Seriously, Jace. Don't you want to settle down and have your own family someday?"

He shrugged. "I think about it occasionally, but I don't think it's the right time. I still have some things I have to get done."

"Like what?"

Jace's voice dropped to a whisper. "Quiet, George."

"What is it?" George whispered, too.

Jace didn't answer as he slipped to the left where the trees were thicker. The not so quiet footsteps grew closer. He could make out the figures of three young boys, but Daniel wasn't with them.

As the leader was almost even with Jace's knees, he reached out and clamped his hand down on the boy's shoulder.

The boy froze and so did his companions.

Jace kept his voice low. "Where you headed, young man?"

The boy didn't answer as he glanced up at Jace. In an instant his face covered with confusion. "You're not Finch," he muttered.

"No, I'm not. Now, will you tell me what's going on?"

"Why should I tell you?" The boy's voice grew defiant.

The boy behind him punched him in the back. "That's the man who shot Mr. Finch in the hand."

Glen looked up as George walked up. "Who're you?"

"I'm George Barnett."

"Are you Daniel's uncle?" The third boy asked.

"Yes, I am. Can you tell me where Daniel is?"

"Why?" Glen asked.

"Because I've come to take him home."

"See, Glen. Daniel said his uncle would come."

"We can discuss all that later," Jace said. "How did you boys get away without Finch catching you?"

"Daniel told us how to use the reins to get out of the hayloft. It worked." Glen seemed to be the spokesman.

"Then what were you supposed to do?"

"Daniel said they was gonna kill us," the third one said.

"Hush, Ivan," Glen ordered.

"Well, it's the truth. Ain't it, Billy?"

"Shore is."

"Are you gonna take us back?" Glen glared at Jace.

George answered. "No. We're not going to take you back. Now, tell me about Daniel. Is he all right?"

"Finch beat him with his whip," Ivan said.

"Damn. He was just getting over the other beating. I don't think he can stand another one."

"Mr. Finch didn't kill him, but he's in a bad way," Glen said.

"Where are you guys headed?" Jace asked.

"Daniel told us to go to his uncle's ranch and he'd help us." Billy's voice was getting teary.

"And I will, but first, tell us where Daniel is."

"He's in the barn. Glen tried to get him to come with us, but he couldn't get up the ladder." Ivan dropped his head. "I didn't want to leave him."

"But he made us," Glen added.

"He did the right thing." Jace reached down and helped Glen to a standing position. The others stood on their own. "Now, tell us exactly where Daniel is."

"He's in the corner of the barn. Finch didn't tie him up again after he cut him off the pole where he whipped him," Glen explained. "They usually lock us inside at night. I don't know if they locked it tonight, but I think they did."

"Is there any other way in?"

"Only the loft. They nailed up the boards Daniel had loosened on the back of the barn to escape the other time."

"Must have thought Daniel was too hurt to try to escape again."

"That's right, Jace. At least we know where he is." He turned to Glen. "You boys go on to my ranch. Tell my wife I told you to come there."

"Will she hit us?" Billy asked.

George frowned. "Of course not. She'll probably give you something to eat and help you clean up a little."

"I'm hungry," Billy muttered.

"Then, take off." Jace pointed in another direction. "Head out that way. You'll get there quicker."

"Thanks, Mister."

The boys didn't waste time. They scurried in the direction of the Barnett ranch.

"Lord, I hope Daniel is going to be all right. I've just discovered my nephew. I don't want to lose him now."

"We'll get him, George." Jace's voice was full of confidence. "Sly should be in place. Let's work our way to the barn. I want to check those boards in the back that the boy mentioned."

~ * ~

Cletus was getting tired in his kneeling position behind the water trowel that sat just outside the corral. His knees were aching and he wasn't sure it was a good idea to be there anyway. The stupid tenderfoot would more than likely come straight to the cabin. He did the first time he came over, fool that he was. Crazy Easterners didn't have sense enough to realize there was danger around every corner in the West. Of course, that cowboy that worked for him was smarter. He'd probably convince the tenderfoot to be careful.

*Hell, if it hadn't been for that damn cowboy shootin' the gun out of my hand, I'd have shot Barnett in the back when he came over here yapping about me scaring his women. Then there would be no question about his nephew or anything else. The women would've sold out and GW could have bought the place for a bargain price. Why does he want that bastard hired hand to stay alive anyway? The world would never miss one smart-mouthed cowboy.*

The snap of a twig caught his attention and he whirled around with his gun raised ready to shoot this time. Didn't matter who it was.

The only thing he saw were a couple of horses moving around. The red dun seemed to be restless. He kept walking around the corral and pawing at the ground every so often. This wasn't unusual for the big horse. He was often restless. The piebald on the other hand, was as calm as any horse Cletus had ever seen. Tonight he was even prancing a little. Not much, but enough to make Finch think something was wrong.

He squinted and looked around. The sound came again, but he could see nothing. He un-holstered his gun and wondered if he should ease to the side of the barn and look around. Then decided if anyone or anything was going to creep up on him, he could see it from his position. Besides, in a few minutes the sounds ceased and the horses seemed to settle down.

He turned back and looked around the yard surrounding the cabin. There was a half moon and he could see pretty well. He did wish it was a full moon and he could see anything that moved. Then he realized that if the moon were that bright, Barnett and his foreman could see him better, too.

*Where are they? I thought for sure they'd be here by now. I want to get inside and relax with my evening jug and a good cigar. It's about the only time my sister will let me drink in front of her.* He couldn't help chuckling. *I wish Inez would give up trying to make me into the man she thinks I should be. I ain't never going to be that sorry bastard our pa was. I don't understand why she still worships the worthless piece of manhood. Sometimes I can't help wondering if'en she was more a wife to him than a daughter.*

He shook his head. *Nah, that can't be true. The bitch killed him. A frown crossed his face. Did she put the poison in his food because she wanted to get rid of the old buzzard or was it because she walked in on him at the neighbor woman's house and found them both naked in the bed while her husband was out plowing the field? Come to think of it, that was when he started getting sick.*

Another noise stopped his thinking. He whirled around again. This time he thought he saw a figure run behind the barn. *Damn, if they're not trying to slip in on me. It's probably that hired hand. If Barnett comes toward the front yard, Duff'll get him. Now I'm going to take care of this one. Won't be nothing GW can do about it if the man turns up dead.*

He slipped his gun out of the holster and crept toward the corner of the barn as carefully and as silently as his over three hundred pound frame would let him. He knew he'd be able to see the side of the barn as soon as he reached the corner.

Plastering himself to the rough boards, he eased his head around and held out his gun. Nothing. There was nobody there and from the view he had of the cleared yard all the way to the woods, nothing was headed in that direction.

He frowned. "I know damn good and well I heard something back here."

When nothing appeared, he holstered his gun and for some reason he looked up. He was surprised when he saw the hoist hanging from the door into the loft moving slowly back and forth. He watched until it slowed and stopped. He knew there was no wind, so what was causing that thing to swing back and forth.

He bit his lip and looked around again. There was nothing suspicious around, but something had made that hoist move. There was no way it would move by its self on a windless night.

Furious, he muttered, "Surely that Injun bastard wasn't trying to escape again."

Whirling around, he went to the door of the barn, pulled out the key and unlocked the door. Grabbing the lantern hanging on a nail on the wall, he lit it and walked over to where he'd left Daniel on the dirt floor. The young man was sprawled on his stomach and he looked to be unconscious. To be sure, Cletus kicked him in the side with the toe of his boot. "You damn bastard, why don't you go on and die?"

Daniel let out a low moan, but didn't open his eyes.

Cletus looked up toward the loft and wondered if he should wake the other boys. He heard a board creek and knew one of them turned over. He decided to let them sleep. After all, he'd deal with them later.

Shaking his head, he blew out the lantern, hung it back on the nail and went out the door. He relocked the barn and took up his position near the water trough.

No sooner had he got in his kneeling position than he felt the barrel of a pistol against his temple.

A low, but stern voice said, "Make a sound and you're a dead man."

# *Nineteen*

A knock at the front door made Gloria frown. "Who in the world could that be?"

"I'll go see, Miz Barnett," Marty got off the bench at the kitchen table where he'd been drinking a cup of coffee Ruby had poured for him.

He drew his gun, opened the door and was surprised to see three small boys standing on the porch. "What do you fellows want?"

They all started talking at once.

Marty held up his hand. "One at a time. I can't understand what you're saying when you all talk."

They got quiet, then Glen said, "Daniel told us to come see his Aunt Gloria."

"Are you friends of Daniel?"

"Yes," they said, speaking all at one time again.

Gloria walked up behind Marty. "Come in the house and tell me why Daniel sent you to see me."

Marty stood aside and the three boys came inside. Their eyes grew big when they saw all the people gathered in the room. For a minute nobody spoke.

Gloria broke the silence. "Would you fellows like something to drink?"

Billy's eyes grew even wider. "You mean you'll let us have something?"

"Of course. Would you like milk?"

"Oh, boy. Milk," Ivan said and swallowed.

"What do we have to do for it?" Glen asked.

"Why, you don't have to do anything except tell me about Daniel. Is he all right?"

"Mr. Finch beat him with his whip," Billy said.

Without being told, Opal had moved to the kitchen and took three glasses from the cabinet. She filled them with milk and decided to put the leftover cookies on a plate. She picked up the cookies and one glass of milk. Ruby stood and got the other two.

"I thought you might want some cookies," Opal said handing the glass to Glen and setting the cookies in front of the three children who had taken seats on the floor.

"I ain't never had a cookie," Billy muttered as he took the glass Ruby held out to him.

"Me neither," Ivan said.

Glen didn't say anything, but he reached for a cookie and gobbled it down. He followed it with a big gulp of milk.

Gloria turned her head and looked at them. "You boys are hungry, aren't you?"

"Yes, ma'am." Glen put his milk down. "We ain't never had nothing this good."

Gloria went into action. "Ruby, go out to the hen house and see if you can find me a couple or three eggs. To make sure she's safe, you can go with her, Marty." She turned to Opal. "You watch Pearl. I'm going to fix these young men something to eat."

"Are we going to have to do some work?" Glen stared at her.

"Absolutely not."

"We don't mind if you want us to do something. We work hard and we don't get much to eat."

"Well, the only thing you have to do tonight is tell us about Daniel."

"Mama, why don't you let me cook something for the boys and you talk to them?" Opal followed her mother to the kitchen.

Pearl moved on the couch and opened her eyes and looked around. "Did I go to sleep?"

"Yes, honey." Gloria moved back beside her daughter. "How are you feeling?"

"I'm fine." She looked at the boys. "Who are they?"

"Friends of Daniel."

"Oh." Pearl closed her eyes and looked as if she were going to go back to sleep.

Gloria turned to the young fellows. "Now tell me everything."

Glen cleared his throat and launched into his story. He told her how Finch had showed up with Daniel and immediately tied him in the barn and whipped him. He then informed her that after they were locked inside, Daniel had called them to him and told them how to escape and to come here.

"Then we run into the men," Ivan said.

Ruby came back inside and joined her sister in the kitchen without saying anything. It wasn't long until the aroma of frying eggs and bacon filled the room.

"What men?" Gloria drew their attention back to her.

"Daniel's uncle and another man. After we told them where Daniel was, he told us to come here. He said you'd let us come in." Glen looked at her.

Billy smiled. "And he said you'd feed us."

"And you have," Ivan finished.

"Well, he was right. I'm going to feed you more than milk and cookies." She glanced toward the kitchen. "Is it about ready, girls?"

"Yes, ma'am." Ruby smiled.

"Do you want to come to the table and eat?" Opal looked at them.

"I think they should wash their hands before they eat." Gloria moved to the sink and filled a pan with water.

Glen kind of laughed. "Daniel's Uncle George said you'd wash us, too."

"Daniel's Uncle George was right. I like people to be clean around me."

When the boys were seated at the table and were eating the bacon, eggs, the leftover biscuits from supper and drinking more milk, Gloria bit her lip. It was all she could do to keep from crying when she saw how nearly starved these young lads were. They were eating as if they'd never get another meal. She made the decision at that moment that they'd never go hungry again. Not as long as she was alive and could do something about it. She was sure George would feel the same way.

~ * ~

"Who the hell are you and what do you want?" Cletus's brave words didn't hide his fear.

"It don't matter who I am, but what I want is the key to the barn."

"I ain't gonna let you steal nothing out'a my barn."

"If you don't want to die for your barn, give me the key. If you don't, I'll shoot you and take it."

Cletus fumbled in his pocket and pulled out the key.

"Now, walk over there to the door and unlock it."

When he did as he was told, he saw George standing at the door. "I might have knowed you'd be behind this."

"Shut up and open the door." Jace pushed his shoulder.

Cletus opened the door.

George rushed inside and grabbed the lantern. Lighting it, he began looking around.

"They said he'd be in the back corner, George."

George nodded and headed in that direction.

"Who told him that?" Cletus was getting some of his bravado back.

Jace ignored him. He looked around and saw one of the poles holding up the roof was covered in blood. He figured this was where Finch did his beatings. Shoving Cletus in the poles direction. "Sit here."

"I don't want to set here. There's blood on the floor."

"I know. Probably blood you caused an innocent boy to shed."

"Innocent, hell. He's an Injun. He's got no feelings."

It took all Jace's willpower not to smash the man's face. Instead he forced him down by the pole. Grabbing a rope from the floor, he began tying Cletus's hands.

"Let me loose. Who do you think you are?"

"What I think is that I've heard all I want to hear from you." Ripping his bandana from around his neck, Jace rolled it into a gag and tied it around the man's mouth. He then proceeded to tie the man to the pole. He hoped Cletus would think about what he'd done here, but he doubted he would. The man seemed to be heartless.

Jace then moved to the back of the barn and found not only George working with Daniel, but Sly was there, too. Keeping his voice low, he asked, "How'd you get in here?"

"Somebody left a horse's reins tied to the hoist. I climbed the wall and came through the loft."

Jace nodded. He wasn't surprised that Sly was so agile. He'd watched him on the ranch and knew the man could move around.

"We've got to get Daniel home, Jace," George said in a normal voice. "He's in bad shape. I'm not sure…" His voice trailed off.

"We'll get him there, George." Jace looked around. "Sly, you go bring our horses to the edge of the woods behind the barn. I'll carry Daniel." George started to say something, but Jace went on. "George, follow me and blow out the lantern. Finch left the key in the lock on the door. Be sure to lock the barn door behind us and bring the key with you. That'll make it harder for somebody to get to him out when they come to look for him."

"I'm on my way." Sly headed for the door. "Them horses will be waiting."

Jace knew there was no need to tell him to be careful. He knew the man would. Carefully lifting Daniel to his shoulder, they headed out of the barn with Cletus Finch glaring at them even when the light went out and the door closed.

Cletus was livid. He sat in the dark tied to the pole and cursed Jace with every word he'd learned through the years. He didn't care what GW said, he was going to kill that man someday. Someday soon. Nobody was going to treat him the way the smartass cowboy had treated him tonight. It was as if he thought he was better than anyone around him. That just wasn't so. He was nothing but a cowboy working on a rundown ranch. It didn't matter if he was a rich cowboy, which Finch doubted. Why would a rich man lower himself to work on a ranch like the one Barnett owned?

As his mind began to clear of his murderous thought, he started to think things would work out anyway. He'd bang the pole until he woke the boys in the loft. One of them would come and cut him loose. They'd be afraid not to. If they didn't, he'd make a sample of him with his trusty whip. He just wished he'd been able to get his hands on his whip when that smart cowhand was pushing him around.

Then he frowned. Could he wake up the boys? If not, when his sister found him in the morning, would she give him a fit because he'd failed to keep the Indian? And what was it with her and that Indian? Why did she hate him so much anyway? He couldn't help wondering if it was because of the Indian brave that had been a friend of their pa's when they were young. Inez had practically worshiped that man. Then their pa had found him and Inez down by the creek. They'd been swimming, but were lying on a blanket when he caught them. They were both naked. Pa had told the Indian he had to marry Inez. But the Indian had another idea. The night before the wedding, he disappeared and was never heard from again. Several months later, Inez gave birth. Their pa said he'd never let a half breed live in his house. While his sister was still trying to recover from the hard birth, their father told fourteen year old Cletus to take the infant and get rid of it. He didn't care if he took it to the Indian village, left it on the church steps or killed it. He just wanted it out of his house.

That un-named infant half breed had been Cletus Finch's first kill.

~ * ~

"Glen, what do you think they'll do to us tomorrow?" Ivan whispered to him across Billy who slept on his quilt between them.

"I don't know, but it might be worth it if we get more good things to eat."

"I know. I didn't know bacon and eggs could be so good."

"How could you? We've never had them before. If we got an egg, we had to steal it and eat it raw."

Ivan was quiet a minute, then he asked, "Why do you think she gave us a blanket to sleep on? We told her we was used to sleeping on the hay in the loft and sometimes the dirt floor of the barn."

"I don't know, Ivan, but I'm glad she did. It feels good instead of the scratchy straw."

Ivan was quiet again for a short time. Then he said, "I hope Daniel don't die. He looked the worst I've ever seen him after a beating."

"I guess it was because it hadn't been long since his last one, but maybe they'll be able to save him. We saw how fast she told her daughter to go to bed and let Daniel have the couch. Then they all started working on him."

"Boys," Sly's soft voice interrupted their conversation. "The Barnetts are good people. They ain't going to do nothing bad to you. Now why don't you get quiet and go to sleep. It's gonna be dawn before you know it."

When they didn't say anything, Sly asked, "Did you understand me?"

"Yes, sir," they both said.

Sly must have caught the fear in their voices because he said, "Now don't get me wrong. I'm not mad. You guys did a good job of telling us where Daniel was and we was able to get him out of that awful place. I even climbed into the loft because you left the reins hanging there. That was a smart thing to do."

"Daniel told us to do it. We didn't have no rope."

"You were very brave and I know Mr. George appreciates it. Now, don't you worry your heads about what's going to happen around here. You might have to do a little work, but it won't be hard. You'll probably gather eggs and feed the chickens and maybe some work around the barn. But Miz Gloria will feed you good and nobody will work you so hard that you'll get too tired."

"Are you shore?" Glen asked.

"I shore am. Now why don't you get some sleep? Mr. Jace will be calling us to breakfast before you know it."

"You mean we'll get to eat breakfast?"

"Of course you will. Nobody expects you to do any work on an empty stomach. Don't matter if that work is easy or hard."

Quiet settled on the loft as the Sly's words sank in. In a sleepy voice Ivan asked, "Glen, are we dead?"

"No, Ivan. We're not dead. What made you think that?"

"Cause if we're dead I don't want to be alive no more. Being here is like being in heaven."

"I know. I feel the same way."

There was no more talking after that, but it took Sly a little longer to go to sleep. He was thinking about those poor boys and what a hard life they'd had in their few years. He decided he was going to tell Jace in the morning that he was willing to work for half pay if he'd take the other half and give it to the Barnetts to keep those three boys in their loving home and away from that awful Finch fellow.

When Opal entered the main room of the cabin, she saw her mother sitting by the couch where Daniel lay. "How is he this morning, Mama?"

Gloria shook her head. "I'm not sure, honey. He's hurt really bad."

Opal walked over and put her hand on her mother's shoulder. "He'll get better. I have faith that you will pull him through like you did before."

Gloria patted her hand. "I'm going to try my best, but we all need to keep praying for him. He's going to need more than my feeble efforts."

"We'll all keep praying." She glanced toward the kitchen area. "Has Daddy gone out?"

"Yes. He said he'd do the milking and then he wanted to ask Jace to go to town after breakfast. We need to get supplies and your father wants to be here when Daniel wakes up. I want you to go with Jace, honey. I need more medical supplies and I'm not sure Jace would know what to get."

Opal couldn't help it. Her heart lurched thinking about being alone with Jace for a trip to town. To cover her feelings, she asked, "What do you need, Mama?"

"I made a list and put it on the table."

Opal nodded, walked over to the table and put the list in her pocket. "I'll go gather the eggs and start breakfast."

In a matter of minutes, she returned with the eggs. Ruby was coming into the room. After her sister inquired about Daniel, she joined Opal in the kitchen.

"Want me to go milk?"

"Papa's doing it, but you can help me cook. Mama looks tired and I think we should do it."

"I agree. I'll make the biscuits."

Opal smiled. "Good. You're better at it than I am."

Pearl came into the room. She also talked with her mother then joined her sisters. "What can I do to help? I'll even go fight those awful chickens for their eggs if you want me to."

Opal chuckled. "Don't worry. Ruby already got the eggs."

Ruby looked at their younger sister. "Your nose looks better this morning. It's not so swollen. It looked like you'd been in a fight last night."

"I was in a fight, Ruby." She glanced at Opal. "Did some boys come here last night?"

"Three of them. They ran away from the man who whipped Daniel."

"Good. I think that was the man who hit me in the nose."

"It probably was."

"You can check in the bin to see how much flour we have. I've got to make enough biscuits for everybody and Opal needs to make gravy to stretch the food."

"Somebody needs to go to town to get some supplies."

"I know, Pearl. I'm going after breakfast." Opal didn't add that she was going with Jace. She didn't want them to start asking questions or to tease her and she knew Pearl would. She sometimes wondered if her little sister didn't suspect that she was having feelings for the handsome cowboy.

But neither sister asked how she was getting to town. Pearl only said, "Good."

"When you finish, Pearl, you can peel some potatoes." Opal nodded toward the potato bin.

"Sure."

By the time the sisters finished cooking breakfast, Marty and Sly came in, followed by Jace and three scared looking boys. When they hesitated, Jace motioned for them to take seats on the bench behind the table.

~ * ~

"Are you sure?" Glen whispered. He wasn't sure at all. He was waiting for somebody to start yelling at him to get to work, but he didn't know what they'd want him to do. Maybe they'd tell him.

"Yes, I'm sure." Jace winked at him. "Now take a seat so the ladies can serve us."

He motioned for his friends to slip on the bench as Jace indicated. He then slid in beside them. Jace and the two cowhands took the bench in front of them.

Glen watched as Daniel's Uncle George walked over to his wife beside Daniel's bed on the couch. They said a few words he didn't hear, then George led his wife to the table and sat her at the end nearest the sitting area of the room. He then took his place at the head of the table. "I wanted my wife to eat with us so she can tell us all at one time how Daniel is doing."

"Good morning, Gloria," Jace said. "I'm glad you're joining us. We've all been wondering about Daniel."

The other men nodded to her.

"Thank you, Jace, and the rest of you fellows. Daniel is still unconscious, but his breathing is strong. I keep praying he'll begin to rally soon. When Opal gets to town today, she's going to ask the doctor to come out here. I want to make sure I'm doing all that can be done for our nephew. It breaks my heart to see him in this shape."

Opal poured coffee for the man and their mother while Ruby gave the boys a glass of milk. They then began to pass the food.

George dished out his eggs and passed the bowl to Glen. The boy didn't seem to know what to do.

When Gloria saw what was happening, she said, "Take a spoonful or two out and pass it on to Billy, Glen."

"Yes, ma'am." His hand shook as he lifted a scant spoonful of eggs to his plate and handed the bowl to Billy.

Gloria nodded at her daughter and Opal moved to take the bowl. "Here fellows, let me dip for you. I didn't realize how hot the bowl was."

She put another heaping spoonful on Glen's plate then on Billy's and Ivan's. She smiled as she put the bowl in her mother's hand.

By then George was putting bacon on his plate. "Looks like there's at least two slices each for you boys," he said. "If that don't fill you up, there're probably be more."

Glen took his two slices as did his friends.

Soon the plates were full and the grownups were talking. Glen wasn't paying much attention to them. He was too busy staring at the food before him. He didn't know if he'd ever seen so much good looking cooked food at one time in his whole life. He sure hadn't seen it at the Finch ranch. Glancing at Billy and Ivan, he knew they were probably thinking the same thing.

Picking up his fork, he wondered if he should take a mouthful. He remembered that one time when the witch had given him a plate. He'd been excited to see some actual food before him. When he picked up his fork to eat, she'd snatched it away and began to cackle just like the witch that she was. She'd then told him he was crazy to think she was going to waste good food on the likes of him. She then threw a stale biscuit at him and went back into the house with the food.

Glen sighed and glanced around to see if anybody was going to grab his plate this time, but they were all busy talking about Daniel and how glad they were to have him back at home.

Billy and Ivan had started eating their food, but they were younger than his eleven years. Ivan was nine as best he could remember and Billy was only six or seven. He wasn't sure. Neither of them could know the danger of trusting these grownups. But the food did look awfully good and it was right there on his plate. Moving quickly, he stuck his fork in the eggs and lifted it to his mouth. Glancing around, he saw that everyone was ignoring him. He then tried to get a second forkful to his mouth. Success. It wasn't long until he was eating one mouthful after another. His plate was almost empty before he relaxed enough to finish his meal without gobbling. He decided he might have to do some hard work after the meal, but at least his belly would be full when he set out to perform his duties to this family.

## *Twenty*

Opal sat a little rigid on the wagon seat. Though she was excited to go to town with Jace, she didn't want him to know how much it thrilled her to be near him when there was nobody else around. Try as she might, she couldn't relax and talk to him the way she did when they were on the range or when he was in the house with the family. Therefore, the first half mile of the trip to town had been covered in silence. Racking her brain as to what to say, she was surprised when the horses reared and the wagon swerved to the side before Jace got the horses stopped.

"What's the matter?" She grabbed the side of the bench seat to keep from tumbling off the wagon.

"Snake," he said as he took the rifle from under the seat. He put it to his shoulder and fired at the coiled rattlesnake.

Opal closed her eyes, but said nothing. She didn't like snakes and the last thing she wanted to do was look at a dead one.

In a matter of minutes, she felt Jace's hand on her shoulder. "Are you all right, Opal?"

She nodded. "I just didn't want to see the dead reptile."

"Well, look in the other direction and we'll move on."

She nodded again and he picked up the reins.

Opening her eyes, she glanced over at him and saw he was grinning. "What's so funny?"

"Nothing."

"Don't tell me that. I know you well enough to know you don't smile like that over nothing."

He put the reins in his left hand, reached over with his right hand and covered the hand she had in her lap with it. "Let me put it this way. The brave Opal Barnett I know faces wild cows, thorny bushes, wild game, and most anything else that comes up when she works on the range. But when it comes to a little old snake—a dead one at that—she crumbles. It's hard for me to take in."

She pursed her lips. "I don't like snakes."

He squeezed her hand. "Then I promise to tell you to close your eyes the next time we run into one."

She blushed. "You're teasing me."

"Just a little." He squeezed her hand again and then took the reins in both hands again. "If you wouldn't sit so close to the edge of the wagon bench, you wouldn't almost fall out when I make a sudden stop."

"So, what am I supposed to do?"

"You need to sit closer to me. After all, I don't bite."

"I don't know about that." She moved away from the edge. "You have nice white teeth."

He laughed, reached over and took her hand again. She didn't resist. "And you, my dear, have a nice beautiful mouth, yourself. White teeth, soft lips and a wonderful smile. That is when you're not frowning because of some silly old snake."

"You're not going to let me forget that, are you?"

"Never. Not even when we're old and gray."

Opal gave him a quick look. What was he saying? Would he really be around when they were growing old? No, she told herself.

It had to be just a figure of speech. She decided to play along. "By then I'll probably be so demented I won't care what you say."

"Then before we grow old, let's enjoy this beautiful day."

"It is nice."

"What do you mean nice? The sun is shining, there's a slight breeze to keep it from getting too hot, nobody is chasing us and I'm riding in this wagon with a beautiful young woman who is holding my hand. I think that makes it more than nice. It makes it a happy time and what more could a man ask than that?"

Opal was getting confused. What was Jace saying to her? Though she liked his words, they scared her at the same time. She decided to change the subject.

"Jace, do you think Daniel is going to be all right?"

He reacted as she thought he would. He grew serious. "I don't know, Opal. I sure hope he does. He was just beginning to feel at home with your family when this happened."

"I'm glad, because he is family and our home is his."

Jace nodded. "I think he'll realize that if he can get through this."

"How could a man like that Mr. Finch treat another human the way he's treated Daniel and those young boys?"

"I don't know. I just know that sometimes the people you trust will turn on you."

Opal got the feeling Jace was no longer talking about Finch. "Do you know people like that?"

"Unfortunately, yes." Jace didn't elaborate.

Opal didn't want to infringe on his private thoughts. She simply muttered, "I'm sorry."

He kind of smiled and squeezed her hand. "I trust you, Opal. If I could tell anyone about it, I'd tell you."

She squeezed his hand back. "Thank you for saying that."

"I mean it." He let her hand go.

Opal felt her hand grow cold. She wished he still held it, but she wouldn't say anything about it. Then she felt almost complete shock when took her arm and looped it in his. He then leaned down and kissed her forehead.

Opal was stunned, but she didn't remove her hand. Instead, she reached up with her other hand and held on to his arm.

He didn't say anything, but he smiled at her. They rode the rest of the way in silence.

He only removed his arm when they entered Wildweed. She appreciated him being so thoughtful. She knew people would gossip if they saw the two of them enter town hugged up. She figured he must have thought the same thing and that was the reason he let her go. She hoped it wasn't because he was tired of having her close to him.

~ * ~

When Duff jerked the gag off, the first words out of Cletus Finch's mouth were, "If it's the last thing I do, I'm gonna kill that damn man."

"Who're you talking about?"

A furious Cletus ignored him. "Where're them rotten boys?"

"I ain't seen 'em, Boss."

Trying to get over the stiffness of being tied to the pole all night, Cletus stretched out his arms. "Well, find 'em. I'm gonna give ever one of 'em a few licks with my whip."

Duff looked puzzled. "Why you gonna do that?"

"For then not getting down here and untying me, you fool. Now go find 'em."

"I'll see if they're cowering in the loft." Duff moved to the ladder and climbed up. "They ain't up here, Cletus."

"Hell, they gotta be somewhere. They couldn't have got out of here."

"Maybe whoever tied you up took them outta here."

Cletus shook his head. "No. I watched the bastards leave and the boys weren't with them. They gotta be here somewhere. Probably scared and hiding."

"Maybe Inez has already put them to work."

"I'll ask Inez."

"You'll ask Inez what, brother?" His sister came through the barn door.

"Where're the boys?"

"That's what I come down here to see. What are you doing here anyway?"

"Never mind." Cletus started out the door, but stumbled.

"What's the matter? Are you drunk again?"

"No, I ain't drunk."

Duff offered an explanation. "That man who works for Barnett tied him up and he's been here in the barn all night."

Inez frowned. "I wondered why you didn't come in and go to bed last night, but I figured you give up on them men coming and went to town."

"They come, Inez." Cletus rubbed his wrists. "They snuck up on me and drug me in here and tied me up."

"Why didn't you yell?"

"Hell, woman. I couldn't yell. They gagged me."

"Well, where're the boys? They ain't done a darn thing around here this morning. I've already decided they ain't getting' nothing to eat today."

"They're not here, Miss Inez."

She frowned at Duff. "What do you mean, they're not here?"

They told her how they'd looked for the boys, but hadn't found a trace of them.

"I've got a feeling you'll find them where you find Daniel," Inez said.

"I think she's right, Cletus."

"Of course I am. Now saddle your horses and go get the boys back. I ain't about to do the hard work that has to be done around here."

Cletus stomped toward the tack room. "I don't only intend to get the boys back, but I'm going to kill every man on the Barnett ranch, including that sorry Injun if he ain't already dead."

"You better not go barreling in there without making a plan. Them folks are smart. They could kill you before you get to them."

"No, they….Hell and damnation!"

"Now what is it?" Duff moved toward the tack room. Inez followed him.

"Those lowdown bastard took our reins and bridles."

"Did you see them carry them out, Brother?"

"No, but our equipment is gone. Who else would've got it?"

Duff nodded. "It looks almost like they had more help than just them two."

"There was a third man, but he was old. I don't think he couldn't been much help." Cletus frowned. "Çome to think of it, he was already in the barn when that man forced me in at gunpoint. How the hell did he get in here? The barn was locked."

"Are you sure?"

"Yes, Inez. I'm sure. They took my key and unlocked it." He began to pace.

"Maybe the old man weren't really here. Maybe you just imagined him. After all, you was under a strain by being held at gunpoint."

Cletus paused. There was fire in his eyes when he looked at Duff. "Shut up that kind of talk. I know what I saw. There was another man in this barn. He even helped Barnett tie me up."

"If you say so."

"I do say so. Now, start looking around and see if you can find the halters. We need to get over to the Barnett place afore he does something with them boys."

"Yes, sir." Duff moved away and Inez followed him.

Cletus saw them whispering to each other and he grew more furious. *Did they think he was crazy? Maybe seeing things that weren't there. But the old man was there. He was a real live person. Or was he? How the hell did he get in the barn if he was real? He couldn't go through the wall. Only a ghost or a spirit…*

Stopping his thoughts before they went on, he grabbed a brush off the shelf in the tack room and flung it at Duff and his sister. "Stop talking about me and get out there and find my horse's head gear."

They scattered, but Cletus was slow following them outside the barn. Now that the thought has entered his mind, he couldn't help wondering if it was possible that the old man was something other than a real live person.

~ * ~

Jace helped Opal back into the wagon after their stop at Doctor Wheeling's small white house on the corner of Main Street near the hotel. At first, he was surprised when the doctor said he'd go right out to the Barnett farm. The healer even said he'd take plenty of supplies so Mrs. Barnett would have enough to care for her nephew for several days.

"Oh, thank you, Doctor Wheeling. That would be a big help to my mother."

"It's no problem at all and please call me John."

"Then you must call me Opal."

"That I will, Opal. I'd heard about your arrival in town and have wanted to meet your entire family."

It was then Jace realized he didn't like all the attention the doctor was paying to Opal. After all, the physician was probably only about thirty or so and as far as Jace could tell, he didn't have a wife. It galled him the way the man had taken Opal's hand and insisted she call him by his first name instead of Doctor Wheeling. It was all he could do to keep his mouth shut and let Opal do the talking to this over-anxious man.

As they departed, Jace still felt irritated when he walked around the wagon and climbed in beside Opal. He thought it better if he didn't say anything about the visit to the doctor. Instead he said in a voice that was harsher than he meant it to be, "I'll leave you at Mayfield's and then go see the sheriff. If that doesn't take long, I'll go to the feed store. I know how long it takes a woman to shop. I'll probably be back by the time you're through gathering the supplies."

She gave him a quick glance and said in an almost whisper, "I'll try to hurry."

He softened his tone. After all, he shouldn't take his frustration out on her. "Take your time. I'll need to look around the store when I get back. There are a couple of things I want to get for the boys."

"Mama told me to get them a shirt and some pants. I'm not sure of their sizes, but I think I can guess at them."

"If you wait until I get back to buy those, maybe I can help you size them up."

"Thank you, Jace."

He stopped the wagon, set the brake and jumped out. He was on the other side to help her down before she'd stood and shook her skirt. She reached out her hand to him, but he ignored it and put his two hands around her waist.

There was nothing she could do, but place her hands on his shoulders as he swung her to the boardwalk. When he sat her down, he smiled. "I'll be back to help you soon."

Before she could answer, he climbed back in the wagon and drove off.

She watched him for a minute, wondering why he'd acted annoyed when they left the doctor's office. Knowing she'd not be able to figure it out, she turned and started inside. A sharp female voice stopped her.

"Hey you, there."

She turned to face the rude woman she recognized from her first time in town. "Did you want to speak to me?"

Neva moved closer to her. Her voice fell to an almost whisper when she said, "I hate to do this, but I must warn you."

Opal raised an eyebrow. "Warn me about what?"

"Just because Jace works at your ranch, don't get any ideas about trying to attract him."

"I don't know what you're talking about. I have no ideas about attracting Jace."

"Don't lie to me, Opal. I saw the way you looked at him when he lifted you from the wagon. Just stop it. Daddy has decided he'll be mine and I'll not put up with you trying to divert his attention from me to you."

Opal wondered why the look in Neva's eyes told her the girl wasn't really interested in Jace. "I assure you that I'm not…"

Neva interrupted her. "I said, don't lie to me. Of course, Daddy assured me you don't stand a chance with him, no matter what you do since we're already practically engaged."

"Jace hasn't said anything about being engaged to anyone."

"Well, Opal, look at me and then look at yourself. Which one do you think Jace would be more proud of when he escorted one of us into a ballroom on his arm?"

Though Opal agreed that this woman was much prettier than she, the words coming from her mouth marred that beauty even if she didn't mean them. They also hurt. Though she knew the woman's name was Greenwood and she was the daughter of an important man, she stared into Neva's blue eyes. Without keeping her voice low, she said, "Listen to me, you stuck-up little twerp. If Jace Renwick would prefer a woman like you over one like me, then he's not good enough for me or any of my friends. Now, get your silly self out of my way. I have shopping to do."

Neva gasped, but didn't reply.

Opal threw back her head, stepped around the woman and marched into the general store, leaving a flabbergasted Neva Greenwood standing there staring at her back as it disappeared through the door of the busy store.

She'd just stepped inside when the Riley twin with the brown hair grabbed her arm. "I can't believe you had the nerve to talk to Neva Greenwood like that."

"I wish I could talk to her like that sometime," the black-haired one said.

Opal blushed. "I didn't realize anyone was listening."

"We were just going out the door and we couldn't help overhearing," the one with black hair said.

"I shouldn't have been so loud. I'm sorry."

"Don't be. I think you were great. By the way, in case you've forgotten, I'm Meg. The brown-headed one is Peg." She pointed to her sister.

"Do you think anyone else heard me?" Opal looked around the store. Several people were gathering items.

"I don't think so," Peg said. "We wouldn't have heard you if we hadn't been leaving."

"Good. I don't want people to think I go around talking unrespectful to others. It just makes me mad when someone acts as if they're better than anyone else."

"Hello, Opal," Hilda Mayfield called from behind the counter. "I'll help you in a moment."

"That's fine. I need to look around a little anyway." She smiled at the twins. "It was good to see you again."

"It was good to see you, too," Meg said. "Can I ask you something?"

"Of course."

"Is that good looking man really interested in Neva Greenwood?"

"I have no idea, but knowing him as well as I do, I don't think so. Of course, Miss Greenwood is a beautiful young woman. I could be wrong. I'm sure many men would like to get to know her."

"When they first look at her, they do," Peg explained, "but when they get to know her better, they lose interest."

"I'm sure when your friend Jace gets to know her, he'll feel the same way."

Opal was feeling a little uncomfortable. "As I said, I have no idea how Jace feels." She started for the back of the store. "I have to look at the boy clothes."

The twins followed her.

"You do like him, don't you, Opal?"

"Of course." She turned. "Now which way are the medical supplies?"

"I thought you wanted boy's clothes?"

"She did, Meg, but she wants medical supplies now." Peg waved toward the back of the store. "I think they keep most of them behind the counter."

"Then while Hilda is busy, I'll go over here and get some cloth for bandages. Mama likes to use soft material for that on a wound."

A man walked up to them. "Hello, Miss Barnett. I'm Floyd Mayfield. I don't think we've met, but Hilda is probably going to be tied up for a while. She told me to see how I could help you."

Opal took a paper from her pocket. "Here's the list of supplies we need at the ranch. I have no idea where to look for everything."

"We were trying to help her," Peg said.

"Well, now that I'm here, why don't you run on home? I'm sure your mama is waiting for that sugar."

"He's probably right, Peg. Maybe we should go."

"I guess so." She looked at Opal as if she didn't want to leave, but decided she'd better. "We'll see you again soon, Opal."

"Yeah. Mama said we could come visit you at your ranch someday. I hope it's soon."

Opal gave them a genuine smile. "Good-by, girls. I'll look forward to seeing you soon."

They bid her goodbye and left.

"Now, Miss Barnett, I'll start gathering up the things on your list and you just busy yourself by looking around at the dry goods and such."

"Thank you, Mr. Mayfield, I will."

As he walked off, a woman walked up and said, "Well, it looks like I shop on the same days that somebody from the Barrett ranch does. I'm Aloma Norton. I've met your mother and sisters, and I assume you're Opal."

"Hello, Mrs. Norton. Mama told me about your visit. I'm glad you came to see her. I hope she'll be able to do a return visit soon."

"I hope so, too."

Opal looked at the little girl who held onto her mother's skirt. "You must be Daphne."

She stared at Opal and nodded.

"How'd you know that?" the little boy asked.

"Well, Heath, I would tell you that I have magic powers, but that wouldn't be the truth. Pearl told me your names after you came to our house for a visit."

He grinned. "I'm going to come see Daniel soon. He takes me fishing. Maybe Pearl will want to go."

Opal nodded. "She probably will, but right now Daniel is not able to go fishing. He's hurt."

Aloma frowned. "What happened?"

Opal shook her head. "Maybe I should tell you later."

Aloma nodded. "Heath, take your sister over there and pick out a candy. I'll get one for each of you."

Heath took her hand and led her away. "Come on, Daphne. Let's get some candy."

After Opal explained what had happened, Aloma said, "I don't believe people as evil as Cletus Finch should be allowed to live."

"That's not all. Mr. Finch was keeping three other young boys as slaves. They managed to escape and come to our farm. The oldest is eleven."

"Oh, my Lord. What will happen to them?"

"I don't know, but Jace Renwick, the man who works for us, is going to see the sheriff about the situation. All I know for sure is that Papa and Mama said there was no way the boys were going back to the Finch ranch."

"Good for your parents."

"Aloma, you might be able to help me. Mama wanted me to get shirts and pants for those boys. I know nothing about young boy's sizes. Would you show me what they'd probably wear?"

"Sure. We'll go by Heath's size. He's ten."

The women found three pair of pants, three shirts and drawers. Opal decided to add a bandana and socks for each of them.

"Will they need shoes?"

"Yes. They were barefoot when they got to the house last night."

"Come here, Heath," his mother called. Turning to Opal she said, "We'll measure the boots to his feet and see if we can't make a good guess as to what might fit."

"I appreciate this a lot, Aloma."

"Glad to do it. Is there anything else?"

"I want to get an outfit for Daniel, but Jace is meeting me here when he finishes at the feed store. I'm sure he'll have a good idea about what size to get."

As if on cue, Jace came through the door. Glancing around, he headed directly to Opal. "How's the shopping going?"

"Very well."

He tipped his hat to Aloma. She nodded and said she'd better get her children and leave. "I don't want them trying to eat all the candy in the store."

When they were alone, Jace said, "Did you get some clothes for the boys?"

"Yes. Aloma helped me since she knows boys' sizes. But I want you to help me get boots for them. I also want to get an outfit for Daniel. Will you help me there, too?"

"Of course. I thought I'd pick up a bedroll for each of the boys. I know they're excited to have blankets in the loft, but I think a bedroll will give them a sense of belonging."

"I think you're right. Mr. Mayfield is getting the other supplies."

"Good."

"What happened at the sheriff's office, Jace?"

"I'd rather not discuss it here. I'll tell you all about it on the way home."

She nodded and they moved over to the shirts and pants.

## *Twenty-one*

Neva took a deep breath, put a pouty look on her face and jerked open her father's office door.

Alton Greenwood glanced up with a frown as his front door slammed. She knew it irritated him when somebody came into his office without knocking. He looked as if he were ready to blast them with words, but held his tongue when he saw Neva march up to his desk. He plastered on a grin. "What's wrong now, my little love?"

"I've never been so insulted in my life."

"Honey, what are you talking about?"

"That Barnett girl talked to me like I was a... a person with no breeding at all. Can you imagine that?"

"No, I can't. What made her do that?"

"I don't know. All I did was tell her what you asked me to tell her."

"What was that?"

"That Jace and I were practically engaged and she shouldn't act as if she could take him away from me."

"Maybe you misunderstood her reaction."

"No, I didn't. She said I wasn't good enough for him, as if she was. Why, Daddy, she doesn't even know how to dress. She had on a dress that I know was at least three years old." Neva hoped her act was convincing her father that she was really upset.

Alton didn't ask her how she knew the age of the dress, which she thought he would. He seemed more concerned about why anyone would attack her. He'd made it clear he thought Neva was the only real lady in Wildweed and all the other women here were always trying to live up to her standard. Of course he'd also made it plain that they would never able to achieve that goal. As he often said, there was nobody as pretty or as cultured as his Neva.

"Calm down, Neva, and try to consider the Barnett girl's background."

"What does that have to do with it?"

"Well, sweetheart, some people just don't know how to talk to people who are so far above their class. The girl probably has never met anyone as beautiful and cultured as you."

Neva pursed her mouth. *This can't be true. Opal Barnett is a pretty woman. Maybe in her way, even prettier than me.* But she couldn't tell her father that. "She thinks she can entice Jace away from me."

Alton laughed. "There's no way in the world that could happen. Jace is besotted with you. No unrefined country girl could turn his head."

Neva forced a grin. "I'm sure you're right, but I just wanted to let you know I did what you told me to do. I let her know not to try to take Jace. I just wasn't prepared for the way she talked to me."

He nodded. "Leave it to me, baby. I'll take care of her for you."

She moved over to him and hugged his neck so he wouldn't see she was shocked at his words. She certainly didn't want him to do anything to hurt Opal Barnett. "I have the best daddy in the world."

"And I have the most perfect daughter." He stood and put his arms around her waist and pulled her close to him. "Now, why don't you go on home and calm yourself down before you make yourself sick over something I can handle for you. I'll see you at home tonight."

She looked up at him. "If I go home, will you promise you'll tell me what you did to get even with the Barnett woman for me?"

He smiled at her and leaned down and kissed her cheek. "Yes, love. I'll tell you."

She pulled away from him and started toward the door. "I'll be waiting at home to see what you say."

"Tell you what. Maybe I should see if I can catch Jace before he leaves town. If I can get him to come to the house for supper, that'll show the girl who he wants." He closed the ledger book on his desk.

"That's a good idea, Daddy." She blew him a kiss and closed the door.

Once outside, she bit her lip and wondered why it made her uncomfortable when her father hugged her. He'd been hugging her all her life, but it seemed he'd been holding her closer lately and she wasn't sure she liked it. There was only one man who she wanted holding her that close and it wasn't her father.

George finished helping Sly and Marty feed the horses. He then turned to Sly. "Would you and Marty keep an eye on the boys for a while? I'm going in the house and check on Daniel."

"Shore, boss. Jace said since we'd finished the branding, we should work on building the bunkhouse. I'll see if they'd like to help us move some of the supplies that are behind the barn over to the site."

George frowned. "I don't know. I think that would be fine for Glen, but Ivan and Billy are so young I'm not sure they'll be careful. There could be nails and other debris on the ground. They have no shoes and I don't want injured feet."

"I heard Miz Gloria saying the other day that she'd like some flower beds in the yard. Why don't I get Ivan and Billy to help me lay a couple out?"

"That's a good idea, Marty. Maybe you and the younger ones could work on that while Sly and Glen work on moving some of the building supplies." He looked around. "Where are they now?"

"In the loft," Sly said. "I think they're afraid Finch will come here looking for them."

"He probably will, so be on the lookout. If you see anybody headed this way, hide the boys immediately."

"Yes, sir."

"Thanks, men. I'll be back out in a little while."

As George started out the door, Glen scrambled down the ladder to the loft. "Mr. George, sir." His voice was timid.

George could tell the boy was nervous, then he glanced up and saw the other two peeping over the edge of the loft. He knew Glen was approaching him for all three of them. He kept his voice gentle. "Yes, Glen."

"We was wondering…that is…we wanted to know how Daniel is doing." His shaky voice gave away the almost terror the boy felt by simply speaking to an adult.

George wanted to take the boy's fear away, but he knew the only way he had to do it was with his actions and his words. "I'm sure you do want to know about your friend. Why don't you come to the house with me and see Daniel for yourself?"

Surprise spread across his face. "You'd really let me come?"

"Yes, Glen. You can come back and tell your friends what you see with your own eyes. That way you won't have to rely on what somebody tells you." George nodded to the boys in the loft. "He'll be back soon and tell you all about Daniel."

Glen didn't say anything until they reached the cabin's back door. "Do I need to wait outside?"

"No, Glen. Come on in." George opened the door and motioned for him to go through. He followed him inside.

Gloria and Ruby were in the kitchen. Ruby was stirring something in a big pot and Gloria was filling pie pans with berries.

"Hello, dear. Is everything all right?" Gloria smiled at her husband and glanced at Glen.

"Everything's fine. We thought we'd come in and check on Daniel. The boys were all concerned about him."

"I see. He's about the same, but he did murmur a little this morning."

"What did he say?"

"It wasn't understandable, but I felt it was a good sign that he might be getting a little better."

"I believe you're right." George put his hand on Glen's shoulder. "Let's go over there and see him."

Daniel lay on his stomach on the couch, much like he did the other time he was hurt. Pearl and Sapphire were sitting on the floor nearby. "Mama told us to stay close so we would hear Daniel if he said something."

"That's a good idea, honey." George took the vacant chair beside the couch, the one he knew Gloria had been sitting in. He motioned Glen forward, then reached out and touch Daniel's forehead. In a low and soothing voice, he said, "You've got to get well, son. You're a part of our family and it won't be the same if you don't get better."

Glen stared at the still form. "Is he going to die?" he whispered.

George took his hand. "No, Glen. We're going to make sure Daniel has the best of care we can give him. Opal and Jace have gone to town. They're going to send the doctor back here to help us make sure Daniel gets better."

"Mr. Finch didn't get no doctor when he beat Daniel before."

"Well, Mr. Finch is no longer in charge of you guys. We're here to make sure none of you ever have to be hurt by him again."

"After Mr. Finch beat him this time, Daniel said you'd come and get him."

"He knew I'd never let that man keep him there."

"I wish we never had to go back there again."

Gloria had walked over to them. She put her hands on Glen's shoulders. "Don't you worry, Glen. You're never going back to that evil man. I don't know what we can work out, but we'll think of something."

"I'll work hard for you, ma'am. I'll do anything you want me to do as long as you don't make us go back there. You can even whip us if you want to 'cause you feed us. The witch never fed us much, but she whipped us a lot."

Gloria knelt down in front of him. "Look at me, Glen." When his eyes were level with hers, she went on, "Nobody on this ranch is going to whip you. Not now. Not ever. We might lose our temper and yell once in a while, but there will be no hitting. As far as food is concerned, as long as the family eats, everyone on this ranch will eat. If you stay here, you'll definitely have to help with the chores and do your part, but you will never be expected to do more than you're capable of doing and whatever needs doing, you'll have help to do it if you need it. That's the way we treat our daughters and Daniel, so if you like these rules, you'll be welcome to stay at this ranch."

Glen did something he, nor anyone else expected him to do. He threw his arms around Gloria's neck and began to sob.

She folded her arms around him and looked over his shoulder at George with mist filling her eyes. George nodded at her and he couldn't help the moisture that began to gather in his eyes.

Before anybody could say anything, Daniel moaned. They all turned to look at him. His eyes opened and he gazed at George for a few seconds. Then in a raspy voice, he muttered, "I knew you'd come get me, Uncle George." His eyes immediately closed and he said nothing else.

"He spoke to me, Gloria." George voice shook with excitement and some disbelief.

"I know, dear. I heard him."

Glen snuffed and said, "I heard him, too."

"I believe that's a sign he's going to be all right." George looked toward the ceiling and said, "Thank You, God. Thank You."

Jace turned from helping Floyd Mayfield place the last of the supplies Opal had purchased in the wagon when a deep voice said, "Hello, Jace."

He turned and nodded. "Greenwood."

"I need a word with you." He glared at Mayfield.

Floyd must have taken the hint because he turned back toward the store. "Thanks for helping, Jace. I'll get back in there and tell Miss Barnett you're all loaded up." He glanced at Alton Greenwood, nodded and disappeared though the door.

"So, what word did you want to have with me, Mr. Greenwood?"

"I think I asked you to call me Alton." Jace nodded and Greenwood went on. "I heard you were in town and I thought it would be a good time to invite you to come to the house for supper. I'm sure Neva would be delighted, though she'll fuss at me because she didn't have time to have Mrs. Kingsley prepare something special for you."

Jace stared at this man. Was he crazy? Why would he think he'd leave this load of goods to eat supper at his house? He tried to keep his voice calm. "Miss Barnett and I need to head back to the ranch."

"I heard she was with you, but there's no reason you can't send her on to the ranch with the supplies. After we have supper and you and Neva had a nice little chat, I'll loan you a horse to go back to the ranch if you feel you must go."

Jace frowned at the man. "Are you seriously asking me to send Miss Barnett home alone?"

"I'm sure she'll be fine."

"How would you feel if some able-bodied cowboy sent Neva on a seven mile trek across the prairie with a ranch wagon loaded with supplies?"

"I'd kill any bastard that treated her that way."

"Don't you think George Barnett would want to kill me if I sent his daughter home alone?"

"Of course not. There's too much difference between the Barnett girls and Neva."

"What do you mean?"

"I hear Barnett lets his daughters ride horses and help out on the ranch just the same as if they were boys. I'm never let Neva do that. She's much too delicate for such a thing."

Jace knew it was hopeless to argue with the man. He moved to the front of the horses and checked their headstalls. Not because they needed it, but he knew if didn't move away from Alton Greenwood, he might just knock some of the man's teeth out.

Unfortunately, Greenwood followed him. "If you don't want to send the woman home alone, send her to the Apple Blossom Café and tell her you'll be detained for a couple of hours."

Jace turned around and glared at Alton. "If Miss Barnett goes to the Apple Blossom Café, I'll be going with her. I don't know how you were raised to treat a lady, but my mama would have had a fit if I didn't do the right thing."

"Don't you see that Neva is the only real lady in this rundown town? She was educated in Denver and she learned how a proper woman should act."

"From what I understand, the Barnett girls were educated in Memphis, Tennessee…"

"But, Jace, don't you see that you're wasting precious time messing around with those Barnetts? You need to find a wife and head back to your ranch in Texas where you can start raising your own family."

Jace had never before been as happy to see anyone as he was when Opal appeared in the door of the general store. He ignored Greenwood and smiled at her. "Are you ready to head home, Miss Barnett?"

She nodded.

"But, Jace …"

Jace moved to the boardwalk and held his hand out to Opal. "Would you like to go to the café down the street and eat something before we head out?"

She frowned at him, but shook her head. "I'm not hungry. I'm sure Mama will have a good meal cooked by the time we get back to the ranch."

"Good. I prefer her cooking to anything we can get here in Wildweed anyway."

"Jace…?"

"Excuse us, Alton, but I think we'll head out now. I don't want it to be too dark when we get home.

Alton sighed. "You will come to supper another time, won't you?"

"Possibly."

"Good. How about Saturday?"

"I'll let you know." He dropped Opal's hand and then put his hands on her waist. He swung her onto the seat as if she were a delicate flower. "Good day, Alton."

Opal stared at him as he walked around the wagon, climbed in, took the reins and snapped them over the horse's back. He didn't speak and neither did she.

~ * ~

They were well out of town when Opal reached over, touched his arm and asked, "Are you all right, Jace?"

He glanced over at her. "I'm fine. Why do you ask?"

"You haven't said a word since we left Wildweed. It seems Mr. Greenwood upset you."

He nodded. "It did a little, but I'm not going to dwell on it."

"Good. It's a long seven miles back to the ranch when there's no conversation." She removed her hand.

"Put your hand back where it belongs."

She turned and looked at him. "What are you talking about?"

"This." He took her hand and looped her arm with his. "Now, that feels right."

Opal giggled, but she didn't remove her arm. "Jace, you're awful. An engaged man shouldn't act this way with another woman."

He looked startled. "What the hell does that mean? Uh…sorry for cursing."

"I forgive you and it means that Miss Neva Greenwood informed me today that she has plans to marry you. You're already practically engaged, she said."

He shook his head. "There's no way I'd ever marry that silly girl."

"I'm not sure she understands that."

"She might as well. Marriage to her will never happen. Not by me, anyway."

"I'm glad, Jace."

His mouth crinkled at the corners. Not a complete smile, but enough to show her that her words pleased him. "Why are you glad, Opal?"

She shrugged. "I'm not sure, but I have a feeling there is something strange about Miss Greenwood. She says one thing, but her eyes say something else. She's hiding something."

"So you noticed that, too?"

"By that, may I assume you've noticed the contradiction in her words and actions?"

"Yes, you may assume that." He reached over and patted her hand. "I'm glad you saw it because I was wondering if I was making it up in my mind."

"You're not."

They rode a way in silence, then Jace pulled the wagon under the shade of a cottonwood tree. He turned and looked at Opal. He never intended to tell anyone why he was in this town, but before he could stop his mouth, he blurted. "Alton Greenwood is the man who killed my father, though he was using another name at the time. I came to Wildweed to make him pay for his crime."

She gasped. "Are you sure, Jace?"

"I'm positive. I just can't figure out a way to prove it."

"Mr. Greenwood is a respected businessman in Wildweed. I know a lot of people don't like him, but it's hard to believe he's a murderer."

Now he felt compelled to tell her more. "Greenwood fits the description of the man who killed Dad. They said he was married and had a small daughter. After he left the goldfield, he changed his name and moved around a while. Then his wife died and he settled in Santa Fe, then Denver. His housekeeper is a woman he moved here from Denver. She was one of his mistresses. From what I've learned, he had several, even before his wife died. He didn't want his daughter to find out, so he put her in school near his sister in Denver. A while back he worked his way here. Some months ago, he sent for his daughter. They've been living in Wildweed ever since."

Opal removed her arm from his, reached up and took his face in her hands. The stubble on his chin was prickly, but for some reason it make her feel warm inside just to touch it. "I'm sorry about your papa, Jace, and I'm sure you're right about Greenwood, but you can't accuse a man of killing your father without proof."

"I know that, Opal. That's why I came here. I've got to find a way to get the proof I need to prove Greenwood is a murderer. I don't care about the interest in the mine he stole from Dad, but I can't let him to get away with killing my father because of his greed."

Opal knew he was telling the truth. Why she said what she did next, she didn't know. "I'll help you find the proof, Jace."

He didn't answer, but his eyes bored into hers. It was if he were looking into her soul. She knew she should remove her hands from his face, but for the moment it was as if she were paralyzed.

The next thing she knew, his arms were around her and he was pulling her close to his rock hard chest. Her mind wasn't working well. All she could think of was how wonderful it felt to be held by this man. *Stop this, Opal. You can't surrender to this man's charms. He has already said he has no plans to marry. All he wants is revenge. You've never been anything but a friend to him. If you don't stop him, he's going to make you his convenient woman of the moment. You know you don't want that.*

But she did want that. Especially since his lips had covered hers. She felt fireworks going off in her head, not to mention the quivers that were racing up and down her body all the way from her feet to the back of her neck. What was happening? She'd been kissed a few times before, but never like this. Never had any man's lips moved her in the way those of Jace Renwick did. She didn't want him to stop and she was sure he knew she was feeling this way.

But he did stop. Abruptly. He pulled away and took her by the shoulders, pushing her away from him. Though he was breathing hard and seemed to be forcing his words, he muttered, "I'm sorry, Opal. I shouldn't have done that."

She smiled at him. "I'm not sorry, Jace."

He pressed his forehead to hers. "Oh, Opal. You're so special. You don't know how long I've wanted to kiss you, but I knew I had no right."

"I think I gave you the right when I kissed you back."

"You father is going to kill me. He made it clear when I came to work for him that his daughters were all off limits. That is, with the exception of Sapphire. He said if I was willing to wait for her, I'd have his blessing."

Opal laughed. "Sapphire loves you."

"I love her, but not in the way…I mean…Opal, please forgive me for my actions. I wish…it hadn't hap…I mean…"

"For heaven's sake, Jace. Don't be so dramatic about it. You kissed me. You didn't take advantage of me or anything. I was a willing participant."

He pulled back and looked into her eyes. "Are you saying you're so used to a man's kisses it meant nothing to you?"

She put her hands on the front of his chest. "Not at all. In fact, I've never been kissed the way you kissed me and if I'm never kissed again, I'll always remember the magic you made me feel."

Jace smiled as his arms went around her and pulled her against him again. "Oh, Opal. I've never had a woman tell me my kiss is something she'll always remember."

"I don't see why not. It was wonderful."

He took hold of her chin and tilted her head so they could look into each other's eyes. "I wasn't going to tell you, but no woman's lips have ever made me as hungry for more as yours. Even if your father does kill me, it'll be worth it just to kiss you again."

Before Opal could agree with him, his hungry mouth was on hers again. His tongue explored her lips and she automatically parted them and invited him in. Again her only thought was that she loved being in this man's arms and feeling his mouth on hers and his hands exploring her back. Even through her dress she could feel the calluses on his hands and yet they were tender against her skin. She couldn't believe she wanted him to move his hands to the front of her body.

Again, he pulled away, but this time he didn't apologize. "We need to head home before I get too carried away."

She didn't tell him how much she wanted to forget going home and finding a place where they could spend the rest of the day in each other's arms. She didn't want to admit that she had hoped the kiss would lead to something more serious and that she wanted him to get carried away. But she said, "I think you're right."

Jace picked up the reins and started the horse. They were leaving the shade of the tree and headed for the road, when he reached over and pulled her close to him. "I'm thinking of riding up to the house holding you in my arm like this."

She glanced at him. "Really?"

"Don't you think it would tell everyone what's been in my mind for a long time?"

"Yes, but maybe we shouldn't spring it on them in such a quick way."

He chuckled. "Maybe you don't want…."

A bullet hit one of the wagon wheels and Opal screamed.

Jace jerked the horse to a stop, and grabbed his gun. At the same time, he was pushing Opal toward the opposite side of the wagon from the origination of the shot.

Another shot went over his head as he dropped to the ground beside her. She watched as he peered toward the small knoll on the other side of the road and waited. If she had a gun, she could help him.

"Can you reach under the seat and get me one of those rifles?"

"I'll get them both." He stretched and his hand pulled the rifles into sight.

Opal reached up and took hold of the stock. She pulled it to her and watched as he felt for the other one. Soon it was in his hand and he glanced at her. "You stay here and guard the front in case they decide to come that way. I'm going to ease to the back of the wagon so I can get off a better shot.

She nodded and laid the barrel of the rifle on the floor of the wagon to steady it from her shaking.

Another shot whizzed by and Opal let out a little scream as she felt a stinging sensation on her shoulder. Blood ran down the front of her dress.

Jace glanced around. "Are you all right?"

She had turned so he wouldn't see she was hit. "I'm fine. That bullet just came awfully close."

"Stay low. I just found out how much I like kissing you. I don't want some outlaw to keep me from doing it again."

"I want you to do it again. Maybe often."

"Very often."

Another bullet went over her head.

Jace fired back.

There was a scream and she knew he'd hit whoever was shooting at them and in a matter of minutes there was the sound of a horse galloping away.

Jace eased back to her. "I think I hit him, but he must not have been hurt enough to keep him from riding away."

She was still turned so he couldn't see her shoulder. As she pushed her gun back under the seat, she said, "I don't think it's bad, but I have a little problem."

"What kind of problem?"

She turned and he tossed his rifle in the wagon, grabbed her and lifted her into his arms. "Damn it, Opal, you're hit. Why the hell didn't you tell me?"

Though her shoulder was hurting terribly, she couldn't help smiling. "Stop cursing, Jace. It's nothing serious."

"Don't tell me it's nothing serious." He lifted her to the seat and climbed in beside her. He began unbuttoning her dress.

She smacked his hands. "Stop that. I said it's not serious."

He put her hands to the side. "Keep your hands out of my way. I'm going to check your shoulder and see how bad you're hurt."

"But…"

"No buts. Sit still."

"Well, at least let me unbutton my dress myself."

"I can't believe you're getting modest with a gunshot in your shoulder."

She began slipping the buttons through the buttonholes down the front of her dress. "It's not modesty. Well, maybe it is." She didn't realize she said out loud the thought that ran through her mind, but she did. "When you undress me, I don't want it be because you want to check a gunshot wound. I want it to be because you love me."

## Twenty-two

Jace swallowed as he watched the buttons slip through their holes. Did she know what she'd just said? He couldn't believe it had come from her mouth. Though Opal had surprised him by responding to his kisses today, he never dreamed she had serious thoughts about him. Love was not a word he could allow into his vocabulary at this time in his life. He was too near reaching his goal. He couldn't let anything or anyone stop him from reaching it. Yet, this woman had stirred him as no other ever had. Then she had to go and get shot. When he first saw the blood on the front of her dress, it scared him so badly he thought his heart was going to beat out of his chest.

"There. Now you can check my shoulder."

He came back to the present. Ripping the kerchief from his neck he began dabbing at her wound. "It looks like the bullet went through. Thank God I don't have to dig it out of you."

"I told you it wasn't that serious."

"Any gunshot wound is serious, Opal. We need to clean it as good as we can and your mother will have to use some of her salve on it. We don't want it to get infected."

"Then I'll say I'm glad this one wasn't any more serious than it is."

He chuckled.

She puckered her lips. "Why are you laughing? You said I had a serious wound and now you're laughing at me. What kind of friend are you?"

"I'm your best friend. Now, tear off some of your petticoat and I'll bandage your shoulder."

"I bought some cloth for bandages. Couldn't we use that? I hate tearing up my petticoat. I don't have that many nice ones."

He began unbuttoning his shirt. "Look, sweetheart, I'm not climbing in the back of that wagon and searching through all those packages for a piece of cloth. If you don't want to tear up your petticoat, I'll use my shirt."

"Oh, for heaven's sake. You're not going to use your shirt." She flipped up her skirt and grasped the edge of her petticoat.

He grinned. "Thanks. I don't have that many shirts and they show when you're wearing them and petticoats don't."

She only shook her head at him.

He watched as she struggled with trying to tear her undergarment. "Want me to help you?"

"I hate to admit that my arm is getting kind of stiff. I do need your help."

He didn't say anything, but reached down and began to tear strips of the white muslin petticoat. "I'm going to need enough to make a sling."

"Want me to stand up and take it off?"

"I think I can get it with you sitting." He didn't tell her that handling her petticoat was making him grow warm. He hoped she wouldn't notice, but he figured since he was also sitting, she wouldn't be able to see the evidence.

He finished the dressing and saw Opal flinching. "I know it hurts, honey. I wish there was something I could do to help ease your pain."

"I'll be all right." She blinked back tears.

Folding his arms around her, he whispered, "I wish that bullet had found me and not you."

"That's a sweet thing to say, Jace, but I'm glad it was me. I can't stand the thought of somebody taking you away from me now."

"I'm not going anywhere. Not anytime soon, anyway." He pulled her tighter to him. "Now lean on me and I'll try not to hit too many ruts the rest of the way home."

After another mile, Opal moved against him and he looked down at her. "Are you asleep?"

"Huh?"

"I just wondered if you were going to sleep."

She didn't answer and he smiled at her. She was breathing steadily and he knew she had drifted off. Good. She needed to sleep all the way if she could. He sifted his position so she would be more comfortable and looked at her shoulder. There was blood seeping through the bandage. Lord, he hoped she would be all right until they could get help. He wondered how he was going to tell Gloria and George how he managed to let their daughter get shot.

He began to mutter aloud. "Maybe I'll say, sorry, George, but I was not there when Opal needed me. She was shot while I was at the other end of the wagon." He shook his head. "That won't work. Maybe I'll say, George if I could change places with her I would. I don't want her to be hurt any more than you do."

Shaking his head again, he said, "Hell, why don't I tell him the truth? Why don't I say, I felt like I was going to die when I looked at her shoulder and saw she'd been shot. I can't tell him that I want to hold her in my arms until she's all well. How can I tell the man that no matter what I try not to, I'm falling love with his daughter?

Will he run me off the ranch? If I have to go, will Opal go with me? If I have to leave, how will I make Greenwood pay for his crime?"

He almost ran out of the road when Opal muttered, "Yes, if you have to go, I'll go with you, Jace."

~ * ~

Though the Barnetts were upset when he brought Opal home with a bullet hole in her shoulder, they didn't seem to blame him. They rushed around and insisted she be put to bed in her room, though she tried to tell them she was fine and didn't want to go to bed. Everyone ignored her. Since he'd carried her into the house, Jace carried her to the room Gloria indicated.

He wasn't prepared to see such a cramped little room with a regular bed on one side and a small cot on the other. There was a small dresser with a mirror above it in the corner. Nails on the wall held their clothes and a small table beside the bed completed the furnishings.

Not saying anything, Jace put Opal on the bed. Gloria rushed around him and began working on her daughter's shoulder. Though he wanted to stay and see how Opal was going to be, he saw there was nothing else he could do, so he slipped out of the room.

George followed him. "What happened, Jace?"

"We were ambushed."

"Do you think it was Finch?"

"It was either him or that man who works on that ranch. I didn't get a look at him, but I'm pretty sure I winged him."

George frowned. "I wish you'd killed him."

Jace couldn't help a small smile spreading across his mouth. "I thought you were a man of peace, George."

"I thought I was too, but when a man's family is at risk, things change. I'm beginning to realize there are times a man has to resort to violence in this part of the country. Talking doesn't always work."

"Being raised in the East, I thought talking was the way to end arguments, too. It didn't take me long to learn differently."

George frowned. "I didn't know you were from the East, Jace."

"I was actually born in Colorado, but my mother moved back to Baltimore when I was seven. I came West again when I was about twenty."

"Will you be going back to Baltimore someday?"

Jace shook his head. "The West is my home now. I intend to spend the rest of my life here."

"I see." George changed the subject. "I'm not comfortable leaving the boys outside without you or me there. I know Sly and Marty will watch them, but as you can testify, those from the Finch ranch can sneak up on you when you least expect it."

"That's for sure."

"Would you mind going out there and checking on them? I'll be out as soon as I see that Gloria is all right taking care of Opal and Daniel both."

Jace wanted to stay close to Opal, but he knew he needed to do as George asked. He nodded and went out the back door.

It wasn't long until George joined them where they were beginning work on the bunkhouse. "I see you have the young boys stacking the short ends of the wood."

"I thought that was a job they could handle." Jace finished nailing a board to what would eventually become the south end of the bunkhouse. "How are the sick?"

"Daniel is the same. Opal wants to get up and come into the parlor, but Gloria insists she stay in bed." He chuckled. "I have no doubt but that Gloria will win that argument. She most always does."

"Opal needs to take it easy. Though her injury didn't look serious, you can't fool around with a gunshot wound."

"That's what we keep telling her." George reached for the hammer and said, "Jace, I see dust in the distance. Do you suppose somebody is coming?"

"Looks like it. Maybe we should get the boys to safety in case it's someone from the Finch ranch."

"I agree." George turned toward the other side of the structure. "Marty, come here, please."

Marty ran up. "Yep, Boss."

"It's getting close to supper. Take the boys into the barn and show them how we like things closed up for the night."

Marty frowned, but didn't argue. He turned and called the three young boys. They obediently followed him into the barn.

As the rider got closer, Jace said, "It looks like a buggy. I don't think Finch or his man would come here in a conveyance like that."

"You're probably right, but let's wait to be sure who it is before we have the boys come back out."

When the buggy was close enough for him to see it well, Jace said, "It looks like the doctor. Opal and I went by his office and asked him to come out right away. Looks like he took his time about it."

"I hope he can help both Opal and Daniel. I'll go inside and see what he has to say."

Jace had to bite his tongue to keep from saying that he didn't want the doctor looking at Opal's shoulder. He was afraid it would give the man more ideas than he already had about wanting to see Opal again—and not in a professional manner.

"Owa!" Jace threw the hammer down and grabbed his thumb.

"You all right, Jace?" Sly asked as he dragged a board toward the end where he was working.

"Mashed my damn thumb."

Sly chuckled. "Stop fretttin' man. It's gonna be fine."

"What are you talking about?"

"Miss Opal. She knows a good thing when she sees it. That slick lookin' doctor won't turn her head from you."

"You're a fool, Sly. I don't have any designs on Opal Barnett."

"If you believe what you're saying, you're the fool, Jace Renwick."

Jace didn't get a chance to argue. Marty came out of the barn with the boys and Sly walked away chuckling.

Picking up his hammer, Jace began nailing the board again. Angry at himself for caring and angry that Sly understood more than he should, he raised the hammer and slammed it toward the nail. He missed and hit his finger again. His 'Damn it' was probably heard inside the house.

~ * ~

Neva thought her father was yelling at her and calling her a slut because she'd lain with Marty Mayfield and he found about it. She flopped over to get his voice out of her head, but it didn't work. The yelling continued.

She opened her eyes and realized she lay in bed in her room while the yelling took place downstairs. She couldn't understand the words, but she knew whoever owned the voice arguing with her father held back none of its anger. Though she wasn't sure what was happening, she knew it was too late for this kind of confrontation. She didn't know what time it was, but she knew it was much too late for company. She remembered going to bed at ten. She was sure of this because the big clock in the hall chimed ten times as she climbed the steps to retire for the night. The angry man must have come after that.

Neva frowned and wished they'd get quiet so she could go back to sleep, then she wondered if her father could be in danger.

Whoever the man yelling sounded mad enough to turn violent.

Deciding she better check without them knowing, she got out of bed, slipped her feet into satin slippers and threw her blue silk robe around her shoulders. She didn't need a light as she eased down the stairs because a lamp burned in the parlor located beyond the entry. The closer she got to the bottom of the stairs, the clearer the voices became.

"I don't care what you said, GW. I wanted him dead and I'm sorry Duff didn't kill him."

"Damn it. I told you not to kill him. I intend to make him think Neva wants to marry him. That way I can figure some way to get my hands on some of his money."

"But the bastard tied me up and left me in the barn all night."

"He could've killed you, but he didn't, so stop whining."

"Hell, Greenwood, you've never been humiliated like I was. If you had, you'd want to kill the bastard, too."

"Not if I knew I could make money by letting him live."

Neva instinctively knew her father wouldn't want her to overhear this conversation. She hurried down the hall and slipped into the linen closet near his study. The thin door allowed her to hear the men plainly.

"You only think of money. Otherwise why would you have us keep slave boys to run your ranch?"

"And you couldn't keep three little brats and one dumb Indian on the place."

"I told you that Injun was a relative of the Barnetts."

"What the hell difference does that make?"

"None, I guess."

"That's your problem. You never think about anything beyond what's happening to you at the moment, Finch. You've got to look at everything and how it will affect your life if you want to be successful."

"How about you? You're only interested in getting your daughter hitched to Renwick. Why else would you want the Barnett woman killed?"

"Well, you failed on doing that for me, didn't you?"

"I sent Duff out to wait for them after we seen them loading things up at Mayfields'. He was supposed to shoot her."

"Well, did he?"

"He's not sure."

"What does that mean?"

"He said he thought he hit her and she screamed, but then Renwick shot him in the arm. He thought it was time to get out of there and take care of his wound afore he bled to death."

"So he didn't wait around to see if the woman was dead?"

"Hell, no. Would you?"

"Stop your damn yelling. Neva is asleep upstairs. She might wake up and hear you."

Finch let out a sinister laugh. "Don't want her to know what a crook you are, huh?"

"Shut up, you fool."

"Why should I? If you don't give me the money I'm asking for, I just might give your precious daughter a visit."

"You wouldn't dare."

"Oh, wouldn't I? How would you like for her to know you've robbed and killed for years to get where you are today? Maybe she don't care, but if I don't miss my guess, she'd be a little ashamed of her pa."

"Listen you son-of-a-bitch. If you ever breathe a word of what you know about me, I'll kill you with my own hands and not blink an eye. You know I've done it before and I'll do it again."

"You might regret that. As I said, you've got a pretty little daughter. Wouldn't want anything to happen to her, would you?"

"You damn son-of-a-bitch, if anything were to happen to my Neva, I'd see that you were tied up by your feet and skinned one section at a time until you finally died."

"You don't scare me, Alton Greenwood, neither does GW Conners, which I know happens to be your real name. I also know you're the man who swore his partner in the Colorado gold mind was killed by raiders when he died from a bullet in the back put there by you."

"You don't know a damn thing. You're just talking big."

"Try me and see. I want a thousand dollars so I can leave here before the law comes down on me for your big idea about kidnapping kids."

"Do you think the law is going to believe a nobody like you?

"Do you want to take that chance?"

There was a minute of silence, then the man's voice went on. "I see by your silence you don't want to chance it. Now get me the thousand dollars I want."

There was a pause and she heard a desk drawer open. "I only have a hundred here. Take that and get the hell out of here."

"That ain't enough. I want more."

"You'll get more, but you'll have to wait until the bank opens in the morning."

Neva couldn't believe what she was hearing. She often suspected her father was ruthless, but she never dreamed he would murder somebody to gain financially. Now she knew he was using her because he wanted to get some of Jace Renwick's money, not because he wanted her to be happy. If he cared about her happiness, he would've let her continue to see Marty. And who was this GW Conners the man accused her daddy of being? She thought she might have heard the name somewhere, but she couldn't remember where.

Knowing the meeting between the two men was nearing its end, she realized she'd better get back upstairs. As quickly and as quietly as she could, she eased out of the closet and hurried down the hall. She climbed the stairs and had just turned down the hall toward her room when she heard the men in the entry. The front door closed and she rushed into her room. Closing the door as softly as she could, she threw her robe on a chair and hurried into bed. She didn't bother to remove her slippers.

It felt like only an instant when her door opened. She closed her eyes and pretended to be asleep.

Her father must have heard something and thought it was she. She had to make him believe she was sleeping. Maybe he did because he let the door close. But she didn't hear his footsteps move away.

She lay almost motionless for several minutes. Again her door opened and she knew he was peering inside again. This time he must have been satisfied because he moved away from her door. It wasn't long until she heard him going down the stairs. Breathing a sigh of relief, she didn't even care if he was headed for Vinnie Kingsley's room as he often did during the night. Especially the nights he'd been upset about something.

Neva took a deep breath and let the conversation she'd overheard play in her mind again. The man called Finch had accused her father of being someone besides the man she knew him as. He also said her daddy had been robbing and killing for years. This was hard to believe. That is, until she heard her father say he wanted the Barnett woman killed. At that point she almost screamed at him, but managed to control her thoughts. Was the man she'd always thought of as a loving father really this cruel man she didn't know? Maybe a man with a name she never realized he had. Without warning, tears roll down her cheeks. No matter what she learned about her father, tonight was going to change her life forever. The only thing she had to do was to figure out what she was going to do with all this information.

When her sobs eased, she began to plan. She decided she'd face him at breakfast and hoped she could make him think she was feeling poorly. Maybe she'd hint that she was having her monthly. That way she might be able to face him without letting him know she was going to ransack his desk as soon as she was alone in the house. It wouldn't be that hard, if things went as they usually did on a Wednesday. He would tell her to rest, and leave for his office as usual. It was the day Vinnie went to the general store for supplies. Neva knew she'd have at least an hour alone in the house to look for something that would answer the questions in her head. She prayed she wouldn't discover that he was as bad as that Finch man had accused him of being and she kept telling herself that maybe the man was just angry and had said the things just to be mean. Everything depended on what she found tomorrow. She'd then know what kind of man her daddy really was—a loving father or a deceitful murderer.

## *Twenty-three*

"Daniel's awake, Mama," Pearl announced when she came into the parlor leading Sapphire. "He grinned at me."

Her mother rushed over to the couch. "Oh, Daniel, you are awake."

He nodded.

Gloria couldn't help herself. She leaned down and kissed his forehead. "I'm so glad you're getting better."

Daniel blushed and muttered, "I'm glad, too."

"Do you think you could drink some hot tea?"

"Dan'el." Sapphire walked up and patted Daniel's head.

"Hi, Sapphire. I'm glad to see you." His voice was raspy.

"Play?"

Gloria chuckled. "I don't think Daniel is able to play today, sweetheart. He'll play with you later."

"Come on, Sapphire. We'll go back outside and I'll play with you."

"Before you do that, Pearl. Go get your papa. He wanted to know as soon as Daniel woke up." Gloria looked back at him. "He's been so worried about you. Now, come on, Sapphire. Let's go get Daniel something to eat."

"Eat."

"Yes, honey. It's been a little while since breakfast so I guess you can have something to eat, too."

Ruby came into the room. She moved beside the couch. "I heard them talking to you. Welcome back to the living, Daniel."

"Thanks, Ruby." His voice was growing weaker.

She moved to the kitchen. "Boy, Mama, you sure gave me a tough job. Do you realize how hard it is to keep Opal in bed when she wants to get up? I told her I'd fix her a tray and serve her dinner in bed in a little while, but it wouldn't surprise me if when I get back she's not out of bed and dressing herself. I didn't know my sister was so stubborn."

"She does have a mind of her own." Gloria handed Ruby a cup of herbal tea and picked up another one. "See if you can get this into Daniel. I'll take one to Opal. She won't argue with me."

Pearl came back into the house. "Papa said he'd be right in."

"Thanks, honey. Now if you'll get Sapphire an apple, I'll see about Opal."

"I bet you're right about her not arguing with you, Mama." Ruby took the tea and moved to the couch again. "I've got something for you, Daniel."

He nodded and tried to get up.

"Don't try to sit. I'll feed you." She pulled up a chair and started feeding him with the spoon.

Pearl and Sapphire followed her and sat on the floor to watch him drink his tea as they ate their apples.

~ * ~

Opal jumped when her mother appeared at the bedroom door and said, "Get back in that bed, Opal."

"Mama, I'm fine. I slept well last night and I want to get up."

"Doctor Wheeling said for you to stay in bed for a couple of days and that's exactly what you're going to do."

"I think he was being too over protective. I swear to you, I only have a little pain now and I want to get up."

"I think he was taken with you and he wanted to make sure you were going to be well by the dance the community is planning in a few weeks."

"What dance?"

"Before he left he told you papa and me about it. He said he hoped we'd come. He hinted that he'd like to escort you."

"I'm not going to any dance with the doctor."

"Why not, Opal? He's a nice looking man and you're getting to the age that men are going to start pursuing you. A doctor wouldn't be a bad match for a woman out here in this country."

"Don't try to push me in the direction of a man I'm not interested in, Mama."

"All right, if that's the way you feel." She handed the cup to her daughter. "Drink this tea and I'll bring you a tray a little later."

Opal took the mug and sipped the tea.

"Now," her mother asked, "Can I trust you to stay in this bed at least for the rest of this day?"

"Yes, ma'am."

"Good. Daniel is better, but he still needs more care than you do."

"Oh, I'm glad he's getting better. Tell me about him."

Gloria told her about Daniel waking up and ended with, "Now you're all caught up on the family news and I'm going to get back in there and finish cooking the mid-day meal for the hands. It's not that long until they'll be in here hungry."

"Mama," Opal said as she started out the door.

Gloria turned. "Yes, dear."

"How did you know Papa was the man for you?"

Startled, Gloria stared at her daughter. "What are you saying, Opal?"

"I just want to know how a woman knows she's met the right man."

"We're not talking about the doctor, are we?"

"No."

"Do you want to tell me who or do I already know?"

Opal dropped her head. "He kissed me, and I felt my whole world turn upside down."

Gloria moved back beside the bed and took her daughter's hand in hers. "Tell me what Jace did to you, Opal."

"He did nothing but kiss me, Mama. In fact afterward, he apologized and said he shouldn't have done it, then told me he'd wanted to kiss me for a long time."

"So he didn't force himself on you?"

She shook her head. "I wanted him to kiss me. He's the one who stopped, not me. I liked it and wanted it to continue."

"My dear child, I have a feeling you're already made your decision about who the man for you is. Now it's only a question of if he thinks you're the woman for him."

"I guess you're saying, time will tell."

"That's right, honey. When a man is about to fall for a woman, he fights it with all his might. He can't imagine himself tied to one woman for the rest of his life and he thinks it would be better for him to pull away from her."

"That's exactly how Jace seems to feel."

"Most men feel that way. It's only when he comes to realize he can't live without her that he'll give in to his feelings. That takes time."

"How much time?"

"It's different for different men. It took your father about three months."

Opal's eyes got big. "Papa didn't love you immediately?"

"Of course he did. He just didn't admit it. I was patient and waited for him to come to his senses."

"So, you're telling me to be patient?"

"That and maybe give him a little push like I did your father."

"How do I do that?"

"I wanted him to make up his mind a little faster so I devised a plan. There was another man who was interested in me at the time. I wasn't at all attracted to him and I never actually went out with him, but I let George think I was considering it. To this day, your papa hates the name Eldon Webber."

"Do you think that was fair, Mama?"

"I don't see why it wasn't. It certainly made your father realize he didn't want anybody else to have me. I knew all along there was nobody for me except him."

"What if Papa hadn't decided to keep you from going out with this man?"

"Then you four girls wouldn't be here today."

Opal laughed. "I'm glad you did it, Mama, but I don't know who I could pretend I like to make Jace want to keep me for himself."

"Now, Opal, I know you're not that dense. Sly told George that Jace cursed and fumed then mashed his finger twice with a hammer while the doctor was here yesterday." Gloria patted Opal's hand. "You think about that while I go finish my cooking dinner."

Neva felt her whole world falling apart as she stared at the paper she held in her hand. How could she have been so blind? No, she didn't completely trust her father. She never had, but this was almost unbelievable. She'd so hoped that when she went through his papers, she'd not find anything to incriminate him in the things the man had accused him of the night before. But she had. Not only did the other papers she'd read prove he was involved in several underhanded business deals, but this one could actually send him to prison or worse, he could hang for it.

The big question now was what to do about it?

She didn't have long to make a decision because she heard a noise in the kitchen and realized Vinnie had returned from her shopping. Shoving the paper in the bosom of her dress and grabbing a sheet of paper, she slipped out of the study. She met Vinnie coming down the hall.

"There you are." Vinnie's voice was a little sharp. "Your daddy told me to keep a check on you since you were feeling poorly."

"I'm much better."

"I can see that. What were you doing in your father's study?"

Neva couldn't help feeling defensive, yet she didn't want to give Vinnie any reason to be suspicious. "Not that it's any of your business, but I wanted a sheet of writing paper."

"What for?"

"As I said, it's none of your business, but to ease your mind I'll tell you. I want to write a letter to a classmate back in Denver."

"I see. I guess that's all right, but you know your father doesn't like anybody messing around in his study."

"I wasn't messing around. I got the paper I wanted and left." Neva waved it at her. "Any more questions?"

Vinnie bit her lip. "I'm not trying to interrogate you, Neva. Your father asked me to keep an eye on you because you were sick this morning. We both noticed how quiet you were. He was concerned and believe it or not, so was I."

"Why would you care about me?"

"I know you don't believe me, but I've tried hard to be your friend ever since I came to work for your father. For some reason, you'd never given me a chance."

Neva swallowed. Should she tell Vinnie the truth? She made the quick decision to do just that. "I knew you and Daddy were lovers in Denver and that's why he brought you here. You were only nice to me because you thought it'd please him."

Vinnie sighed. "You're so wrong, Neva. Yes, your father came to me in Denver, but it wasn't because we were lovers. I'm from a very poor family. When my brother was hurt in a farm accident, he had to be put in a special home. There was no way my folks could pay the doctor bills. You father paid for Grant's care and I swore I'd serve him as long as it took to pay him off. My brother would have died and that's why I'm loyal to him. It would have been nice if you and I could at least have been pleasant to each other."

Neva wasn't ready to accept this explanation. "I'm not sure I believe you, Vinnie. I know my father sometimes goes to your room at night."

With a sad look on her face, Vinnie stared at Neva for a minute, then turned and went toward the kitchen without saying anything else.

Neva was surprised. She expected the housekeeper to argue with her, but she couldn't worry about Vinnie's reaction. She had too much to do before her father came home. She hurried to her room. After she spent enough time there to make Vinnie think she'd written a letter, she put on her gloves and hat then headed downstairs. Now she had to think of something to tell Vinnie that would keep her from getting suspicious. It also had to be good enough to keep her father from coming to find her.

~ * ~

The back door opened. Glen, Ivan and Billy followed by Jace came into the kitchen. "Hello, Gloria."

She was shocked to see him in the middle of the afternoon, but she nodded. "Hello, everyone. Why are you gentlemen coming in this time of day?"

"We thought we'd take a little break." Jace smiled at her, hoping she'd catch on to the fact he didn't want to tell her in front of the guys.

She must have because she said, "Why don't you fellows go over and say hello to Daniel. He's awake."

Billy's eyes got big. "He ain't dead?"

"No, honey. He's very much alive."

"Come on. Let's go see," Glen said.

The three boys walked over to the couch and she turned to Jace with a question on her face.

He spoke in an almost whisper. "I thought I saw somebody spying on us from the trees leading to the creek. I wanted them to be safe and I didn't think you'd mind."

"Of course not." She glanced at them and spoke in a louder voice. "I made cookies for supper. How would you boys like a sample?"

"Yes, ma'am," they said in unison.

"Ruby," Gloria called down the hall. "Will you come help me a minute?"

"Yes, Mama," Ruby called back.

She smiled at Jace. "She's been trying to entertain her sister. Lord knows Opal's harder to keep in bed then Sapphire when she's not sleepy."

"What can I do?" Ruby looked at Jace, but didn't ask why he was in the house in the middle of the afternoon.

"Ruby, I want you to get milk for the boys. Daniel, too, if he wants it and serve them all cookies."

"What about Sapphire and Pearl?"

"I'll get them in." Jace moved to the front door and called them.

"Jace!" Sapphire came running as fast as her little legs would carry her and Jace swooped her up in his arms.

Pearl followed. "What do you want, Ruby? Mama said for me to play with Sapphire so Daniel could rest."

"The boys are here to see him and Mama is giving them cookies."

"Cookie." Sapphire touched Jace's nose and wiggled.

He sat her down and she plopped on the floor. She looked at the boys and said, "Set."

"I think Sapphire is telling you fellows that, to get the cookies and milk, you have to sit in the floor," Jace explained. "Why don't you sit around Daniel's bed, then you can talk to him?"

They immediately dropped to the floor beside Sapphire.

Gloria handed Ruby a plate of cookies. "Jace, why don't you go make sure Opal stays in bed while Ruby is busy helping me?"

His eyebrow shot up. Was Gloria actually going to let him go into the bedroom and see Opal? He didn't take time to question it. He nodded and said, "Yes, ma'am," as he headed down the short hall.

As he stepped through the bedroom door, he didn't think Opal had ever looked prettier. Her long hair was pulled back and tied with a yellow ribbon and her white gown had lace around the neck. He wanted to run up to the bed and wrap his arms around her, but he managed to curb his urge.

"Hi, Opal."

She dropped the book she was thumbing through and looked at him. "Jace, I'm surprised to see you. Is everything all right?"

"Everything's fine. I brought the boys in and your mama is giving them cookies. I thought I might as well check on you while I was here."

"I'm fine. Just itching to get out of this bed, but I promised Mama I'd stay here today. I'll be up tomorrow."

"You look good, but don't rush it. You lost right much blood. That'll make you weak."

"I'm not rushing it, but I can't lie around in bed for a week. It's important that I go to town to buy some pretty dress material."

He frowned. Women sure had strange reasons for not listening to people. What in the world did cloth have to do with her getting well? His curiosity got the better of him and he asked, "Why in the world is buying dress material so important?"

"John told me about a dance coming up soon. I wanted to make something new to wear, but as much as I have to work, I can't spare much time sewing every day. I figure if I get the cloth now, I'll have time to make the dress even if I only have a short time to work on it each day."

Who the hell was this John who was telling her about a dance? He felt his temper rising, but he managed to control it. "Who's John?"

"For heaven's sake, Jace, you know him. John is the doctor who came to see Daniel and me."

Jace's frown grew deeper. "Why's he telling you about a dance?"

She laughed. "We were just talking and he mentioned it."

It was all Jace could do to keep from exploding. He knew it was ridiculous. He had no claim on Opal. Sure he'd kissed her, but that had been a mistake. It hadn't meant anything to either of them. Well, at least it probably didn't mean much to her. He'd had a hard time keeping his mind off her soft lips and sweet body ever since he'd lost his head and done it. Now he couldn't stand the thought of another man holding her and kissing her in that way. Especially that swarthy doctor. He couldn't help sounding sharp when he asked, "Did he invite you to attend with him?"

She smiled and shrugged. "No, but he's coming to see me again tomorrow. Maybe he'll ask me then."

He couldn't hold it back any longer. "I'll be damned if I'll let you go with him!"

She turned her head and looked confused. "I don't understand, Jace. I don't think you have any right to say who I do or do not go to a dance with. I figure you'll be escorting Miss Greenwood."

"I will…"

Ruby ran into the room. "Jace, Mama said to get you. Somebody's coming up to the house in a buggy and they're coming fast."

## Twenty-four

Opal had promised her mama she'd stay in bed for the day, but she couldn't help jumping up as Jace ran out of the room behind Ruby. She went to the window and watched as a horse, with dust swirling around it, came to a stop in front of the house. She couldn't believe her eyes when she saw an upset Neva Greenwood driving the fancy rig.

"What in the world?" She muttered and watched as Jace leaped off the porch and hurried to the side of the coach.

He said something to Neva, but Opal couldn't understand the words. Neva replied and the two of them fell into a conversation.

Opal frowned when the pretty woman reached into the front of her dress and pulled out a paper. She handed it to Jace and he looked at it. His face went from interest to shock to anger in a matter of seconds. Opal couldn't help wondering what the paper could possibly say to make his countenance change so quickly and radically. She also wondered why Neva had come to see Jace. From the exchanges between them, it was clear that this was exactly what she had done. Maybe the girl had been right to threaten Opal to stay away from him. It was probably true that Neva wanted Jace. It didn't matter how much Opal loved him. He might like her, too, but there was no way he'd choose her over the beautiful Neva. Even her mother's trick wasn't going to work on him. Sure he seemed a little upset because she'd mentioned the doctor, but he'd dropped the issue and practically run out of the room as soon as Ruby announced the buggy's arrival.

Opal sighed and tears filled her eyes. Maybe this had been prearranged. He could have been expecting Neva. She turned from the window because she didn't want to watch the two of them together any longer. It hurt too much. *I might as well go back to bed and forget about him and about all the dreams I've had since lying in this bed thinking about the kiss we shared. I might as well give up. There's no way I can compete with Neva, no matter what I do. Mama might have won Papa by making him jealous over another man, but that trick's not going to work with Jace. Not in this situation anyway.*

~ * ~

Marty couldn't believe his eyes as he stared at Jace helping Neva out of the buggy. Why in the world was she here? She wasn't the type to be paying a call on people who lived on a rundown ranch. Her father would have a fit if his precious daughter lowered herself to visit people he thought of as peasants.

"Hey, Marty. Take hold of this damn board. I can't hold it up for you all day."

Marty shook his head and grabbed the end of the board. "Sorry, Sly. I was just surprised to see Jace with that woman."

"Do you know her?"

"Yeah. It's Neva Greenwood."

"Ain't her old man that fat rich fellow in Wildweed?"

"Yeah. He's the one."

"Thought so. He's the one who told me about the job here."

"He hates me. He don't want me anywhere near his daughter."

"Well, I be damned."

"What do you mean by that?"

Sly chuckled. "I just mean if'en you and Jace don't get your mind off women and watch what you're doing, somebody's gonna git hurt. Then I'd have to finish this bunkhouse on my own and I sure as hell don't wanna do that."

"You're not gonna have to do that."

"Then you be careful and don't hit your thumb with the hammer."

"I don't plan to."

Sly laughed, but said nothing.

Though he tried to concentrate on what he was doing, Marty's mind kept thinking of the way she smiled when Jace put his hands around her waist and helped her to the ground. Hell, he could've just took her hand. Why'd he have to touch her body? Nobody but him should ever touch Neva, but her father had made it clear she wasn't going to have anything to do with a shopkeeper. He figured the old man would feel the same way about a ranch hand.

Marty didn't care. He knew Neva loved him as much as he did her and he was going to have her as his own someday. The one night of passion they'd shared wasn't enough for him. He wanted that woman with him for the rest of his life. He just had to figure out how he could get her away from her domineering father. And keep men like Jace Renwick away from her until he could make his move.

"Owh!"

Sly shook his head. "I told you that you was gonna mash your finger."

"Shut-up and nail the damn board, Sly."

~ * ~

Opal heard Jace introduce Neva to her mother and the rest of her family. Her mother insisted on serving the visitor a glass of lemonade. While the people in the other room were chatting, she looked up and Jace was coming in her door.

"Why are you coming in here? Your girlfriend is in the other room." She kept her voice low so those in the parlor wouldn't hear her.

He grinned and walked up to the bed. "Don't tell me you're jealous of Neva Greenwood."

She flipped back her hair. "Of course not. I have no claims on you or anyone else."

He eyed her. "Not even the doctor?"

Lifting her chin, she said, "Not yet anyway."

"You better not ever have any designs on him."

"I don't see it's any of your business, Jace Renwick."

"Oh, yes it is." He leaned over her and his dark eyes gazed into hers. "Get this through your head, Opal Barnett, and don't forget it. No matter what I have to do in the next few days, you're going to belong to me and nobody else."

She swallowed, but couldn't speak.

He went on, "Did the kisses we shared mean nothing to you?"

She could barely breathe. "Of course they meant something. I just thought you weren't interested in me."

His head moved closer to her and she could feel his warm breath on her face. "I've been interested in you since you offered me water the day I rode up to your ranch."

"Oh, Jace." She reached up and touched his face. His cheeks were covered with afternoon stubble, but she thought she'd never touched anything that felt so good. It made little shivers fill her body in places she didn't know could have feeling and certainly not shivers. There was nothing in the world she wanted more than to believe him. Could she?

He kissed her then. A wonderful soft kiss that made her toes tingle. A kiss that she wanted to go on forever. If he was telling her the truth, she'd be the happiest woman on earth. If he wasn't, at least she was happy for the moment.

He pulled away. "Now do you believe Neva means nothing to me?"

"I want to."

"Then do it. She's here because she found some information that I need to prove her father was a party to my dad's death."

"Can you prove it now?"

"I have to have more and I've got to figure out a way to get it."

"Jace, is this really what you want to do?"

"Yes, Opal, it is."

"Then I guess you have to do what you think is best."

He leaned down and kissed her again. "I'll be right back."

"Where are you going?"

"I'm going to bring Neva in here. She has a story to tell you."

Before she could tell him she didn't want to hear anything Neva Greenwood had to say, he went out the door.

Almost instantly he returned. "Neva wants to talk to you, Opal."

"Hi," Neva said in a shaky voice.

Opal nodded.

"I'll leave you ladies alone, but I'll be back shortly."

"You don't have to go, Jace."

"I think it's best." He nodded to her, paused a minute then leaned over the bed and gave Opal a quick kiss.

She was so flabbergasted she wasn't able to say anything to him as he slipped out of the room. Blushing, she glanced at Neva and saw the woman smiling at her. Since she didn't know what to say, she waited for her visitor to break the silence.

"First of all, Opal, I want to apologize to you."

Opal lifted an eyebrow. "Oh?"

"Yes. I know you think I'm a bitch and I have to admit that I acted like one."

Stunned, Opal said. "You came across as stuck-up, but I wouldn't call you that."

Neva chuckled. "Then you're the only woman in Wildweed who wouldn't."

Opal smiled and Neva went on, "I've been awful since I moved here from Denver. I didn't want to come, but Daddy insisted I move here. He thinks that way he can control my life and I was letting him do it until now."

"Until now?"

"I've learned some things about my father and it seems he's not the man I thought he was."

"I'm sorry."

"Thank you." Neva sighed. "But I didn't come here to complain about my father. I want you to know that it was never my idea to try to attract Jace's attention."

"Oh?"

"My father thinks he's a rich rancher from Texas and he wanted me to make Jace think he wanted to marry me because of the money. I was never interested in the man."

"I can't believe any woman wouldn't be interested in Jace."

"Maybe a lot of them would be, but my heart belongs to somebody else."

"Really?"

"Yes, but Daddy has made it clear I'm never to see him again. Now I don't even know where he is. I suppose Daddy ran him out of town."

Opal knew by the woman's eyes that she wasn't lying. Her heart went out to her. "Don't give up, Neva. You can probably find him on your own."

She shook her head. "I don't see how. Besides the fact that I don't have any money of my own to run off looking for him, I have no idea where to begin."

"Maybe there's some way I can help you."

"It's hopeless, and shortly even Daddy will see that."

"What do you mean?"

The edges of Neva's almost perfect mouth turned up. "I'm not ready to say, but I appreciate the offer to help me. Now, please let me finish my apology."

"You have nothing else to apologize for."

"Oh, yes I do. Because my father thought you were interfering in my quest to rope Jace into marriage, a man that works for him shot you."

Opal's eyes got big. "You must be kidding."

"I wish I were, Opal."

"Did you know?"

"Not until last night. I woke up and heard the man and my father yelling at each other in his study. I know I shouldn't eavesdrop, but I slipped down there and heard the man tell Daddy that he shot you."

Opal frowned. "I never dreamed you wanted Jace bad enough to let someone kill me, Neva."

"I didn't know anything the shooting. I told you, I didn't want Jace. Daddy thinks he's rich and I guess he thought he could get his hands on Jace's money."

"Jace hasn't said anything about being rich."

"I don't know about that, but I know my stupid mistake was going along with my father's plan. I don't care for Jace in that way, but I knew if I married him, it would be an answer to my problem."

"What problem could marrying Jace possibly solve for you?"

Neva hesitated, then looked around as if she were making sure they were alone. Finally she looked into Opal's eyes and whispered, "I'm with child."

## *Twenty-five*

Jace's mind was whirling as he walked toward the barn. He'd only scanned the paper Neva had given him and he wanted to get to his room where he could read it again. This time more closely. Yes, the paper had given him help in proving a case against her father, but it wasn't enough. He needed more and, if Alton Greenwood had kept this, he'd more than likely kept the one thing that would prove beyond any doubt that he was a murderer.

"Hey, Jace. Hold up."

"Yeah. What is it, Marty?" He stopped and watched as Marty approached him in determined steps.

"What the hell is Neva Greenwood doing here?"

Jace frowned. "What business is that of yours?"

He looked as if he was holding back his anger. "Neva's a friend of mine."

"So?"

Marty couldn't seem to control himself any longer. He glared at Jace. "You touched her."

"What are you talking about? I didn't touch the woman."

"Yes, you did. You can't deny it. I saw you."

"You're crazy."

"No, I'm not. Damn it, Jace, you put your hands on her waist and lifted her out of her buggy. I saw you do it."

"For god's sake. I helped Neva out of her buggy. Any gentleman would've done the same thing."

"You didn't have to touch her waist. You could've taken her hand. You just wanted to get your hands on her."

Jace couldn't help it. He chuckled. "You've got it all wrong, Marty. Let me assure you, I have no interest whatsoever in Miss Greenwood. She's not my type at all."

Marty frowned. "I heard in town that her daddy wants her to marry you."

"I can't help what Greenwood wants. I have no intention of marrying his daughter."

"Are you sure?"

"I'm positive. If I wanted to marry anyone—and notice I said if—I'd want it to be Opal Barnett."

"Opal? Really?"

"Yes, really. Now, why don't you get back to work and forget about Neva. That woman's bad news for any man."

Anger reared its head in his eyes again. "That's not so. She's a wonderful girl. People around her just don't appreciate her."

Jace frowned. "Sounds to me like you may know something about her I don't know."

"Damn it, Jace. I love her."

"You're kidding."

"No, I'm not. I knew it the first time we were together."

Jace frowned again. "Then why was her pa pushing her to marry me?"

"Because he thinks you're rich and he doesn't think I'm good enough for her. He said he'd never let his daughter go out with a lowly shopkeeper. That's one reason I came to work here. I want to prove to him that I'll make her a good husband."

"I hate to tell you this, Marty, but being a cowhand is a step down from shopkeeper. I don't think Greenwood will be any more impressed with this job, but if you love the girl, don't let her daddy's opinion deter you from going after her."

"You mean…"

Before he could finish his sentence, a shot came from the direction of the woods. With a look of surprise on his face, Marty glared at Jace for a second, then his eyes closed as he fell forward.

Jace caught him before he hit the ground.

~ * ~

Alton sat behind the desk in the downtown office he used to keep business deals from taking place in his home. He busied himself reading the week old Phoenix paper. Nothing much exciting seemed to happening there, which surprised him. Usually there was something about trouble at the mines or another story about the search for Geronimo who was a thorn in the side of both the Mexicans and the US Army.

The door opened and slammed back against the wall, causing him to drop the paper and open his mouth to yell at the intruder. He changed his mind when he saw a furious Inez Finch standing there. He kept his voice level. "What are you doing here?"

"I came to warn your sorry ass about a couple of things."

Alton lifted an eyebrow. Though he was used to foul language when he was around men, it surprised him to hear it coming from the lips of a woman. Even a woman as lowdown as Inez Finch.

"And what are you warning me about, dear lady?"

"If anybody shoots my brother because of that fool, Duff, I'll hold you responsible."

"How can you do that, woman? I can't control who hates your brother enough to kill him."

"You're the one who got him into all this mess."

Alton didn't ask her what mess. He knew. "Your brother is a grown man. He should be able to take care of himself."

"He can't. He come home drunk as a skunk about two o'clock this morning and passed out. I've had to take care of him all his life. I'm still doing it and you better remember that."

"What are you trying to say?"

"Just that I know when we're being used. Cletus is gullible. He'd let you get him into a mess he can't get out of."

Eying her, Cletus dropped back in his chair. "I'm not responsible for Cletus. For you or Duff either, for that matter."

"I know that. I also know when it comes right down to it, you'd let us all be strung up to save your hide. But I've made sure that's never going to happen. If we go down, you go with us."

Alton frowned at her. Surely she wasn't smart enough to keep some proof of what was going on at the ranch. But he couldn't be positive. He decided to change the subject so she'd relax enough to tell him what had happened. "Tell me, Inez. What has Duff done that puts Cletus in danger?"

She walked over to the chair in front of his desk and took a seat without being invited. "I told him not to go, but even with his gun shot, Duff wouldn't listen. I know it was nothing but a scratch on his arm, but it had to hurt him some. He said he didn't give a damn how much it hurt or if you wanted your prissy daughter to marry Renwick, he owed the man for shootin' him and he was going to get him today. He said he was gonna get that Barnett woman, too."

"What did the fool do to get even with them?"

"He went after them. I tried to talk him into waiting until dark, but it didn't do no good. He was too mad at Renwick and that woman to listen to anything I said."

"Why didn't Finch use force to stop him?"

"I told you he was passed out. I tried to stop him, but Duff was like a crazy man, no matter what. I come to tell you about it."

Alton hit his desk with his fist. "Damn fool."

"I called him that, too."

"When he gets back to the ranch, if he don't get himself killed, send him to see me. Cletus, too."

"I told you Cletus is passed out."

"He's got to wake up sometime."

She stood. "Now I've warned you that I'm going to make you pay if Cletus dies, so I'll be going."

"Now, Inez, don't think like that. I'm sure Cletus will be all right." He hoped the man would. He actually wanted to kill Finch himself and had planned to when he came to get more money this morning. Now he knew why he hadn't shown up. It didn't really matter. He'd do it yet. Then as soon as he had things the way he wanted them in Wildweed, he would be free to take Neva away.

"Cletus better be all right." She leaned toward him. "The other thing you need to know is that I've got to have some help at the ranch. With Duff's arm hurt and Cletus refusing to do any of the work, it's all fell on me. I've been milking the cow, feeding the chickens and slopping the hogs. It's wearing me out. You got to get some more young'uns out there to do the work. The barn needs mucking and the hay's gettin' low. And Cletus won't clean it. I can barely get him to feed the livestock. Ain't nothing been done out on the range."

Alton nodded. "I see why you're frustrated, Inez. I'll see what I can do about getting you some help. I'll also have a talk with Cletus and Duff when they get here. I don't think it's fair that they put all the work on you."

She sighed. "I never expected you to be this understanding."

"Of course I am. I want that ranch to start paying its own way soon."

She nodded. "Then I better get back to the ranch. By the time I get there, that cow will probably be bellowing her head off."

"Hang in there, Inez. I'll get you some help soon."

"I'll be expecting it, GW." She went out the door and slammed it behind her.

Alton stared at the closed door. *I'll have to get rid of that woman when I do her brother. I'm sure her threat to ruin me has no merit, but there's no reason to take a chance. I knew he and Duff had to go, but I planned to spare her. Well, no longer. Nobody will be any wiser when she turns up dead. Accidents happen at ranches all the time.*

Pulling his watch from his brocade vest pocket, he saw it was pushing ten o'clock. *I need to run home and get that account book. I'll still have time to balance it before I go home for dinner.* He shook his head. *I sure hope Neva's feeling better. She was so out of sorts this morning I'm not looking forward to her ill temper. If she's still out of sorts, I'll tell Vinnie I won't be home for meals today. That'll give me time to go out to the ranch and straighten stupid Cletus out.*

~ * ~

Gloria ran to the back door and saw Jace ease Marty to the ground in a swift movement, then kneel beside him. Jace then grabbed his gun and fired in the direction of the woods. She saw Sly come running from the construction site and George from the barn, both with their rifles in their hands.

"What's happening, Mama?" Ruby asked over her shoulder.

"I don't know."

"Can I go see?" Pearl came running up.

"Of course not." Gloria's voice was a little sharp. "Go keep Sapphire busy."

They heard George's voice yell, "Get him out of the line of fire, Jace. I'll cover you." He was hunkered down behind the well and he fired in the same direction Jace had.

Gloria figured if Marty had been shot it was probably dangerous to move him, but Jace didn't hesitate. He picked him up and headed to the house. It was closer than the barn.

"Mama, what's going on?" Opal came from the bedroom leaning on Neva.

Ruby turned to her sister. "Somebody's attacking us, but papa is fine. Looks like Marty's hit. Jace is bringing him in."

Gloria met him at the door. "What's going on, Jace?"

"Somebody's shooting at us. He's been hit. I can't leave him outside."

"Of course not. Bring him in." She stood aside said, "Grab a quilt, Ruby. We'll have to put him on the floor."

"Put him here," Daniel said as he rolled off the couch. "I'm better. Is there some way I can help?"

Jace placed Marty face down on the spot Daniel vacated. "Sit close to the front door and keep a sharp eye out. Are you a good shot?"

"Yes."

Ruby returned. "Where do you want me to put the quilt, Mama?"

"Beside Daniel."

"Should I get the gun, Jace?" Ruby asked.

"Yes, get it and give it to Daniel. He's going to watch the front door. We'll keep the back covered." He turned to Gloria. "Do what you can to help Marty. I'll be back as soon as I can."

"What can I do to help?" Opal asked.

Jace looked at her. "We've got it covered. You get back in bed."

"But…"

"Listen to him, Opal," her mother said. "I've got to take care of Marty."

"Be careful, Jace," Opal said.

He gave her a quick smile. "I will." Then he was out the door on the run.

"Where are the boys?" Daniel asked.

Ruby handed Daniel the rifle. "Papa took them to the barn. I'm sure they're safe there."

"Good." He turned his attention to the front yard.

Gloria turned to the sofa and dropped to the chair they kept there. She reached down and turned Marty's face from the wall to face her. That way she'd know if he woke up.

"Oh, no," Neva cried and ran to the couch. "It's my Marty. He can't die. He can't." She dropped to the floor on her knees.

Gloria put her hands on Neva's shoulders. "He's not dead, honey, but I've got to take care of him. If you want to help, go get some water and some towels so I can clean his wound. Ruby will show you where

~ * ~

Greenwood came out of his study carrying the account book he'd forgotten that morning. "Vinnie," he yelled.

She came into the hall. "Yes?"

"Where's Neva?"

"She went into town to mail a letter."

His face filled with fury as he glared at Vinnie. "What the hell did you mean by letting my daughter go running off like that?"

For once, Vinnie decided she was going to stand up for herself. She wasn't going to let him get away with yelling, or worse still, hitting her like he often did. She was going to fight back. "I didn't let her because she didn't ask me. Like I said, she came into the kitchen and said she was going to mail a letter."

"Why didn't you take it to the mail for her?"

"I offered to, but she said she was feeling better and wanted to get outside for a little while."

"So you just let my sick baby go off by herself?"

"Your *baby* is fine."

"How the hell do you know? She could pass out and…"

"Women seldom pass out from her ailment."

"Are you a doctor now?"

"No and neither are you. What Neva has is natural for a woman."

"Damn you, woman. Don't you know Neva's special? She doesn't react like other, tougher girls."

He headed toward her and she saw his hands ball into fists. She backed up and took a deep breath. "Do I have to spell it out for you? Neva was starting her monthly. Sometimes it leaves a woman out of sorts for a day or so. She'll have cramps and feel irritable. This happened to her this morning."

Alton stopped and looked at her with a frown. "How do you know all this?"

She saw his fists relax and so she relaxed a little, too. He wasn't going to hit her this time. She lowered her voice and said calmly, "I'm a woman."

He turned to walk out of the room, but hesitated and looked at her again. "Did she say anything about going someplace besides mailing a letter?"

"No, but you know Neva likes to spend time in town. She probably ran into a friend or went to the dressmaker or the general store. I'm sure she'll be home soon."

He nodded and left the hall saying, "You're probably right this time. I'll be back for dinner."

Vinnie breathed a sigh of relief and went back to the kitchen. She had no idea if Neva's problem was her monthly, but it was a good explanation. The beast would never know the difference.

And regardless of what Neva or the citizens of Wildweed thought, Alton Greenwood was a beast of the first order. She should know. She'd practically been his slave for five years. Yes, he had paid her brother's medical expenses and paid for the special doctor and nurse to care for him, but she'd paid, too. Dearly. Not only did he expect her to be a good housekeeper, she had to be willing and able to satisfy his manly needs anytime he wanted to come into her room, and to her way of thinking, his needs were often bizarre.

Unbeknownst to Alton or his spoiled daughter, there were many times she plotted how she could rid herself of this man. She knew she'd never do it, but there was no fault in thinking how good life would be if Alton Greenwood were to die in his sleep. Then she'd remember Grant and his problem. She couldn't do anything to change her fate because her brother would be the one to suffer. She'd promised her father on his deathbed that she'd always see that Grant was taken care of.

All of this was a burden that she didn't think was fair for a twenty-one year old to bear. But as she'd been told, life was not fair. With another sigh, she stirred the beans and prayed that someday things would change for her.

## *Twenty-six*

The first thing Jace noticed when he walked into the house behind George was that Ruby and Gloria were cooking, Daniel was back on the couch, Opal was dressed and in one of the rocking chairs near the window and though the rest of the family was scattered about the room, Marty and Neva were nowhere in sight.

Before he could comment, Gloria turned from the stove and asked, "Did you catch them?"

"No, but we're pretty sure who it was." George walked over and gave his wife a kiss on her cheek.

"It was Finch, wasn't it?" Opal asked.

Jace nodded. "We think so, and what are you doing out of bed?"

Gloria answered for her. "Marty is in pretty bad shape and getting up exhausted Daniel. I didn't know what else to do, so I put Marty in the girls' bed and Daniel back on the couch. Neva insisted on taking care of Marty."

"Why would she do that? I didn't think Neva cared about anybody except herself." Jace looked confused.

"I think there might be more to Neva than people think. She told me she was in love with Marty," Opal explained.

Jace shook his head, but said nothing else.

George had a frown on his face. "If Marty has their room, where are the girls going to sleep?"

"We're going to make pallets and sleep on the floor here." Pearl's grin showed her excitement about the plan. "I think it's going to be fun."

Jace looked at Opal and knew there was no way he could sleep in his comfortable bed tonight knowing she was sleeping on a quilt in the floor. He spoke before he could change his mind. "I don't think they should have to sleep on the floor, especially since Opal has the gunshot wound. She and Ruby can sleep in my bed."

Gloria looked at him. "Where would you sleep?"

"In the loft with Sly and the boys."

Gloria hesitated. "I don't know."

"Jace is right, honey." George slipped his arm around his wife's waist. "Opal doesn't need to be on the floor with her injury and they'll be perfectly safe in the barn. Jace has fixed it so he can lock up his room by dropping a board across the door at night. Nobody can get to them unless they unlatch the door by lifting it from inside."

"Then I guess it's settled." She pulled away. "Call Sly and the boys. It's time to eat."

Jace still didn't think Gloria was happy about her daughters sleeping in the barn, but she wouldn't argue with her husband. As for him, Jace liked the idea of Opal being in his bed. He just wished he were the one to be in it with her.

~ * ~

Vinnie sat the plate of fried chicken, potatoes, green beans and corn on the table in front of Alton. "I hope this suits you."

"You know I like it fine, but Neva would rather have it baked or something like that."

"I baked Neva a piece. If she's hungry when she gets back, it'll be here for her."

Alton frowned. "Be back? Where is she?"

"As I told you, she went to post a letter and said she might do some shopping. She even said she might have dinner at the Apple Blossom Café."

"I thought she hated that place."

"She said somebody told her they had something like Beef Wellington, whatever that is."

He nodded. "Sounds like something Neva would like."

"I'll go get your coffee."

"Why don't you get a plate for yourself and eat with me? I don't like eating alone."

"If you wish."

In a matter of minutes, she returned with the coffee and a plate. She sat at his left because she knew the seat to his right belonged to Neva.

Alton broke the silence that followed after he ate most of everything on his plate. "This is very good, Vinnie."

"Thank you." She smiled at him, but didn't tell him she'd prepared his favorite meal because she wanted him to be in a good mood when she asked her question. Now seemed to be as good a time as she was going to have. "May I ask you something?"

"Of course, my dear." He jammed the last spoonful of beans in his mouth and gnawed the meat off the chicken bone.

She took a deep breath for courage. Looking at him as pleasantly as he could, she said, "It's been over a year since I've been to Denver to visit Grant. Do you think we could go before the weather gets bad?"

His eyes grew dark and glared at her. "Why would you want to do that? The last time you saw the boy, he didn't even know you."

She couldn't let him see her cry and she fought back the tears. "But I knew him."

He put down his fork. "Now you've gone and ruined this wonderful dinner. I don't want to talk about an insane boy while I'm having my meal."

She dropped her eyes and in spite of everything she did, a tear slid down her cheek.

"Are you crying?"

She shook her head, but she could tell he knew she was lying. For some reason, it always made him demand she lay with him when she cried. It seemed to give him a feeling of power. She had no doubt he'd demand she do so today. She wasn't wrong.

"I think I'll go lie down and let my dinner settle. I plan to meet some businesspeople tonight and I might be late. If I'm not back, you and Neva go on and eat your supper and go to bed." He stood and held out his hand to her. "In the meantime, it'll do you good to rest a little yourself. When you feel better, you can come back down and clean up."

Vinnie felt as if he was up to something, but she had no idea what, or what she could do about it if he was. Though she dreaded going to his room with him, she took his hand without complaint. She knew if she said a word, he'd be rougher with her than he usually was and from the dark look in his eyes, she didn't think he was going to be satisfied with simply knocking her around a little. She wanted to keep it as easy on herself as she could so she decided to let him have his way.

~ * ~

It was late that night and Jace still hadn't gone to sleep. The boys wiggled and turned on their bedrolls and Sly snored like a dying mule. But that wasn't the main reason he couldn't sleep. He had that auburn-headed woman who was snuggled in his bed on his mind and no matter how he tried to tell himself she didn't really matter to him, he knew she did. The thoughts of her with that sneaky doctor wouldn't go away. What did she see in him anyway? Sure, he was successful and could give her a good living. And though he hated to admit it, Wheeling was a decent looking man. Maybe even one women would think of as handsome. He wondered if Opal thought the man was good looking.

That thought made him frown as he turned over. He had to get this off his mind. The bunkhouse was nearing completion and he had a lot of work to do tomorrow. Since the shooting, he needed to go into town to report it to the sheriff. Though he'd wanted to go to the Finch ranch and face the men, George had talked him out of it.

"I don't need you to do something that will land you in jail, Jace. We need you here. I'd like to go shoot both of those men, but let's do this legally and let the law handle it."

"I know you're right, George, but those bastards need to pay for what they've done. Marty is a nice young man. He didn't deserve being treated that way."

"That's true and they will pay. There's no doubt that Marty's shooting wasn't an accident. I expect they'd like to kill every man here, then take the boys and Daniel back as slaves." George had shaken his head and added, "And it's no telling what they'd do to the women. Still, I don't think we should do anything about it without going for the sheriff."

Jace had finally agreed, but he had no intention of letting it go past tomorrow without getting those men arrested. Nobody was going to do anything else to hurt this family. Especially Opal. Hell, he might as well admit it. He loved the woman no matter how much he tried to fight it.

He started to turn again on his bed when he heard a strange noise. Not a regular night noise, or a prey animal after food. This was a man's voice. Though it was only a whisper it had floated in the window at the end of the loft.

Jace didn't hesitate. He jumped up, grabbed his gun and hurried to the window. The sight he saw made his blood run cold.

Three men with torches were setting fire to straw or hay they'd placed around the edge of the cabin.

"Fire!" Jace screamed and headed down the ladder to the barn floor. He ran to the door and shot in the direction of a figure at the end of the house. The man fell and his torch rolled out of his hand.

The other two figures ran to the front where their horses were hitched. Jace followed and clicked off a couple of rounds, but they managed to mount and ride away. Jace didn't follow. It was more important at the moment to make sure the people in the house were safe and then put out the fire.

George came out of the house and Gloria followed.

"Get everybody out, George!" Jace yelled as he headed toward the door.

"I'll get…." Gloria started.

"You go help Ruby and Opal start bringing buckets of water. George and I will get everybody." He went in the back door.

"Can you walk?" Jace asked when he saw Daniel was sitting up on the sofa.

Daniel nodded.

"Get out of here. The house is on fire."

George went down the hall and into his room. He grabbed the baby and she began to cry.

Neva came out of the room where Marty lay, still unconscious. "Somebody help him!" she cried.

"We'll get him. George, give Neva the baby and help me get Marty. Maybe we can lift the mattress and that way he'll not be hurt by us picking him up."

In a matter of minutes, the house was empty. The blazes were lapping at each end of the cabin and a window broke from the heat in the room where Marty had been. Jace saw the buckets were moving quickly and the fire had been doused near the steps, but little flames kept popping up. He ran into the barn, grabbed a horse blanket and ran back to beat the flames as the others brought water. It took almost an hour, but by working together, they managed to put the flames out.

Jace turned to Gloria. "Will you go in and see if it smells too smoky in there for people to go back in? If you can, open all the windows and doors so it can air out."

"I'll help her, Jace." George took Gloria's hand.

Nobody had paid any attention to the man lying near the edge of the porch until they started inside.

Glen moved to the body and stared down at it. "Is he really dead?"

Jace moved beside the boy and put his hands on the boy's shoulder. "Yes, Glen. He's dead."

Glen nodded. "I wish it had been Mr. Finch, but I'm glad Duff's dead. He was mean, too."

"What do you mean?"

"Mr. Finch was meaner, but Duff was bad. He'd beat us sometimes and he'd steal the food whenever Miss Inez would actually feed us something decent."

"I'm glad you got away from those people, Glen. I'm glad all of you did."

"Me, too." He grinned. "I hope we never have to go back there."

"You don't have to worry about that. You'll never have to be around Cletus Finch again. Attacking the Barnetts tonight sealed his fate."

"How?"

"There's no way he can get away with this. Everybody knows Duff works for him and it'll be easy to prove he was here when we were attacked. I just wonder who the third man was."

"Maybe it was GW," Glen mumbled.

Jace raised a surprised eyebrow. He had no doubt that Glen had unwittingly answered that question correctly.

~ * ~

The next morning, Jace drove the wagon with Neva sitting at his side. George sat on her other side.

"Are you sure this will work, Jace?" George asked.

"I hope so."

Neva sighed. "Opal and I discussed it. We're sure Jace can get to the bottom of everything if he can get Daddy to trust him."

"What if your father doesn't trust him?"

"Don't worry about that, Mr. Barnett. I'll handle Daddy."

"Do you think you can?" George didn't look convinced.

"It's worth a shot," Jace said. "Opal is a pretty smart girl and she worked this whole plan out with Neva."

"Opal is smart, I'll give you that, but why would she want to work out a plan to trap Greenwood and help you with whatever you're up to?"

"Oh, Mr. Barnett, I know you're not blind."

He frowned. "What do you mean?"

"Why, anybody with eyes can see that Opal and Jace are crazy about each other. I'm surprised you didn't know that."

George continued to frown.

Jace swallowed and wasn't sure what to say. He wasn't ready to confess the way he felt about to Opal to anybody, much less her father. He felt that if he were going to discuss it with anyone, he'd talked with Opal about it first. Finally he said, "Of course, I like Opal. We're friends. I like all the Barnetts and hope they're friends with me, too."

"Now, Jace, don't try to say you're not interested in Opal the way a man is about a woman he wants."

"Drop it, Neva."

"But…"

George butted in. "Let it go, Neva. I'm sure whenever Jace wants to say something about his personal feelings, he'll do it in his own time."

They were approaching the edge of Wildweed. Jace pulled the wagon to a stop. "I think you should get out and untie your horse, George. I'll meet you at the saloon after you see the sheriff and I deliver Neva home."

"He won't tarry." Neva adjusted her bonnet. "As soon as we're able to find the information he wants, I'll be going back with you. Though Opal and Ruby promised to look after Marty, I'm not going to be away from him for very long."

Neither man argued with her.

George jumped from the wagon and mounted his horse. He saluted them as he rode off toward town.

Jace looked at Neva. "Are you ready to…"

"Just a minute, Jace. I'm sorry if I talked too much in front of Mr. Barnett. It's just that I know how much you and Opal love each other. I hate to see you trying to hold your feelings back. I sure learned my lesson by not letting everybody know I loved Marty."

"It doesn't matter, Neva. I'm sure Opal doesn't feel about me the way you think."

"Oh, yes she does."

"Did she tell you so?"

"No, she didn't have to. I could tell by the way she looks at you."

He shook his head and at the same time snapped the reins over the horses. "Are you ready to go see if we can convince your father that I'm the most honorable man in Arizona?"

## Twenty-seven

Alton Greenwood was furious. "What the hell do you mean Neva isn't here?"

"If you'd come home for supper last night, you'd see she hadn't come home."

"Why didn't you go find her?"

"I walked into town and went to all the places I thought she might be. Nobody had seen her. I didn't know anywhere else to look so I came back here and waited."

He slammed his fist down on the table, making the water splash out of his glass. "Why didn't you tell me when I came in?"

"I didn't hear you come in. I must have fallen asleep."

He shoved the dining room chair back and approached her. "You whore. How could you fall asleep with my daughter missing?"

"I didn't mean to." She backed away.

Alton backhanded her across the mouth and she stumbled, hitting her shoulder on the corner of the buffet. "If anything happens to my daughter, I'll kill you for not taking care of her."

"That hurt, Alton."

He reached to slap her again, but she backed away and he missed. "You'll call me Mr. Greenwood. We're not on a friendly basis. You're only here to do the work and to keep my bed warm when I need you."

"You're an evil man, Alton Greenwood. I hate you."

He laughed. "Do you think I care?"

"If you weren't paying for that special doctor for my brother, I'd walk out on you this minute."

"You'll never go anywhere as long as I keep paying that bill either. You know you brother will die without those treatments and if you leave, you'd be the one killing him, not me."

Before she could answer, Neva's voice came through the front door. "Daddy! Daddy! Are you here?"

Alton whirled around and hurried to the parlor as Neva entered. "Where the hell have you been, girl?"

"Oh, Daddy!" She ran to him and threw her arms around his neck.

Alton's face took on a dark look as Jace came into the room. "What did you do to my Neva?"

"Jace didn't do anything, Daddy. If it wasn't for him, I'd be dead."

Alton frowned. "I don't understand. What's going on?"

"Do you think Vinnie could get me a glass of water or something? I feel kind of parched."

"Vinnie!"

"I'm right here, Mr. Greenwood. I'll get Neva something to drink."

"Let's sit down, Daddy, and I'll explain everything."

"Sorry I accused you of hurting Neva, Jace," Alton muttered as he dropped to a chair.

"I would've probably thought the same thing if it'd been my daughter." Jace took a seat on the settee beside Neva.

Vinnie came in with a tray. She had water, coffee for the men and there was a cup of tea. "I thought you might like a cup of tea, Miss Neva."

"Thank you, Vinnie. That would be nice." She took the tea.

"You're welcome." Vinnie served the coffee to the men and started to leave.

"You might as well stay in here, Vinnie." Alton's voice came out as a command. "I know you're going to be lurking behind the door listening anyway."

Vinnie bit her lip and took one of the straight chairs near the door.

"Now, Neva, let's hear your story."

"Well, yesterday after I wrote my roommate from school, I went to mail the letter. I felt a lot better and it was such a pretty day I decided to ride out into the country. I went farther than I intended. I was turning around to come back when the horse was spooked by a rattlesnake. It took off running out across the prairie. I had dropped the reins and had no way to control it. I was terrified and don't know how far or how long the horse ran, but it must have hit a hole or something, because I was thrown from the buggy and hit my head. I must have been unconscious because when I woke up I was at the Barnett ranch and Mrs. Barnett was taking care of me."

"Who found you?"

Jace took up the story. "Sly, one of our hands, found her. He didn't know what else to do, so he took her to the ranch. She was lucky she was found as quickly as she was."

"I'm glad somebody found you," Alton said, "but how did Jace save your life?"

"I'm getting to that. It was late by then and Mrs. Barnett wouldn't let me leave…"

"She kept you against your will?"

She frowned at him. "Let me finish, Daddy."

"I'm sorry, sweetheart."

"As I was saying, Mrs. Barnett said she was afraid that if I left, it might injure me more. She said they'd watch me until morning then send for the doctor or bring me back to town."

"Well, at least the woman was thinking of your welfare."

"Daddy, if you'll quit interrupting me, I'll finish my story." He nodded and she went on. "The Barnett girls were so nice. They slept elsewhere and let me have their bed. I was sleeping well until it happened."

"What happened?"

"That awful Finch man and the man who works for him set fire to the cabin. Oh, Daddy, can you believe it? They were going to burn everybody alive. If Jace hadn't woke up and got us all out of the house, we'd all be dead." Neva began to cry.

Alton's face turned a pasty white. "I can't believe…"

"It's true, Daddy. Jace was a hero. He even shot one of the men."

"It was the man who works on Finch's ranch. That's how we knew who set the fire." Jace explained.

"Mr. Barnett has gone to tell the sheriff and Jace brought me home because he knew you'd be worried."

"I wanted to get Neva home as soon as possible, but I thought after you saw she's fine, you might want to talk to the sheriff yourself. You have more weight in this town than George Barnett does, and I figure the sheriff will certainly want to investigate if you talk to him."

"I'll do it, but I don't want to leave Neva just yet."

"I'll be fine, Daddy. Please go make the sheriff go after that awful man." She turned toward Jace. "You'll stay with me until Daddy gets back, won't you?"

Jace slid his arm across her shoulders. "Of course I will. And Alton, don't worry about her in case the sheriff wants you to ride out to the Finch ranch with him."

Alton nodded and stood. "He probably will want me to. In fact, I'll see that Finch pays for trying to hurt my precious Neva."

As soon as Alton left the room, Neva jumped up. "Vinnie, what happened to you? You have a big bruise on your face."

She placed her hand on her cheek. "I ran into the door."

Neva shook her head. "Daddy hit you, didn't he?"

Vinnie's eyes got big. "I…uh…"

"You don't have to answer. I know he did. Why do you let him get away with doing that to you?"

"You know he pays for the doctor to take care of my brother. He'd quit paying if I decided to leave. That's what we were arguing about when you came home."

"I see." Neva stood. "All right, Jace, he's gone. Come with me and I'll show you where the papers are."

"What's going on, Miss Neva?"

"I've discovered my father is not the man I thought he was, Vinnie. He's mean and he's cruel. Jace thinks he murdered his father. If he did, I want to know."

Vinnie stared at them with disbelief on her face. "He's going to be awfully angry if you start going through his things."

"So, let him. I have to know the truth." She nodded at Jace and he followed her to Alton's study.

"Where do we start?"

"The paper I gave you came from the bottom drawer of his desk."

Jace opened it. None of the papers related to anything he wanted. He put them back and opened the middle drawer. An opened letter caught his eye. He scanned it and frowned. "Miss Vinnie, didn't you say Greenwood paid a doctor to care for your brother?"

"Yes."

"What is your brother's name?"

"Grant Kingsley. Why?"

Jace handed the letter to Neva and she frowned after reading it. "Vinnie, Daddy has been lying to you."

"How?"

Neva gave her the letter. Vinnie read it and then gasped. "Oh, no! Could there be a mistake?"

"No, Vinnie. That letter is from the doctor. Your brother died over a year ago."

"But your father said…that scoundrel. I've been begging to go back to Denver to visit Grant. He kept saying he would take me, but he was lying. No wonder he wouldn't let me go." Vinnie burst into tears and ran from the room.

"I'm sorry she had to find out that way." Neva bowed her head toward the floor. "Daddy really is evil, isn't he? He not only has Vinnie keeping house and cooking, I know he slips into her room at night and I often hear her crying."

"I'm sorry about that, Neva, but try to remember why we're here. You want to be with the man you love and I need to find the proof I need. Can you think of anywhere else we should look?"

"Nowhere except the drawers in that cabinet."

They were looking through the last drawer when Vinnie came back into the room. Her eyes were puffy, but she'd quit crying. "Have you found what you need?"

"No, Vinnie. Do you know anywhere else Daddy might have hidden some papers?"

Vinnie hesitated only a minute before saying, "Come with me."

They followed her up the stairs to Alton's room. She opened the door and stepped inside. "I caught him here one day putting some papers in his dresser. It's the middle drawer on the right. It has a false bottom. He told me if I ever told anyone about it he'd kill me. He meant it."

Jace opened the drawer, removed the clothes, then the false bottom. There were more papers than he thought they had time to go through. He took them all and resealed the false bottom. Neva and Vinnie refolded the clothes and put them back in the drawer. It didn't look like it had been disturbed at all.

"We better get out of here before Daddy comes back."

"I agree."

Vinnie looked at them. "Can I come with you?"

"I don't think…"

Neva interrupted him. "Maybe she better come. If by chance Daddy finds we've discovered his hiding place, he might hurt her."

Jace nodded. "Then, let's go."

"I'm supposed to meet George at the saloon. Do you mind if I run in there and see what he found out at the sheriff's office?"

"Not at all."

They didn't have to go to the saloon. They met George headed in that direction.

"What happened?" Jace asked.

"The sheriff's getting a posse together to go to the Finch ranch."

"What did my father say about that, Mr. Barnett?"

He lifted an eyebrow. "I haven't seen your father, Neva."

"He said he was coming to the sheriff's office."

Jace gritted his teeth. "He's gone to the Finch place to warn him."

"Then we better get there," George said.

"I'll get these ladies to the cutoff, then they can take the wagon to your place."

"I'll tell the sheriff what's happening."

Jace nodded, shook the reins over the horses and headed out of town as fast as he dared push the horses. When George and the sheriff caught up to him, he pulled the wagon to a stop. He handed the reins to Neva and said, "Guard those papers with your life."

"I will."

"We'll meet you back at the ranch." He then jumped out of the wagon and mounted his horse. The three men then rode away.

~ * ~

Opal sat up in Jace's bed with several pillows behind her back. "Thanks for bringing me something to eat, Neva."

"I asked your mama to let me do it. Vinnie was sitting with Marty and I wanted to talk to you." Neva sat on the rocking chair that somebody had brought down from the house.

"What about?"

"Our plan worked. Daddy never dreamed Jace and I were pretending to be interested in each other."

"Good. I'm glad he swallowed it."

"I don't know about him, Opal. I thought my father loved me, but now I'm not so sure."

"What do you mean?"

She reached for the papers she'd put on the bedside table. "I'll tell you later. Let's go through these so I can get back to Marty."

"So you found the proof Jace needed?"

"I think so." She reached for the top paper. "We didn't have time to look at them, but I'm sure there are things here my father would rather nobody ever see. I thought you and I would look at them. It'll keep you busy until Jace comes back."

Opal started to say they shouldn't look at them until Jace arrived, but she was curious. Besides, if she found the proof, he wouldn't have to look for it. "Where should we start?"

Neva grinned and handed her the paper. "What's this one about?"

"This looks like something to do with a family named Conners."

"A man accused my father of being named GW Conners the other night. Let me see that."

Neva studied the paper. Opal watched as a tear trickled down her cheek. "I can't believe this."

"What is it?" Opal kept her voice soft.

"Alton Greenwood was my father, but he was killed when I was three years old. My mother married GW Conners, but after he got into some trouble in Tombstone, he changed his name to Alton Greenwood and my mother let him do it. She must've decided it would be easier to let him keep the name for some reason. I never dreamed he wasn't my real father. Mother never told me the truth and I wonder why. I was almost twelve when she died. She should've told me."

"So the man we know as Greenwood is not your father?"

Neva looked as if she was fighting back tears. "That bastard is going to have to answer to me about this. No wonder I haven't trusted him since I've been in Wildweed. I tried to be the daughter he seemed to want, but there was always something not right with him. I knew it the minute I came here to live. I wanted to go back to Denver, but he refused to let me. When I think back on some of the things he's done and said, I can't help but wonder what his plan was for bringing me here."

"Maybe he just wanted his daughter close to him."

"But, I'm not his daughter, Opal. And right now I'm thankful for that." She put the paper aside and reached for another one. "Let's go on."

The next two papers told them nothing, but when she picked up the third one, Neva gasped. "Oh, my goodness!"

"What is it?"

"Poor Vinnie. I always thought she was Daddy's housekeeper because she wanted to be, but this proves he blackmailed her into coming with him. My mother had just died when he signed a paper saying he'd support her brother Grant until his death as long as Vinnie did everything he asked her to do, including letting him into her bed whenever he desired." She looked at Opal with disgust in her eyes. "She was only fifteen years old at the time. That makes her only three years older than me."

"If you want to quit looking at these, we will. You don't have to put yourself through this, Neva."

She shook her head. "No, it's time I found out who I claimed as a father since I was a little girl." She put the paper down and took another one.

"Oh my, Opal look at this. It seems GW or whatever his name is, bought a ranch in the name of Edward Renwick." She handed the paper to Opal.

Opal frowned. "Do you suppose Edward is some of Jace's kin?"

"I don't know, but it sounds logical."

By the time they got to the end, they had all the proof Jace needed to put so-called Alton Greenwood's neck in a noose or at least put him in prison for the rest of his life. Neva stacked the papers on the table and stood. "I'm going to check on Marty. I'm anxious to see him and hold his hand, whether he knows I'm there or not."

"You really do love him, don't you, Neva?"

"I do. I can't wait for him to get well so we can get married."

"So you plan to marry him no matter what your father...I mean...Mr. Greenwood says?"

"That man's not my father and he has no control over me any longer. I honestly don't care what he says. I don't even care if I ever see him again." At the door she paused. "I'm sure Jace will come to see you as soon as he gets home and I'll see you later."

# *Twenty-eight*

Alton decided if he ran into Jace later he could come up with some good reason why he didn't go to the sheriff's office. He had to get to the ranch and get rid of Cletus and his sister before Jace and Barnett and possibly the sheriff headed there. There was no way crazy Finch wouldn't cave in and tell them who the third man was who tried to burn down the Barnett cabin.

When he thought about it, his blood ran cold. *Damn that stupid Cletus. Why did he have to try to get rid of the family that way? What if he'd burned up my beautiful Neva?*

There's no way he would let himself accept any of the responsibility of what had taken place. Sure, he wanted to get rid of the Barnetts. If burning their house would have done the trick, he'd do it again, but next time he'd make sure Neva wasn't there. Besides, Cletus should have run them off a long time ago.

After seeing how attentive Jace was to Neva when he brought her home, he was afraid she might actually want to marry him. He couldn't let that happen. No man was going to have Neva except him. Somehow Jace would have to meet an accidental death; he and Neva could go to Texas and claim Jace and Neva were married and she'd be able to claim a section of that big ranch.

He couldn't help being a little excited. As soon as it all worked out, it would be the right time to put Neva in the position he'd been grooming her for since she'd been that pretty little blond girl who used to climb on his lap and let him hold her close to him and tell her fairy tales. She'd never be in danger again. She'd be loved and protected by him for the rest of her life and he'd love her in the way he'd wanted to since she first began to develop as a woman.

His mind was still full of jumbled plans when he came in sight of the ranch. He decided he'd better be careful going in. He knew Duff and Cletus had been cousins or something and if they knew Duff was dead, they might just blame him, though he knew it wasn't his fault. The man should have been more careful. They might think they had to defend Duff. Somehow he'd have to shift the blame to Barnett, though he actually knew Jace was the one who shot the man.

Hitching his horse to the post near the front steps, he couldn't help noticing how rundown the farm was beginning to look. There was grass growing up in the path to the barn, chickens were running loose in the yard, there was trash thrown about and a cow was bellowing in the barn.

"Get out here, Cletus."

Inez came out on the porch. "He's asleep."

"Hell, he better wake up. I came to warn him the sheriff is on his way out here."

Her expression didn't change. "Why?"

"Damn, woman. Barnett knows who burnt his house last night. Did you think he wouldn't report it?"

"Why ain't Duff come back? Cletus said he probably run away?"

"I see Cletus didn't tell you the truth."

"What should he have told me?"

"Duff is dead. Barnett killed him."

Inez grabbed her mouth. "Oh, no."

Alton climbed up the steps and went into the cabin, leaving her standing on the porch looking stunned. Inside, he yelled, "Cletus, get your ass out of that bed. The law is on its way out here."

Heavy feet hit the floor. "Who the hell is yelling in here?"

"It's me, you fool." Alton stuck his head in the door. "The sheriff's on his way."

Cletus grabbed his pants. "What are we gonna do?"

"I'm going to get away from here and I figure you'd better do the same. If you don't, you know they'll string you up for trying to burn out a whole family."

"I'll be damn if they string me up by myself. If they get me, you'll go with me."

"Then let's get out of here."

"Where are we going, GW?"

"There's a line shack on the back of the property here. You can hide out there until it's safe to leave town. You better take Inez with you. They'll probably arrest her, too."

"Why the hell would they arrest me?" Inez came into the room.

"You've condoned what Cletus and Duff have done. Besides that, you kept those boys here and I'm sure they're going to check into that."

"Like Cletus said, if I go down for that, I'm taking you with me."

"We don't have time to keep arguing. If you don't want them to catch us here, we better get going."

In less than twenty minutes, the three of them headed across the back of the property. Inez was fussing, but she wasn't interested in getting caught at the house. She did insist on taking a small valise with her. Alton couldn't believe it, but she said she had to have her own nightgown to sleep in. He shook his head, but went out of the room when she packed it.

Cletus hitched the work horse to the farm wagon and she threw her bag in the back. She drove the wagon and the men took their horses. They cut across the pasture and headed toward the back of the ranch. Alton knew it would take an hour or more to get to the line shack, but he had no intention of going that far. They were almost a mile from the ranch cabin when he dropped his horse back behind Inez's wagon.

Cletus reined up and turned to look at him. "What's wrong?"

"I think my horse has picked up a rock. I need to get it out. Go on and I'll catch up with you."

Cletus nodded and moved forward behind the wagon.

Alton waited until he was several yards away. He then eased the rifle from the scabbard and aimed. The bullet hit Cletus in the back and he tumbled from the horse.

Inez jumped up and screamed, but didn't have a chance to say anything.

The second bullet went into her stomach and she fell over the seat with her head hanging into the bed of the wagon.

If he'd had time, Alton would've checked to make sure they were dead, but he knew somebody could've heard the shots. They weren't that far from the Nortons' place and he could possibly be working out on the range.

He shoved the gun back in the scabbard and turned his horse. He had to hurry back to town, but he'd take a route where he wouldn't be seen. Barnett and the sheriff would come by the road, so he'd circle around the open fields. It might be quicker anyway. He needed to make sure Jace didn't have too much time alone with Neva. He'd make sure the man left as soon as he arrived. *I'll then be alone with my beautiful untouched Neva. We'll head for Denver tonight and when we arrive, I'll show her how much I love her and always have. Though my sister might try to protest, she'll eventually agree that the best thing is for Neva and me to get married as soon as possible.*

~ * ~

"Pa, did you hear those gunshots?"

"I sure did, son." Sam Norton stopped nailing the fence wire back to the post and looked in the direction of the foothills.

"It was a signal for help, wasn't it?"

"Seems so, Doyle. Two shots are the accepted signal for help around here. 'Course I don't know what anybody would be doing in that direction unless they're cornered by a bear or wolf or some other strange creature." He propped his hammer against the post.

"Maybe they fell off their horse and broke a leg like I did two years ago."

Sam chuckled. "Could be. Go grab our horses and we'll check it out."

Doyle ran to the two horses they'd tied to a scraggly bush close to the fence. They mounted and it didn't take them long to reach the murder area where Cletus Finch lay on the ground and his sister lay in the wagon. Both of them were in pools of blood. Cletus's horse had wandered to the grassy area where the wagon had stopped. Both horses were grazing as if nothing had happened.

Doyle hesitated when he saw the man on the ground with blood all over him. "Is that the Finch man?"

"Looks like it." Sam dismounted, looped his reins around a cottonwood limb and walked over to Finch's body. He felt his wrist.

"Is he dead, Pa?"

"Yes, he is, Doyle."

"How about that woman in the wagon?"

"I think that's his sister."

"Reckon what happened?"

"I don't know, son, but I better check her." Though he figured she would be dead, too, he walked over to where she was in the wagon bed. He was surprised to see her breathing. Her breaths were ragged, and she gasped for air between each one, but she was alive. He snatched the bandana from around his neck and placed it on the hole in her stomach.

Without looking away from her, he yelled, "She's alive, Doyle. Head to the Barnett ranch and see if you can round up some help. There's nobody at our house but your mama and she can't leave the children."

"I'll be right back, Pa." He looked relieved that he was being allowed to leave.

Sam turned to his patient. "Ma'am, can you hear me?"

She mumbled something.

"I didn't understand what you said, but don't try to talk. My boy has gone for help."

She shook her head and this time he understood her to say, "Ain't no use. I ain't gonna make it."

"Sure you will." Though he didn't believe what he'd said, he wanted to reassure her if he could.

"No, I won't. You need to listen." Her voice was raspy.

"Please save your strength, Miss Finch."

"No, Norton. Now listen to me." She coughed.

"All right, but don't waste…"

"Damn it, I said listen." After that she went into a coughing fit and blood gushed out of her wound around his hand.

Sam swallowed. "All right, I'm listening."

It took her a minute to gather enough strength to say, "There's a satchel back here and it has some papers in it. Make sure Barnett gets them to the sheriff."

He frowned. "Why?"

"Barnett has the boys. He'll know what to do."

"If that's what you …"

"Promise me."

"I promise, but…"

She gasped a couple of times.

Sam mashed harder on her wound. "Miss Finch. Miss Finch. Inez."

She opened her eyes and gave him a lopsided smile. "Don't fret. It ain't so bad. Dying, I mean." With that she closed her eyes, took one last gasping breath and slipped out of this world.

For a few minutes, he sat there and looked at her. He couldn't help thinking what a wasted life she had led. Not only her, but her brother, too. Their greed and their hate for their fellow man had brought them nothing in the end. He couldn't help wondering why some people chose to live that way.

Climbing from the wagon, Sam moved to the horses. He figured the easiest thing to do was bury them here where they were killed, but he didn't particularly want them resting on his ranch for eternity and he was sure Barnett would feel the same way. They would have to be taken to town and buried in the graveyard outside of Wildweed. He removed the blanket from Finch's bedroll, moved to his side and wrapped him in it. He didn't bother to check the man's pockets or remove any of his clothes. He'd leave that to the undertaker.

Moving back to the wagon, he found the satchel Inez had told him about. He moved to his own horse and hooked the handle on his saddle horn. Going back, he took the blanket that was spread across the seat. It had blood on it, but he knew it didn't matter. It was going to be bloody when he wrapped her anyway.

By the time he had both Cletus and his sister laid out in the bed of the wagon, he heard horses approaching. He turned as his son entered the sheltered area. Two men he hadn't met pulled their horses in behind Doyle. Without being introduced, he figured one was George Barnett and the other was the Jace Renwick he'd heard of.

"Pa, I ran into these men headed for the Finch ranch, so I brought them here."

"That was the right thing to do, Doyle."

There were quick introductions and Sam said, "I'm sorry we had to meet under these circumstances. My wife said she really liked Mrs. Barnett and your daughters."

"Gloria enjoyed her visit and hopes they can get together again soon."

"That'd be nice. I know the women around here get lonely."

"As soon as we get a bunkhouse built and a few other things done at my ranch, we'll have you over for Sunday dinner. Gloria is a great cook."

"I can vouch for that," Jace added.

Doyle looked at the bodies in the wagon. "Pa, I though Miss Finch was alive."

"She was, Doyle, but she died shortly after you left."

He kind of shuddered. "I'm glad I wasn't here."

"Do you have any idea what happened here, Norton?" Jace asked.

"I'm not sure. At first I thought maybe one of them shot the other, then I realized that was impossible. There were no guns anywhere that had been fired. Finch's was still in its holster and Miss Finch's was under the wagon seat untouched. There's no doubt in my mind that somebody shot them both. But I have no idea who it could have been."

George asked, "Do you think it could've been Greenwood, Jace?"

"I'd bet money on it."

"You don't mean Alton Greenwood, the big businessman in town, do you?"

Jace nodded to Sam. "One and the same."

Sam looked puzzled. "What in the world would he have had to do with a man like Cletus Finch?"

"I saw Mr. Greenwood at the Finch ranch one day, Pa."

They all looked at Doyle.

"Tell us about it, son."

"Well, one day me and Daniel had gone fishing and we was coming back from the creek. Daniel grabbed me by the shoulder and pulled me behind a bush. When I asked him what was the matter he said Mr. GW was headed to the ranch and he didn't like him 'cause he beat him once. I looked at the man and told Daniel that was Mr. Greenwood. Daniel said he guessed that was why Mr. Finch called him GW."

"That settles it. We need to get to the ranch. I'm sure he'll go there as soon as he gets home and finds Neva and me gone."

"I agree." George looked at Sam. "I'll send Sly, a man who works for me, to take them to town, if that's all right with you."

"That's fine with me, George, but I think I'll pull the wagon down to my barn. I don't want some animal to get to the bodies."

The men shook hands and Jace and George headed to the ranch. Sam turned to Doyle. "Son, you should go ahead and warn your mama that I'm bringing these bodies in. I don't want her to be too upset about it."

Doyle nodded as Sam tied his horse and Finch's to the back of the wagon. He was trying to figure out a way he could help out at the Barnett ranch as he climbed on the wagon seat and headed home. It was then he remembered the man needed a bunkhouse.

~ * ~

Neva jumped when Marty said, "Hello, beautiful."

She threw the paper she was reading to the floor and leaned over him and kissed him on the lips. "Oh, Marty, my love. You're awake."

"There's nobody I'd rather wake up and see than you."

"I'm glad you're with me, but I can see you're in pain."

He nodded. "Where am I and why am I here?"

"You're in the Barnetts' house because you were shot. Mrs. Barnett and I have been taking care of you."

He frowned. "I remember seeing you talk to Jace, but why? What are you doing here?"

"I had some information for him."

Marty frowned again and this time he couldn't hide the moan that escaped from his lips. He did manage to say, "Your father's going to be furious."

"We'll discuss that later." She patted his hand. "Now, I'm going to get Mrs. Barnett. She said she had some laudanum she could give you for pain."

Gloria appeared at the door. She had a bottle and a spoon in her hand. "I thought I heard talking in here."

"He woke up, but he's really hurting, Mrs. Barnett."

"I figured as much." She moved to the side of the bed and filled the spoon with liquid from the bottle. "Open your mouth, Marty."

"I don't think…" He didn't finish his sentence because Gloria stuck the spoon in his mouth and he had no choice but to swallow.

She smiled at him. "Now young man, I'm going to get you some soup and Neva will feed you. Then you need to go back to sleep for a while."

"But I want to know…"

"Neva will explain everything." She smiled at him again and left the room.

Marty reached out and took Neva's hand. "I'm not only in this bed nursing a gunshot wound, but I'm totally confused. Please straighten me out."

Neva was about half way through the explanation when Ruby came in with a bowl of chicken soup and set it on the small table beside the bed. "Mama said for you to eat this."

"Thank you, Ruby," Marty said.

"You're welcome." She went out the door.

Neva pulled her hand out of his and stood to put pillows behind his back. "I think you can eat better sitting up."

He moaned, but managed to sit with his back on the pillows.

She picked up the bowl and began spooning it into his mouth.

"It's good, but go on with your story."

She continued to talk and only finished as he took the last spoonful of soup. She could see he was fighting to keep his eyes opened. She dabbed his mouth with a towel and then removed the pillows. "I think you need to rest now."

"I don't want to go to sleep. You might leave." His words were getting slurry.

"I won't leave, Marty."

"Good…I…" His eyes closed.

Neva leaned down and kissed his forehead. "I have a lot more to tell you, my love, but I want you feeling better when I do."

~ * ~

Alton saw the Norton man and his son heading to the area where he shot the Finches. He knew he'd have to work fast to get Neva and leave town until all this blew over. He'd then return alone and close out all his businesses here. He'd sell the ranch and pocket the money. Everything else could be handled from Denver or wherever they decided to settle.

Of course there was the matter of Vinnie. He'd tell her he just got word that her brother had died and she was no longer obligated to him in any way. He grinned to himself. He'd even give her a few dollars and tell her to go make a new life for herself somewhere besides Denver. He didn't want Neva ever to know he'd used the woman as his personal whore for the years she'd been with them. Neva wouldn't question him. She never liked Vinnie anyway.

He didn't think it was dangerous to leave Jace and Neva alone together for a little longer. He'd go to his office and gather all the money he had hidden there. Then he'd take what he could out of the bank. Of course, he could have a bank in Denver send for the rest after they were settled.

Yes, it was all going to work out fine. He'd insist that Neva pack light and promise her new clothes when they got to Denver. He'd gather a few clothes and the papers he had hidden at the house and they'd be gone when the sheriff started asking questions about the Finches. As far as Barnett was concerned, there was no way he'd ever know he had anything to do with the fire at his ranch.

He'd wait until they reached a luxury hotel in Denver to bring Neva to his bed. It would be wonderful. Just the way he'd imagined it so many times. He and his beautiful virgin would love each other forever and she'd never know that having her as his own was the reason he'd killed her mother.

## Twenty-nine

"I can't believe I let you two talk me into bringing you back to Wildweed with me."

Neva looked at Jace's face with its frown. "If you hadn't let us come, we'd have hitched up the buggy and come on our own."

"She's right," Vinnie said. "It was the only smart thing to do."

"I could've handled it and you two would've been safe."

"We're safe now." Neva folded her arms across her chest. "GW Collins or whoever he is won't dare hurt me. He thinks I'm the most beautiful virgin in the world."

Jace frowned. "What makes you say that?"

"He made the mistake of writing some of his fantasies down. Opal found them when she was studying the papers we took from his dresser."

"What did he say?"

"I'd rather not repeat it."

"Why didn't you or Opal say something about it?"

"We decided you had enough to think about with finding the proof he was the man who killed your father."

Jace glanced at her. "How do you feel about putting the man who raised you behind bars for the rest of his life?"

"He deserves to pay for the crimes he's committed."

Vinnie broke into the conversation. Her voice sounded as if she were about to cry. "I'm not sorry to say I hope the bastard hangs."

Neva reached over and placed her hand over Vinnie's clinched fist. "I'm so sorry I wasn't a better friend to you, but I truly thought you were with us because you wanted to be. I never dreamed he'd blackmailed you into being his servant. I didn't know the black-hearted man who was supposed to be my father."

"I could have been more open with you when you came to Wildweed to live with your father."

Neva bit her lip. "Do me a favor, Vinnie. Don't call him my father again."

"I'm sorry. I promise I won't."

Jace changed the subject. "We need to decide what we're going to say if we don't beat Greenwood back to the house."

"We could tell him we went for a drive," Neva suggested.

"Would he believe you took your housekeeper with us?"

"Probably not."

"You could tell him someone came by and said he'd had an accident and you and Neva felt you had to check it out. Then tell him I insisted on coming along," Vinnie suggested.

Jace nodded. "Maybe that would work."

"I'm counting on him not being home yet," Neva said, "but in case he is, we'll go with Vinnie's story."

"We're coming up on his house, so we'll soon see if he's there or not. Remember now, if he's not there, we're going to act as casual as we can when he comes back."

"And I'm going to find an excuse to leave and go get the sheriff when you and Neva engage him in a conversation."

"That's it."

He pulled the buggy into the small barn in the back and they climbed out. He patted the horse's neck. "Hang in there, boy. We have to leave you harnessed so Vinnie can use you when she goes for the sheriff."

They entered the house through the back door. It was quiet, but it would be if Alton were there alone. To be sure he hadn't returned, they hurried through the downstairs and were relieved to find it empty.

"There's still some fire in the stove. I'll chunk it up and make some coffee." Vinnie hung her bonnet on the peg at the pantry door. "I think there are some cookies left from yesterday."

"That sounds good. It'll look more natural if we're acting casual when he gets here." Jace took a chair in the adjoining sitting room.

Neva sat on the settee facing him and looked as if she were trying to relax.

Vinnie had just served the coffee and cookies when there was a noise on the front porch. "He's here," she whispered.

Jace had a view of the front hall and noticed that Alton stashed a satchel behind the hall tree. He hung his hat on the tree and came into the sitting room. "Well, looks like you two are having a nice snack."

"It's delicious," Neva said, but she didn't look at him.

"You've been gone an awfully long time, Greenwood." Jace put his coffee down. "What took so long?"

"The sheriff headed out to check the Finch ranch and I knew Neva was here with you." He grinned at her. "I thought she might like some time with you alone so I went to the office and worked for a while."

"I see." Jace picked up his cup and drank.

"Would you like some coffee, Mr. Greenwood?" Vinnie asked in a voice that Jace thought she was trying to control.

"Yes, Vinnie, I would." He moved to the settee and sat beside Neva.

Jace saw her cringe, but she didn't say anything. She did make it look as if she were reaching for the cookies when she moved away from him and closer to the end of the fancy couch.

He could reach her, though, and he did. He patted her knee. "How'd my beautiful Neva spend her afternoon with Mr. Renwick?"

Vinnie came into the room and handed him his coffee. She then started toward the back door.

"Where you going?" Alton asked.

"I left some clothes on the line. I'm going to get them in."

He nodded and turned back to Jace. "I suppose you'll be leaving now that I'm home?"

Neva looked frightened, but Jace gave her a big smile. "Neva has invited me to stay for supper. I'm looking forward to it. Vinnie said he planned to cook a big beef roast. As a rancher, I suppose you know my favorite food is well-cooked beef."

Alton looked as if he didn't know what to say and Neva took advantage of his hesitation. "I thought you and Jace could talk about his ranch in Texas. He said he has some things he wants to make you aware of."

"Well, sweetheart, maybe we could do that another time." He reached over and put his arm around her shoulder. "I've worked hard today and I'm a little tired. Jace could join us at another time."

"Don't be silly, Daddy. We can't un-invite a guest." It was obvious Neva's smile was forced when she patted his hand. "If you'll excuse me, I need to go out for a few minutes. I'll be right back."

Before he could object, she stood and hurried out of the room.

As soon as she was out of sight, Alton turned to Jace. "I'm not trying to be rude, but I don't think this is a good day for you to stay for supper."

Jace's eyes bored into his. "I'm sure you don't think so."

Alton frowned. "What…"

Jake continued to glare at him. "Did you think I wouldn't find out?"

"I don't know what you mean, Jace. I'm only asking you to leave because I wanted to give Neva a wonderful surprise tonight."

"May I ask what?"

"I shouldn't tell you, but she wants to go back to Denver. I've decided this is a good time to take her. I wanted to surprise her with the news."

"I don't know what gave you the idea she wants to go to Denver. She seems to think her life is going to be here with the man she has fallen in love with."

His face took on a furious look. "The only man my Neva loves is me."

"Of course she loves you. You're her father. But there comes a time in a young woman's life when she wants the love of a man her own age, not an old man like her pa."

Jace could tell the man was furious by the way his face reddened and his eyes blazed. "I'll have you know I'm Neva's stepfather. I married her mother when she was only three years old, but that's beside the point. Nobody can ever love that beautiful virginal girl the way I can."

Jace raised an eyebrow. It dawned on him that this man had more than a fatherly interest in Neva. It didn't seem possible to him that a father, even a stepfather, would feel this way about his daughter. No wonder Alton wanted Jace out of here. He had something planned and whatever it was wouldn't be good for the young woman. Now he was glad he didn't plan to leave. He certainly wouldn't go now, no matter what Greenwood said. Neva would be left at this man's mercy if he did.

Before he confronted Alton about his father's death, Jace decided to see if he could discover what the man had planned for Neva. She'd discovered the proof he needed to prove Greenwood killed his dad. He owed her for that.

"How could you deprive Neva of finding her own happiness in this world? Beautiful young women don't want their fathers planning their futures as you seem to be doing."

"Well, if you must know the truth, Neva's not interested in you. I only pushed her to make a play for you because I thought we could use some of your money. Now, I realize we don't need it. I can make enough money to support her for the rest of my life."

"So you want Neva to live with you until you die?"

"Of course."

"How are you going to keep her from running away with a man her age?"

"I'm going to marry her, you fool. She'll be my virginal bride and we'll be happy together."

Before Jace could say anything, Neva ran into the room. "You, fool!" She screamed. "I'd never marry you. That's the most disgusting thing I've ever heard. I thought you loved me as a daughter."

"Neva, calm down. I knew when I saw you that first time after you returned to my sister's house from school that you'd grown into the woman I'd always thought you'd be. I knew then we had to be together and if you'll think about it, you'll agree."

"You're crazy. I loved you because I thought you were my father. Now I find that's a lie. You're an imposter. Why did my mother ever let you use my father's name?"

"That's not important, Neva." He smiled at her. Or was it a leer? "Since he won't leave for me, why don't you ask Jace to go and we'll discuss our future?"

"I have no future with you. I intend to marry the man I love."

"There's nobody you could love more than me. I knew that the minute I set eyes on you…"

"I know you tried to keep me from it, but it didn't work. I fell in love with Marty Mayfield."

"Don't be ridiculous. An experienced man needs to teach a pure innocent girl what life is all about. Marty Mayfield wouldn't know how to even approach a woman like you, much less teach you about love."

For a moment Neva didn't speak and Jace wondered if she was thinking over what the man was saying. He knew she wasn't when she said, "So you think I'm an innocent virgin?"

He grinned at her and nodded. "Of course I do, darling."

"You're such a fool." Neva looked at him as if she wanted to bash his head in. "Let me enlighten you. Marty Mayfield has already taught me what love's all about."

"You can't be serious. You've never been with a man."

She glared at him. "Oh no? Then tell me how and why I'm carrying Marty's child."

Alton lunged toward Neva, grabbed her shoulders and began shaking her hard. "No! If you're telling the truth, I'll kill you, you little tramp. I didn't want any man to touch you except me."

Jace had kept quiet during the exchange, but he jumped up and jerked Alton backward. "Take your hands off her."

"Why should I? She doesn't want you either." He was almost screaming.

"I know." He shoved Alton down on the settee. "Now I have a question for you."

"Get the hell out of my house. I'm not answering any questions you have. I need to talk to Neva alone."

Neva glared at him. "I'm not staying here with you."

"Why not?"

Neva didn't answer.

Jace heard steps on the porch. He knew Vinnie would have the sheriff wait at the door and listen. It was time to ask his question. "Tell me, Alton Greenwood or really GW Collins, why did you kill David Renwick and steal his Colorado gold mind?"

"I did no such thing. Where did you get such an idea?"

Jace took a paper out of his vest pocket and waved it at Alton. "Right here."

"Where did you get that?" he roared.

"I must say you keep good records. It shows here where you paid a man at the assayer's office to say the mine was worthless and how you conspired with the two other men to take over the mine. Of course after you murdered my father, you made sure the other two thought the mine gave out, too."

"I don't believe you're David Renwick's son. Your brother in Texas said you were born and raised there, so stop trying to horn in on what belongs to me."

"That so-called brother is a man whose life I saved. He'd tell you anything I asked him to. Besides, I've never been to Texas. Like you, I lied."

Alton jumped up and pulled a gun from his coat. "You dirty son-of-bitch. I've killed one Renwick. Killing another one will be no problem."

"No!" Neva screamed. "I never dreamed you were so evil."

"Oh sweetheart, you don't know how evil I can be." He waved the gun at Jace and jerked Neva to him with his other hand. "I'm getting out of here and I'm taking her with me."

Neva began kicking and flailing her arms. "Turn me loose."

He laughed an evil laugh. "Shut-up, you stupid little tramp. I'll teach you to lay down with a bastard like Marty Mayfield. Maybe I'll turn you loose when I'm through with you."

The sheriff's deep voice said, "You'll drop that gun and turn her loose right now, Greenwood."

Alton raised his gun, but as he fired Neva grabbed his arm and his shot went wild.

Alton fell to the couch with blood spurting out of his chest. The sheriff hadn't missed.

### *Thirty*

Opal opened her eyes and saw Jace smiling at her. She snuggled close to him and ran her hand through the dusting of dark hair on his chest. "What are you grinning about, my love?"

"Just admiring my beautiful wife and thinking what a lucky man I am." He nuzzled the top of her head and breathed in the smell of lilacs.

"I think I'm the lucky one." She giggled. "I knew the day you rode up and asked for a drink of water there was something special about you, but until our wedding night, I didn't know how special."

"My goodness, in two weeks, my wife, who used to be so shy and retiring, has turned into a brave-talking woman."

"When I'm in the arms of the man I love, I feel brave."

"I hope you still feel that way when we get moved."

"I have faith that I will. In fact, I'm looking forward to moving to our ranch, but I'm going to miss our special room here in the barn."

"So will I, but I think Vinnie is going to put it to good use."

"Are you mad because I insisted we take this bed to our ranch?"

"Of course not. It's a special bed. It's where I first made love to my wife."

"I'm glad Neva and Marty gave her one of the beds from their house in Wildweed."

He laughed. "Can you believe that as soon as Marty found out he was going to be a father, moving back to town and working in his uncle's store sounded like the perfect job for a new husband?"

"And with the money Neva inherited, they decided to re-do the entire house. She told me she didn't want a thing in it that reminded her of Alton Greenwood."

"Things worked out for the best, didn't they?"

"Yes, Jace. I know you wanted him to pay for what he did to your father and he did, but I'm glad you weren't the one who killed him."

"So am I." He leaned over and kissed her. "Now that Sly and the boys are all moved into the new bunkhouse Sam Norton brought neighbors to finish building, we have the barn to ourselves. Let's take advantage of it."

"Don't you think we should get dressed and get this bed on the wagon to move to our ranch?"

"We've got time."

She slipped her arms around his neck. "Then let's take advantage of that time."

He moved over her. "We're going to do just that, sweetheart."

~ * ~

"Are they ever coming to breakfast?" George looked at Gloria. "I'm hungry."

"They'll be here soon, honey. Have some coffee while you wait."

"I bet I know what they're doing," Pearl said as she handed Sapphire her rag doll.

George looked shocked. "I'm sure you don't know any such thing."

"Oh, yes, Papa. I do."

"How could you know, little sister?" Ruby tried to keep from laughing when she asked.

"I heard them talking when I went to the barn with Vinnie to milk the cow."

Gloria looked at George and he only shrugged. She turned to Pearl, "Honey, you know you're not supposed to eavesdrop on other peoples' conversations."

"I know, Mama, but I couldn't help hearing it. Jace told Opal they needed to make a list of what they needed to buy for their ranch and I bet they're making that list."

Every adult in the kitchen let out a relieved sigh. Gloria said, "I bet you're right, sweetheart."

George cleared his throat. "Well, when all those papers he and Neva found were sorted out, and Jace learned he owned a mine in Colorado and the ranch Finch was living on, I suppose they could buy anything they needed."

"I hope the boys don't go live at that ranch with them."

"I don't think they will, Pearl. They want to stay here with Daniel." Her father smiled at her.

"Good. I kind of like playing with Glen."

Gloria looked out the window. "Speaking of Daniel, here he comes. I wanted the whole family to be here for this breakfast."

"What about the boys and Vinnie?" Ruby asked.

"Vinnie is in the cook house that was built on the end of the bunkhouse preparing their breakfast now," her mother explained.

Daniel walked in and spoke to everyone.

Gloria walked over and gave him a kiss on the cheek. "You don't know how good it is to see you looking so well."

He smiled. "Thanks, Aunt Gloria."

She grinned at him. "It does my heart good to hear you say that."

"Dan-il!" Sapphire dropped her doll and ran to him.

He scooped her up. "Hello, Sapphire."

"Looks like her affection has switched from Jace to you, cousin," Ruby said.

"I don't mind."

The door opened again and Jace and Opal walked in. "Good morning, everyone." Opal was beaming.

Sapphire squealed, "Jace" and wiggled out of Daniel's arms. She ran toward Jace holding up her hands.

He picked her up and swung her in a wide arc in the air. "Hello, my little love."

She giggled and planted a big kiss on his cheek.

"Well, now that Sapphire has greeted all the men in her life, shall we gather at the table and have our family breakfast?"

"Gloria's right. I know this is our last breakfast with all of you living on this ranch, but I pray it won't be the last meal we share." George moved to the table and held his wife's chair.

"Don't worry, Papa." Opal kissed his cheek. "Jace assures me he wants to come here and eat at Mama's table often."

"Then let's join hands and give thanks for the wonderful nephew and son-in-law who have joined our family."

~ * ~

Jace put his arm around Opal and pulled her close to him. "Well, sweetheart, it's the first night we get to sleep in our own bed in our own home. How do you feel?"

"I feel wonderfully blessed."

He smiled. "So, do I, my love."

As she liked to do, she ran her fingers through the hair on his chest. "I always had faith that I'd find where I was always meant to be in this world and this is it."

"Even though it's not a riverboat going down the Mississippi?"

"Oh, Jace. How did you know about that?"

"I heard you and Ruby talking about it one time."

She laughed as she rolled on top of him. "That was a silly girlish dream. I wouldn't give up what I have now for all the boats on the Mississippi River."

He looped his arms around her and kissed her chin. "Then I guess you're not going to like my plan."

She leaned back and looked at him in the moonlight. She wondered if she'd ever get tired of looking at his handsome face. She didn't think so. "What plan is that, my husband?"

"I need to go back to Baltimore and clear up all my dealings. I thought if you'd like, we might just take a cruise on the Mississippi while we're in the East. But if you don't want to…"

She leaned over and nibbled his ear. "So you plan to take me with you?"

"I thought we could call it a delayed honeymoon."

"Then it's settled. Anyway, you might as well get used to the idea that anywhere you go, I'm going, too."

"Even to hire hands and buy feed and stock for this ranch and to make sure your papa has the right kind of help to keep his place up?"

She giggled. "Maybe. After all, I know how to ride a horse and shoot and how to run down strays."

"Then I guess I'll have to appoint you the foreman around here. How much do I have to pay you?"

"How about we always discuss my pay at night when we're relaxed?"

He pulled her tighter. "Shall we start tonight?"

"Sounds good to me." He rolled her over and smiled down at her. "This is going to be your first payment. Of course, you know I get to share it with you."

"I wouldn't have it any other way."

He kissed her and they continued the transaction with action—not words.

# *Meet*

## *Agnes Alexander*

Agnes Alexander has published hundreds of short stories and articles. In 2011 she decided to concentrate on writing what she most likes to read, Western Historical Romance *Valissa's Home* published in 2013 her first western with Wings ePress. *Opal's Faith* is the 2nd one with Wings.

A life-long resident of North Carolina, she counts traveling as one of her passions. She has visited 48 of the 50 States and says Alaska and Hawaii are on her bucket list. Of course, she loves to read, but tries to limit herself to one or two books a week. Besides traveling and reading, Agnes enjoys jewelry making, watching old movies and spending time with her family.

She can be contacted at

www.agnesalexander.com